INFERNO SPHERE

OBSIDIAR FLEET BOOK 2

ANTHONY JAMES

Illustration © Tom Edwards
TomEdwardsDesign.com

Follow Anthony James on Facebook at facebook.com/AnthonyJamesAuthor

CHAPTER ONE

THE HADRON BATTLESHIP *ES Devastator* emerged from high lightspeed travel, spilling rapidly-decaying particles of energy in its wake. The *Devastator* had travelled across a vast span of deep space – coming from Pioneer eighty days distant – to Roban out on the frontier of Confederation territory. The Hadron was packed with the latest Obsidiar processors, which had calculated the journey down to the millisecond and deposited the vessel a mere thirty thousand kilometres above the planet's surface.

The Hadron's bridge was the shape of a trapezium, tapering towards the front and surprisingly compact given the colossal size of the warship. With almost everything automated, twelve main crew was all it took to operate this five thousand metre juggernaut of engines and weapons.

Admiral Henry Talley stood on the warship's bridge, his eyes locked onto the main sensor feed. A projected image of Roban hovered in the air, ephemeral, yet somehow beautifully real. The planet's rotation was too slow to detect and Talley stared at the daylit side as though he could find answers to the dozens of questions which beset him.

"It looks stunning," said Lieutenant Emily Mercer, sitting in front of a complicated bank of sensor and comms equipment to one side. "Unspoilt jungle and blue lagoons."

Talley looked across. Mercer was young – no older than her late twenties, with blonde hair and finely-etched features that earned her more than her fair share of attention. She was a damned fine comms officer, though it wasn't the time for her to be staring at trees and lakes.

"Eyes to your console, Lieutenant," snapped Talley. "I need scans of the area."

She blinked. "Scans, sir? This is a Confederation planet."

"Just check," he ordered. There were many things his crew were unaware of.

"We're being hailed by the Imposition class *Furnace*, sir. It's coming around the far edge of Roban. They seem surprised we're here."

"They will be. And shouldn't that be *ES Furnace*, rather than simply *Furnace*?"

"That's the name they've transmitted," Mercer said, with a look of puzzlement. "What's wrong, sir?"

Talley didn't answer directly. "Bring them up on the screen. It's a while since I last saw the *Furnace*."

The *Furnace* was fifty thousand kilometres away – close enough for the *Devastator*'s sensors to produce an image of near-perfect clarity. The cruiser was just as Talley remembered it – two thousand five hundred metres of wedge-shaped alloy, bristling with missile batteries. It had a rounded dome at the front and rear where the particle beams were housed, whilst its thick armour plating was pitted and scarred from high-speed flight through asteroid belts and dust storms. It was a fighting ship through and through.

"They have locked onto us, sir," said Commander George Adams in the rasping tones of a man who smoked and drank too much when he was off-duty. "Our countermeasures are prepared."

"We won't be needing them just yet. Lieutenant Mercer, get me a channel to their bridge."

"I'm establishing a connection."

"Would you like me to activate the stealth modules?" asked Lieutenant Joe Johnson. "They're warmed up and ready to go."

"Hold for the moment. There's no way that could be seen as anything other than a preparation for combat and since they're on the Space Corps network, they'll know exactly where we are anyway."

"Sir."

Talley remained standing, ignoring the concentrated stares of his crew. As far as they knew, this was simply a standard patrol visit to the Confederation's most distant planet. There'd been a few questions – probing as much as they dared. After all, the *Devastator* wasn't usually sent out on routine trips such as this one, especially not with five thousand of the Space Corps' highly-trained soldiers jammed into quarters designed to hold less than half of that number.

With the recent events on Atlantis, Talley wasn't expecting to be here for long. The Vraxar had come to the Confederation, putting the problems with Roban and Liventor into perspective.

"I've got Captain Kit Mills," said Mercer.

"Bring him through."

The connection was perfectly clear with no background hum, such that it was difficult to be sure the comms link had been made. Talley cleared his throat.

"Captain Mills, why have you targeted the *ES Devastator*?"

"We were not expecting you." Mills sounded nervous, as well he might. The *Furnace* was the most powerful ship stationed at

Roban, but against the *Devastator* it was comprehensively outgunned.

"We were not expecting you, *sir*," said Talley. He waited.

"I don't report to you, Admiral Talley," said Mills, the tremor in his voice even more apparent.

"What do you mean you don't report to me? I am an Admiral in the Confederation's Space Corps. You will stand down at once, Captain Mills and provide me with a full explanation as to why you have targeted a warship on your own side."

"Roban is no longer part of the Confederation," said Mills, almost finishing his sentence with an automatic *sir*. "Nor is Liventor."

Talley was fully briefed on the declaration of independence, but it seemed appropriate that he give Mills a hard time about it, since the man had effectively stolen several trillion dollars' worth of asset from the Space Corps fleet. In addition to his irritation about this rebellion, Talley was both pissed off and worried about the news from Atlantis. *Humanity really doesn't need this crap,* he thought angrily.

"Your declaration of independence does not make us enemies, Captain Mills."

"You have arrived without warning into our airspace, Admiral Talley." Mills sighed audibly. "We are standing down."

"They are no longer targeting us, sir," said Commander Adams. He was a hard man and his face showed no recognizable emotion.

"This is something of a mess, Captain Mills."

"You do not have permission to remain so close to Roban, Admiral Talley. I must ask you to return to lightspeed."

"You know I can't do that."

"They've scrambled two Resolve class light cruisers and three Crimson class destroyers," said Mercer. From the look on her face, all thoughts of Roban's natural beauty were gone.

The additional hardware wouldn't make any difference to the outcome of an engagement.

"Time to intercept?"

"Less than a minute, sir."

The situation was escalating far quicker than it needed to, as if the Council of Roban were determined to show their resolve in a battle they certainly didn't need to fight.

"Captain Mills. Please speak to whoever commands you and advise them the situation here is getting out of hand."

Mills was evidently very keen to follow this suggestion. "I will inform them immediately, Admiral."

The connection went dead. Talley glanced around the bridge and saw expressions of dumbfounded shock. He wondered if he should have done more to prepare them. They were going to get a double dose of unwanted news in the near future.

"Lieutenant Mercer, contact the light cruisers and the destroyers. I want to be absolutely certain they will not do anything rash."

Mercer and Ensign Gav Banks got on with it. The approaching ships were still on the Space Corps network and therefore easy to reach. The two comms operatives spoke quickly and quietly as they frantically did their best to keep on top of the situation.

Talley crossed his arms and drummed his fingers against his bicep. Outwardly he looked calm, but his jaw muscles clenched and unclenched. He reached out with one hand and opened up the topmost of his private messages.

The Confederation Council will not accept the secession. Situation volatile. Hostilities must be avoided. Await further instructions but expect recall at short notice. Duggan.

Talley grimaced. This wasn't a situation that demanded a military mind – it was one for the politicians to resolve. The presence of the *Devastator* wasn't likely to do anything other than inflame what was turning out to be a precarious situation.

The Vraxar, on the other hand, most definitely required a military mind and Talley itched to be on the return journey. Having read the report on how effective the *ES Lucid* was against the alien warships, it made sense to have the *Devastator* available as soon as possible, instead of using it to pressurize a couple of minor planets out here on the fringes. Orders were orders and for the moment, he'd need to keep the battleship near to Roban.

"Sir, I've checked out the assets based on Liventor," said Banks. "They have the Galactic class *ES Rampage* stationed there, as well as a dozen or so smaller craft."

Commander Adams raised an eyebrow. "The *Rampage* is ancient."

"It's been recently refitted on New Earth," said Talley.

"One final reprieve for the old girl?" Adams replied.

"There's a streak of the sentimental in you, Commander."

"Me, sir? Never."

The *Rampage* was something of a legend in the Space Corps – it had suffered catastrophic damage on more than one occasion, yet never quite enough for it to be written off and dismantled. It was a tough old bastard, but it was a surprise to find it had been given another refit. With money drying up for new warships, the fleet was gradually becoming older and smaller.

"Where is it?"

"I don't know, sir. It went offline ten minutes ago according to the *Juniper*'s logs, along with the Imposition *ES Thunder*."

"Running silent," said Ensign Callie Sykes. "They could be anywhere."

"Not anywhere, Ensign. They're coming here."

"Given what the records say about the *Rampage*'s engine output, that's three days travel. The *Thunder* is a little slower."

"They'll coordinate to ensure they arrive at the same time."

"The *Rampage* might swing it in their favour," said Lieutenant Dan Poole. "In combination, they could have the firepower to defeat us."

"*Defeat* is the wrong word to use, Lieutenant. It will be a disaster if we are required to fire our weapons."

Poole fixed Talley with his blue-grey eyes. There was no sign of insubordination in them. "We must consider every eventuality, sir."

"Of course."

Mercer waved for attention. "I have Councillor Nicholas Alexander on the comms, sir."

"I'll speak to him."

"Admiral Henry Talley," spoke the rich, politician's voice of Councillor Alexander.

"Councillor."

"You're a long way from home, Admiral."

"I belong everywhere within the bounds of Confederation Space, Councillor."

"We have formally seceded from the Confederation in order to form the Frontier League, as is our right under the terms of our constitution."

"A constitution the Confederation does not accept the legitimacy of." Talley bit his tongue, realising he was being drawn into an argument which would go nowhere and achieve nothing.

Alexander evidently thought the same. "A discussion for another day, Admiral. As it stands, we are at something of an impasse. We don't want you here and you refuse to leave."

"Our default position should be neutrality until our disagreements are resolved."

"You are correct, Admiral. The Confederation does not want to count oppressed worlds amongst its number, whilst we do not wish to see the results of our hard labour shipped off to the Origin Sector without adequate recompense."

Talley was well aware of the reasons behind Roban and Liventor's dissatisfaction with their relationship to the rest of the Confederation. It was multi-faceted, but much of it came down to money and recognition – the usual issues. On these two planets it was huge news. Elsewhere, it hardly even got a mention, in spite of how important the major Gallenium mining operations out here on the frontier were to the other planets.

"I have been ordered to remain in orbit about Roban, Councillor. You must be aware the Confederation Council will engage in talks, rather than attempt immediate suppression."

"I am aware of nothing until it happens," said Alexander smoothly. "We have yet to receive an acknowledgement of our grievances, let alone a commitment to negotiate."

Even without the appearance of the Vraxar, the Confederation Council wouldn't give Roban and Liventor an easy ride - a fool could see that. As it was, the alien threat was a much, much higher priority. Fleet Admiral Duggan had done his best to keep news of the Vraxar from getting out to the frontier, though it was something of a tall order to keep it totally under wraps.

"Nevertheless, the ES Devastator must remain here."

"Then you won't mind our own warships escorting you for the duration of your visit. I trust you will not try anything which might appear to be against our interests, such as subverting the cores on the Furnace in order to take control of the warship. We will be watching very closely for any such activity."

Talley had no intention of making promises. "We will remain stationed in orbit until I am ordered otherwise. These Robani spaceships are welcome to accompany us."

"Very well, Admiral."

With that, Councillor Alexander was gone. Talley swore

under his breath - he'd been dumped into a bad situation. He returned to his seat in order to consider how best to proceed.

"Get me a comms channel to Fleet Admiral Duggan," said Talley, after a few minutes' consideration. "A private channel."

Mercer didn't bat an eyelid. "I'm making the request." She hummed tunelessly for a few seconds, a habit which could have been irritating but somehow was not. "That didn't take long. I'm sending him through."

Talley checked his earpiece and then motioned he was ready.

Fleet Admiral John Nathan Duggan sounded alert and with a tone to his voice which gave the impression he wasn't in a good mood. His accent was unidentifiable, suggesting he'd spent his life on more than one planet.

"Henry, the situation is not a good one," said Duggan, cutting to the chase.

Talley smiled grimly. "We have discovered as much, John. They seem eager to confront us."

"Are you outmatched? They might be tempted into doing something particularly stupid if they believe they have the upper hand."

"It's still in our favour, though they have more warships inbound from Liventor."

"The *Rampage.*"

"They've taken it off the comms network, but it doesn't take much to work out where it's headed."

"It's one of the few remaining Obsidiar-cored ships in the fleet."

"I'm aware. It's not long out of the shipyard – for once it's a shame they didn't remove the core. Now the *Rampage* is here and involved in a rebellion against the Confederation."

The Space Corps tried to cling onto every Obsidiar core for as long as possible. On this occasion it was coming back to bite them.

"*Unfortunate* doesn't adequately describe it. We will need the *Rampage* on our side when the Vraxar return."

"Is there time for diplomacy with the rebels?"

Duggan laughed without humour. "I am willing to take a gamble and leave you out there for a short while. The projections team believe we have a few months until the Vraxar manage to crack the *ES Determinant's* memory arrays and find out where our other planets are located. Unfortunately, there are complications, the details of which I will send you shortly."

"Not enough to provoke an instant recall of the *Devastator*?"

"It's worse than that – you simply won't be able to return in time to influence events. Besides, the frontier problem remains and this is our single chance to enact a swift resolution and prevent the rebellion from becoming a distraction in the coming war. In the immediate term, my worry is that Roban has a hotshot captain on one of their ships who might think attacking a Space Corps Hadron is a good move."

"Have you checked the profiles of the officers based here?"

"Of course, but rebellion does funny things to the mind. It can turn the most pacifist of individuals into gun-toting maniacs. In other words, I'm not resorting to guesswork."

"They have accepted the *Devastator's* presence in orbit for the time being – with an escort."

"Keep it stable, Henry. You'll be screwed if anyone starts shooting, even if it's not your fault. It'll be exceptionally hard to keep you sheltered if it goes wrong."

"I assumed as much."

"The Confederation Council are crapping themselves and they are looking to the Space Corps to get them out of a hole."

"They've given you free rein to act?" asked Talley in disbelief.

"Not quite free rein. There's oversight, but it's distinctly hands-off."

Talley knew Duggan well enough to realise this was just another burden to be shouldered without complaint.

"What do you want me to do?"

"I'm not going to give you an easy ride. I want you to get me a win, Henry. Pull something out of your hat so we can move away from the Tallin sector. You might not know it, but you're the best man for the job – better than any of these so-called diplomats we employ."

"Resorting to flattery now?"

"I know you're immune to it. I have every confidence you'll manage. I want the *Rampage* back and I want the release of the six Interstellars they have docked. Most of all, I want the whole rebellion to just go away."

"The Interstellars have become important?" That could only mean one thing.

"The Council have made the decision to evacuate Atlantis. I want those spaceships."

"Even if I'm ordered to use force." Talley made the words fall somewhere between a question and a statement.

"It won't come to that. The *Devastator* is the only ship we've got there. I've recalled the ones we had on the way - we need to keep them close to our centre." said Duggan. "I've got to go. We'll catch up when you get back."

"It's overdue."

Talley ended the connection and removed his earpiece. The others of his crew looked uncomfortably at each other, as though daring someone else to speak first. It was Commander George Adams who took on the duty.

"What's going on, sir?" he asked earnestly. "It seems like everything's going to shit, if you'll pardon the expression." Adams was burly and with the flattened nose of a brawler. Looks were deceiving and he possessed a fierce intelligence.

Talley considered how much he should tell the others. In the end, there was little point in keeping too many secrets, since the cat was pretty much out of the bag.

"Which piece of bad news do you want first? The very bad news, or the exceptionally bad news?"

CHAPTER TWO

CAPTAIN CHARLIE BLAKE stared at the blank viewscreen with a certain amount of trepidation, waiting for it to illuminate and for the person at the other end to determine his fate. Meeting Room 73 on the *Juniper* was icy cold and the stark metal walls seemed to magnify the chill. A glance at the square wall clock told Blake he was one minute early.

At exactly the pre-arranged time, the viewscreen lit up. The image shimmered and then stabilised, with faint static the only sign of the immense distance between New Earth Central Command Station and the orbital.

There was a man visible. He was an old man with short-cropped hair, unstooped despite his years and with a piercing gaze. Fleet Admiral John Nathan Duggan was standing in his office, with an air of calm which was surprising given the threat hanging over the Confederation.

"Good morning, sir," said Blake.

"Captain Blake," Duggan acknowledged. "Let's get on with this, shall we?"

"Of course."

"The allegations against you are serious. Captain Kang accuses you of jeopardising the entire Response Fleet Alpha operation. We lost several of our warships, along with their crew and troops."

"Yes, sir. I am truly sorry for our losses."

"So am I, Captain Blake." Duggan stared directly through the screen. "I relieved Captain Kang of his position an hour ago and dismissed him from the Space Corps. The man was an absolute disgrace. If I could in good conscience hire him again with the specific intention of firing him for a second time, I would gladly do so."

Duggan's veneer of calm remained, but it was easy to tell he was seething below the surface.

"I was expecting to be subjected to a greater scrutiny," Blake admitted.

"You were." Duggan smiled thinly. "I've had a team of fifty combing through the audit logs of the warships in Response Fleet Alpha. There was only one conclusion."

"I am pleased the truth was apparent, sir."

"I also had the same team examine the combat logs of the *ES Lucid*. You did very well in the circumstances."

Blake knew when it was best to keep his responses short. "Thank you."

"You are now the only captain in the Space Corps below the age of seventy-two who has been involved in a real engagement with an enemy fleet and come out of it with a confirmed kill. Three confirmed kills in your case."

"The *Lucid* packs a real punch, sir."

"That it does. Unfortunately, it'll be in the shipyard for several months until it's returned to a fully operational state."

"We don't have much left that can challenge the Vraxar."

Duggan reached out a hand and grasped the tiny sensor which was relaying the image. He twisted it around until it was aimed out of the window in his office. At first, Blake wasn't sure what exactly he was meant to be looking at. Then, he saw a shape, hovering in the grey of the New Earth skies outside Duggan's office.

"Which ship is that, sir?"

"The *Lucid*'s sister ship – the *Abyss*."

"It's waiting to land?"

"We have only one docking trench here with the facilities to fit an Obsidiar core. You can't see it from my window, but they're working on the ES *Maximilian*. I'd initially recalled a number of smaller ships. After further reflection, I decided to wait a few additional days so we could install the cores on our larger vessels."

"How much Obsidiar do we have?" asked Blake. Information such as this wasn't widely available and he was curious.

Duggan's hand pulled the sensor back into its original position. "You'd think the answer to that would be straightforward," he replied. "Unfortunately, it is not. In theory, we could install cores into approximately fifty of our warships. However, there are new technologies in the labs which are in touching distance of viability and these will place a new set of demands on an Obsidiar core."

"In other words, each warship will need a larger core?"

"Precisely. The *Maximilian* is going to be fitted with a two hundred thousand tonne cylinder, which is similar in size to that carried by the *Devastator*. I hope to have new technology prototypes available to drop in soon, which will take advantage of the extra power."

"We're going to run out of Obsidiar very quickly."

"There're never enough of the things you value the most, Captain. I long for the days in which Gallenium was the most precious resource known to the Confederation. You don't need to destroy planets to extract the stuff. To make matters worse, some of our technologies will result in the destruction of the Obsidiar they employ."

"We need to find a new source, sir."

Duggan smiled grimly. "A fine plan, Captain Blake. However, the means continues to elude us and I do not wish to be the man who orders the destruction of a hundred planets in the hope we can somehow stumble upon some fragments."

Blake wanted to say more on the subject, but he could see the Admiral didn't wish to continue the discussion. He changed the subject.

"What are the current estimates on the Vraxar capabilities, sir?"

"Thousands of warships. They defeated the Estral, though you learned it was a close call. With or without Neutralisers, we can't defeat them."

"Maybe they were weakened in victory."

"That's a straw we're clutching at."

"The Space Corps has four hundred and twenty active warships," mused Blake.

The numbers didn't add up in the Confederation's favour, especially given how many vessels in the fleet were either old or the smaller, less effective destroyer types.

"We estimate the Ghasts have in the region of three hundred," said Duggan.

"Will they join us?"

Duggan looked pained. "We'll see."

"Even combined, seven hundred warships wouldn't be enough, sir. With or without Obsidiar cores."

"As it stands, you're correct."

It seemed like Duggan was happy enough to talk and it was too good an opportunity to pass up.

"You have something in mind, sir."

"Our tech labs are capable of producing many powerful

weapons if they're given the time and funding. The Vraxar have come for us at a time when several avenues of research are combining into something we may find useful."

There was an underlying caveat. "If only we had enough Obsidiar?"

"As always."

With a flash of insight Blake realised why he was still here in the meeting room, instead of being dismissed to his usual duties.

"What is my next assignment, sir?"

"I'm that obvious, am I?" asked Duggan. This time there was genuine humour in the smile. Then, the smile vanished. "If you were the leader of the Vraxar, come to conquer new worlds, what would you do after you'd left Atlantis?"

"I'd go somewhere out of the way until I could extract useful information from the *ES Determinant*'s data arrays."

"You wouldn't need to go far," said Duggan. "In fact, it would be for the best if you stayed as close as possible."

"For all they know, our next planet could be six months' high lightspeed travel away from Atlantis."

"Regardless, you'd still remain close to a known point of reference."

The meeting room felt suddenly colder. "Have we found them?"

"Look at this," said Duggan.

The image on the viewscreen changed from showing the Fleet Admiral's office, to a zoomed-in picture of a barren planet or moon, with no clear indication where it might be. A shadow flickered over the planet's surface and then disappeared just as quickly. The viewscreen resumed its feed from Duggan's office.

"One of our deep space monitoring stations picked that up five days ago. If we hadn't upgraded the station to Obsidiar processing units, the sensors would have missed it."

"I assume you're telling me it's Vraxar."

"Analysis of the recording suggests it's not Ghost," said Duggan. "It's definitely not one of ours, therefore we must assume it's likely to be Vraxar."

"Where was the sighting?"

"Just another planet somewhere out in space. It's approximately three days' out from Atlantis, which makes it close enough to use as a temporary base, yet far enough away that it wasn't likely to be found."

"Except we *did* find it."

"We found it through luck, Captain Blake and I am not a man who likes to rely on luck. At the moment, I'll take whatever I'm given."

"When do I leave?"

"Don't be so eager. I picked you because you've seen action and that makes you the most experienced captain I have available. I don't need arrogance."

"Apologies. I wish to do whatever I can to help, sir. I've seen these bastards and smelled their stench. If there's a way to stop them, I'll be at the front of the volunteers' queue."

Duggan appeared satisfied with the answer. "I believe you and you're about to get a chance. The *ES Blackbird* is due to enter local space above Nesta-T3 in the next three hours. There's no time for it to dock with the *Juniper*. Instead, you'll be waiting for it in a shuttle. You're going to investigate the sighting and gather as much information as possible."

Blake felt a thrill of excitement. "Yes, sir."

"I've assigned a crew. Get out there and get us some intel, Captain Blake. We're relying on you."

"I'll do my best."

"You'll need to. If this really is Vraxar, they're only three days from Atlantis. My projections team told me we'd have months until the *Determinant*'s data arrays were cracked, so I'm not pleased to find the enemy waiting on our doorstep. If they decide to make a punitive strike for whatever reason, there's little we can do to stop them."

"Is Atlantis unguarded, sir?"

"Not quite. We're outgunned though and a planet is an easy target. The reality is, I'd hoped the Vraxar would have travelled much further away than they have. This sighting is bad news. If they've left significant forces, Atlantis will continue to be in real immediate danger."

"That danger will never go away while the Vraxar exist."

"The Confederation Council approved an evacuation. The first two Interstellars will arrive in three days."

"Do the people know?"

"Not yet."

"Where are they going?"

"Somewhere out into deep space, to a location selected at random by a processing unit on the *Juniper*. They will stay there for a time until we can construct temporary shelters on another Confederation world."

Blake added up the numbers. "Two Interstellars can't carry everyone."

The response was short and invited no further questions. "No."

With that, Blake was dismissed. The viewscreen went blank, leaving him to sit for a short time gathering his thoughts. The faraway sounds of operations on the *Juniper* were the only intrusion onto the silence.

He pushed himself upright and headed for the door. There was an information panel in the wall adjacent and he paused to access it. A check on the latest orders assigned to his personnel number showed there was a shuttle reserved for him at a docking iris two levels down from his current floor. The Space Corps was nothing if not efficient when it came to administrative tasks.

A lift carried him down the two floors. There were other

people with him, but he hardly noticed their presence, nor they his. A short walk later and he entered the red-lit docking room – it was a long, narrow space with a plain metal floor extending to the left and right. There were circular docking irises every eighty metres or so. A couple of soldiers strolled nearby, gauss rifles over their shoulders. Otherwise, there were few people to be seen.

Blake found Docking Iris 32. He climbed six steps onto a platform and stopped in front of the door. There was a fractional delay while a node from one of the *Juniper*'s many processing arrays decided he was in the right place at the right time. The door spiralled open, allowing him access to a long, claustrophobic corridor lit in the same deep red. He stepped inside and the thick door closed behind him. He sniffed - there was an out-of-place smell of coffee, and persons unknown had discarded a trio of plastic cups onto the floor.

With a tut, Blake walked along the corridor. At the end, a second iris opened allowing him access to his designated shuttle, which was currently latched onto the *Juniper*'s hull.

The shuttle was one of the older, compact models, with care-worn seats designed to be tolerated for short distances only. The floor was particularly grubby and several rows of seats had been ripped out at the rear of the passenger bay – a sure sign this vessel had been used to transport a piece of ground artillery in the past. There was one additional passenger, a person whom Blake recognized. Not so long ago, the appearance of this person would have caused his heart to fall.

Now, he discovered he was actually pleased to see Lieutenant Caz Pointer.

"Hello, sir," she beamed.

"Hello, Lieutenant."

"This is all very secretive, isn't it?"

"You've not been told?" He cursed inwardly. Of course she

hadn't been told, since he'd only learned their destination himself a few minutes ago.

The smile left Pointer's face when she saw Blake's expression. "I'm not going to like what you're about to tell me, am I?"

"No, Lieutenant, probably not."

There was a grinding, shuddering thump, followed by a momentary sensation of free-fall. The shuttle's navigational computer piloted the craft away from the *Juniper* and off towards its pre-programmed destination. Inside, the two occupants mulled over the hand fate had dealt them.

CHAPTER THREE

"ALIEN BASTARDS *AND* A REBELLION," said Lieutenant Poole, scratching his stubble-covered neck with thick fingers. "I don't know which end of the universe I would prefer to be at. On balance, I think we're wasted out here."

"We're definitely wasted," Talley agreed. "Of all the times this Frontier League could have chosen to break away, they managed to pick easily the least convenient."

"Is it significant?" asked Lieutenant Mercer.

It was a good question. "Ultimately, it probably doesn't matter one way or another," said Talley. "The Confederation embraces free will and if these two planets see their future elsewhere, there's little we can do about it in the long term. In the short term, they've stolen the *ES Rampage* and they're keeping us out here when we would be much better placed in the Garon sector."

"Doesn't this mean they'll need to negotiate their own treaty with Ghasts separately?" asked Sykes. "They could end up with less than they have now. Plus, they'll lack the protection of being within the Confederation."

"Every rebellion is two-thirds hope and one-third action, Ensign. Throw off the yoke and pray it all works out nicely in the end."

"You don't sound sympathetic," rumbled Commander Adams.

"I represent humanity first and the Space Corps second," smiled Talley. "I can understand why they have chosen to act in this way. Whether or not I agree with them is something I will keep to myself."

"I hope it doesn't come to violence," said Ensign Banks. "I have cousins on Liventor."

Talley tried to hide his surprise. The crew and soldiers onboard had been carefully vetted to ensure they had no ties with either of the two planets. Somehow Banks had slipped through. Talley was saved from having to respond by an interruption from Ensign Alice Chambers.

"And I have family on Atlantis!" she said angrily. Chambers was usually reserved and she'd said nothing while Talley gave details of the recent invasion. It looked as though she wasn't able to contain herself any longer.

"There were few civilian casualties..." he started. The look on her face stopped Talley mid-sentence and he realised he should have been far more circumspect – for some reason the thought that his crew might have family on Atlantis hadn't even occurred. "Military?" he asked.

She nodded, a tear running down her cheek. "Teklo station."

The four main military installations had been effectively wiped out during the Vraxar attack, with few survivors. Whoever Chambers had there, it was likely they were dead.

"I have access to the records," said Talley softly. He sat at his console. "Who am I looking for?"

"Derrin Chambers. My brother."

It didn't take long. "Missing," he said. "It'll be weeks until there's anything like certainty on most of the personnel."

"Thank you for looking," she said.

"Do you need time?"

Chambers shook her head. "I'd prefer to remain at my station, sir. It'll be easier that way."

"You can speak to me whenever you wish."

She nodded her head once in acknowledgement.

The conversation was over and the crew turned their attention to the task of keeping the *ES Devastator* at a state of readiness. Talley ordered the battleship into a slow orbit at an altitude of fifty thousand kilometres. The sensor view of Roban showed the planet's surface pass by underneath – a semi-tropical paradise which was home to over a billion people.

The rebel fleet shadowed them, keeping in a loose formation only two thousand kilometres behind – at such a short distance, any engagement would be brutal and resolved in moments. Talley was aware of this and paced amongst his crew, ensuring they were ready to activate the *Devastator's* extensive array of offensive and defensive measures immediately. He hoped he was only going through the motions until wiser heads prevailed and the two sides could reach a swift, amicable settlement.

As it transpired, he was caught on the hop an hour or two later by something unexpected.

"Sir," said Mercer with an admirably straight face. "I've just received a message from a group referring to themselves as the Frontier Council. You've been invited to dinner."

"Will they be joining us here on the *ES Devastator*?"

"No, sir. You're asked to visit them on the surface in five hours."

Talley raised an eyebrow. "They're getting bold."

"They're waiting for a response, sir. What should I tell them?"

"Any indication what's on the menu?"

"No, sir."

He sighed and ran a palm across his military-short grey hair. "Tell them I accept the invitation. I will, of course, bring a small entourage."

"I've let them know," said Mercer. "They've sent through details of your destination."

Talley wasn't particularly interested in where he'd been invited - what *did* interest him was the verbal sparring he'd be required to participate in once he got there. He didn't relish the idea one little bit.

"Here's where you're going, Admiral, sir! I've got you an image feed," said Mercer. "Looks nice!"

"It's a bit prettier than a standard government building," admitted Talley, looking at the sensor image of a huge, four-storey white-walled rectangular construction set within several acres of cultivated gardens. He'd half expected to see a carbon copy of the grey, concrete administration blocks which housed officials across the Confederation. For some reason, the sight of the building on Roban was an indication of how much the people here wanted to forge their own path.

Lieutenant Poole had something to say and was blunt enough that he didn't bother waiting. "Sir, you cannot commit yourself to this venture. What if they take you prisoner?"

"There is no benefit for them in doing so, Lieutenant. Therefore, I must treat this as exactly what it is – a meeting with some of the most important people behind the second biggest crisis the Confederation has faced in many years."

"No pressure, then, huh?" said Ensign Sykes, leaning back in her seat and stretching luxuriously. Sykes was dark-haired, dark-eyed and with an attitude that drifted towards insolence. Talley smiled thinly and didn't respond.

"The trip will take you a couple of hours from leaving the bridge to arriving, sir," said Ensign Banks, trying to be proactive.

"Thank you."

Little happened during the next three hours. The *ES Devastator* circled the planet and six rebel warships followed. The Frontier warships occasionally attempted an intrusive scan of the battleship's weapons systems or engines, which the crew were able to fend off without effort. In truth, the rebels could likely access the design plans and specifications for the *Devastator*'s most recent refit, so these probing scans were only for show – they could easily find out the battleship's capabilities.

There was one important detail they wouldn't find, any mention of which was purposely redacted from the usual records - the *ES Devastator* still carried its Obsidiar core, and a much more potent one than that on the *Rampage*. Talley had no plans to tap into it, but it was comforting to know it was there if needed.

With time to spare, Talley read through his queue of messages. Many of them were easily-skipped, whilst a few needed to be read twice. He came across one from his wife, which contained a short video of his daughter's twelfth birthday party. Megan had been inconsolable to learn her Daddy wouldn't be there, since he always pulled out the stops to be off duty on her birthdays. Guilt tugged at him.

At last, the time came to leave. Mirrors were in short supply on fleet warships, so Talley checked out his appearance without one. His dark blue admiral's uniform was pristine – they did something to the material to ensure it remained crease-free and clean even if it was subjected to a direct missile strike. The occupant would be vaporised, but the suit could be handed on to his or her replacement. He smiled inwardly at the thought and ran a hand over one cheek – there were early signs of stubble, even though he'd shaved not six hours before. It would have to do.

"Commander Adams, you have the *Devastator* until I return.

You will not take hostile action under any circumstances, which includes attempts to rescue me if my hosts decide to detain me against my will."

Adams didn't need to have everything spelled out. He saluted crisply. "Yes, sir. No hostile action. If events dictate, I'll take the *Devastator* to a place of safety."

Talley nodded. "Good."

With that, he turned on his heel and walked towards the exit door. The thick alloy blast door opened automatically, letting in a waft of cooler air from the passage outside, along with the usual comforting metallic scent. The equipment on the bridge gave out plenty of heat, ensuring it was always a few degrees warmer than everywhere else on the ship and it was often a relief to get away from it.

The interior of the battleship was relatively compact. The internal rooms and corridors were tucked deep inside the hull and extended for no more than two thousand metres. The vast proportion of the vessel's bulk was made up from several billion tonnes of the precious metal Gallenium. When the atoms in this material were correctly aligned they could produce power in unbelievable quantities, allowing ships like the *Devastator* to travel further and much, much faster than anything in the past.

It took less than ten minutes for Talley to reach his destination, his hard-soled boots producing a muted thud against the ultra-dense material of the floors as he walked. The passages were lit in a cool blue-white and they had no decoration whatsoever, the grey metal bearing no paint. He passed several groups of soldiers on the way. There was little for them to do to pass the time, other than hit the gym or watch replays of their favourite films or TV shows.

The rear bay was the largest open space on the battleship. The ceiling was a few metres high and the floor of the bay was a couple of hundred metres along each side. There was no direct access for personnel – each of the four shuttles was boarded through an iris door which led to an airlock and then onto the shuttle by another iris. It cut down on the risks of someone being accidently exposed to the vacuum of space, especially when the shuttles were docking regularly.

Talley's escort was waiting for him – twenty soldiers stood at attention near to the docking iris for Shuttle One. They were dressed in the latest issue flexible grey polymer spacesuits which covered their entire bodies. The suits had a mirrored visor, which could be slid into place to make them completely airtight, whilst making the occupants look practically identical to each other.

Lieutenant Tom Richards stepped forward, the suit unable to disguise his powerful frame.

"Sir, the men are ready."

"Thank you, Lieutenant. We will depart at once."

"Yes, sir. Are you expecting any trouble?"

Talley looked at the gathered soldiers. They carried the latest low-recoil plasma repeaters, which had short, thick barrels protruding from a heavy magazine of ammunition, attached to which was an ergonomic handle. The plasma repeaters looked ungainly, but they could burn a hole through most things and were not yet widely-distributed. The troops also had gauss rifles slung over their shoulders and wore grenade belts. They weren't taking any more chances than those already forced upon them by Talley's decision to visit the surface.

"I'm not expecting trouble, Lieutenant, however I see you have prepared for it. Let's go."

Talley boarded the shuttle. The passenger bay had seating for over a hundred – more if you wanted everyone to stand. The bay was twenty metres long and ten wide, with the same type of blue-white lighting used throughout the Space Corps. The seats were padded, though showing signs of wear and tear. At the rear of the bay was the angular shape of a mobile heavy repeater, floating on its gravity engine and clamped in place. Richards had evidently wanted a little more assurance than just hand-held weapons and the shuttle's nose-mounted cannon.

Though he wouldn't be piloting the shuttle, Talley entered the cockpit. There was seating for three, in front of a bank of screens and the controls used for piloting the vessel. He took the furthest seat from the door. A man he recognized as Rank 1 Trooper Lance Andrews entered. The Space Corps persisted with its insistence that rank and file soldiers be known only by their surname during normal address. It was archaic, but any change in the approach didn't seem likely to come soon.

"Good afternoon, sir. I'll be your pilot today," the man said.

"Take us out as soon as you can. I don't want to be late for dinner."

Andrews didn't ask questions. He warmed up the shuttle's gravity drive and activated the external sensors, to show the *Devastator*'s docking bay bathed in strobing red lights. The bay door slid smoothly downwards into a gap between the battleship's armour plates, revealing the blackness of space. A few stars twinkled in the distance, the effect exacerbated on the viewscreen.

"Detaching gravity clamps," said Andrews.

There was a heavy, metallic thump, alarming to first-time travellers and of no consequence to the experienced. The shuttle pulled away from the bay wall and headed nose-first out of the battleship.

"We're being followed?" said Andrews. "I'm reading six Space Corps vessels in close proximity."

"Ignore them. Take us to Roban."

"Yes, sir."

The pilot fed power into the engines until they were at full thrust and the shuttle sped away from the *Devastator*.

"Looks like a nice place," said Andrews, unable to take his

eyes away from the sensor feeds of Roban. "I've never been here. Maybe I should come back when the Corps no longer wants me."

Talley didn't want to respond, so he remained quiet. He checked the navigational computer – there were twenty minutes to go until they landed. Whatever happened in the next few hours, he was sure it was going to be rather more significant than a plate of Robani partridge in a shallot sauce.

CHAPTER FOUR

THE *ES BLACKBIRD* was a beautiful craft. It was a smooth, flattened, tapering cylinder which ended in a point. The overall appearance was that of a bullet from an ancient rifle, albeit one that measured twelve hundred metres in length. As it happened, the *Blackbird* was something close to ancient itself, having seen more than forty years of service. The passing years did nothing to take away the incredible design, though it now possessed an unmistakeable air of age.

"This thing can still fly, right?" asked Pointer, following Blake through the passages leading to the bridge.

"Don't be fooled by the age. They keep the *Blackbird* right up to date."

"Stealth and speed, huh?"

"A winning formula."

"And a bigger lump of Obsidiar than anything this side of a Hadron battleship?"

Blake smiled to himself. Pointer had clearly been doing some research into the Space Corps fleet. Her near-death experience on the *ES Determinant* and subsequent encounter with the

Vraxar was turning her into a much better officer. *And much more agreeable company,* spoke a voice in his mind.

"Where did you find that out?" he asked.

"I have my sources," she said.

"I'm sure."

They reached the bridge. It was more compact than a Crimson class destroyer, meaning there was little floorspace. Four advanced, compact consoles were arranged across the room – the captain and weapons officer's were to the fore, with the other two placed to the sides and slightly further back. The air was cool, though not to excess and the greens of the display screens joined with the whites and blues of the ceiling lights. The cockpit of the *Blackbird* was the strangest mixture of cutting edge and anachronistic – the equipment was the best of the best, but the smell of new technology wasn't able to disperse the feeling of age.

There were two unfamiliar officers awaiting their arrival.

"Lieutenant Jake Quinn – engines, sir!" said the first. This man was tall, slim and reminded Blake of the now-deceased Commander Cain Brady who had perished on the *ES Determinant*. The likeness was so strong Blake was sure there must be a family connection.

"Lieutenant Dixie Hawkins – weapons, sir!" said the second. Hawkins was dark-haired, with eyes of slightly different hues. Her skin was smooth, but something told Blake she was older than she looked. She exuded competence.

The rest of the formalities didn't take long and soon Blake found himself in the grip of a narrow-sided leather chair which creaked softly as if it was oiled only yesterday.

"Lieutenant Quinn – do you have the details of our destination?"

"Yes, sir. The *Juniper* sent them over just before your shuttle docked."

"Lieutenant Pointer, let the *Juniper* know we're leaving."

"All done, sir."

"Bring the fission engines to a state of readiness and send us on our way."

The warmup took only a few seconds – quicker than Blake was expecting. The transition to lightspeed was decidedly rough, inducing nausea and an unpleasant cracking from several of his joints. When the sensation passed, he checked out the status of the life support modules. They were operating at peak efficiency.

"What the hell?" he finally asked.

"First time on the *Blackbird*, I take it?" said Hawkins with a hint of satisfaction.

"Yes. Haven't they upgraded the life support units?"

"We're carrying the best the labs can produce, sir."

There was only one conclusion to draw from that. "How long until we get to Cheops-A?" he asked.

"Twenty-one hours." There was definite satisfaction now.

"Fleet Admiral Duggan said it was approximately three days travel. I take it we're a little faster than average?"

"We have the Space Corps' first and only Obsidiar drive fitted," said Quinn. "They dropped it in a few weeks ago."

"And now we're faster by far than anything else in the fleet," added Hawkins. She gave a rasping laugh. "Those transitions sure aren't nice."

"Something to get used to," said Blake. He gave an exaggerated rub of his palms. "Now that you've had your fun, let me have mine by telling you where we're going."

Five minutes later and Lieutenants Hawkins and Quinn were sitting in shocked silence. Blake had a little sympathy for them. The top brass had maintained a shroud around the details regarding the Vraxar, hoping to buy themselves some time to make a few decisions without distractions. Their efforts hadn't even achieved the status of being partially successful and only resulted in continuous, harmful speculation. The Vraxar attack was a very open secret and in Blake's opinion the time to come clean had passed several days ago.

"The Vraxar want to kill everyone," he said. "The Space Corps' primary goal has never been exploration. We've always been a defence force and you've been called upon to do some defending."

Blake quickly realised he'd misjudged them.

"I'm not complaining, sir," said Hawkins. "It's just that you've removed the last tiny element of doubt that everyone in the Corps has been clinging to. I joined up to fight, but I damned well prefer peace."

"You've confirmed the beginning of war, sir," said Quinn. "And when did any bunch of aliens want to do something other than kill as many of us as possible?"

"That's what they're here for again," said Pointer. "The Vraxar expand or they become extinct."

"Is it true what they say?" asked Hawkins. "Do they make you into some kind of metal-flesh soldier?"

Blake sighed. "The ones we fought were exactly that. I have no idea if we saw a representative sample."

The questions came and Blake did his best to answer them. There'd been no specific order regarding secrecy, so he couldn't see the harm in telling what he knew. Everyone in the Confederation was going to find out soon enough, assuming they didn't already know.

Eventually, the words dried up, leaving Blake to the task of acquainting himself with the specifics of the *ES Blackbird*. The interfaces to pilot Space Corps vessels were mostly identical across the entire fleet, but there were usually differences in the armaments and other capabilities. Every captain was trained to fly every ship with minimal issues. Naturally a fresh-faced rookie wouldn't be put onto a battleship, but in theory it wouldn't be a problem for such a captain to fly the vessel.

"Sixteen Obsidiar processing cores, two Shatterer tubes, two Shimmer launchers, half a dozen cut-down Lambda clusters, a few heavy repeaters and a stealth mode," said Blake after a short time checking his console. "Along with a fall-back energy shield."

"The stealth modules are probably different to the ones you're used to," said Quinn. "These ones are designed to be a little more robust."

"Well, we're not going to start shooting anything," said Blake. "It makes sense if we can hide." He frowned. "What's this *predictive flight modelling* option on the engines panel?"

"New calculation routines," said Quinn proudly. "The theory has been in place for a couple of decades, we've just lacked the ability to put it into practice."

"Yes, yes, but what does it do, Lieutenant?"

"In a nutshell – if our sensors get a good enough look at a departing spaceship, this new software tries to predict where they'll end up based on their energy expenditure, vector and numerous other factors."

"Does it work?"

"In testing it works great on fleet vessels. Against anything else, nobody knows. It's not quick either, sir. It'll eat up as many processing cycles as we can throw at it and might still take hours."

"I like it," said Blake. "Anything new is to be applauded. There's something else here – on the weapons panel."

Hawkins stepped over to look. "I don't have that option, sir. What is it?"

Blake tried to access the unknown weapon's subsystem. "You don't have clearance to see it and I don't have clearance to use it or to find out what it is."

He wasn't a man determined to subvert authority just for the sake of it, but he liked a challenge. He attempted to access the weapon by a different means.

"Still blocked." He looked closely. "I can see the date stamp for when it was installed – four days ago. One day after our monitoring station detected activity at Cheops-A."

"We only came onboard three days ago," said Hawkins.

"I don't like secrets," said Blake. "Come out of lightspeed, I want to speak to someone."

"Yes, sir," said Quinn. "Switching from fission drive to gravity engines."

Blake was so accustomed to smooth lightspeed transitions he'd already forgotten how different the *ES Blackbird* was. It was too late to belay his order and the spaceship dropped shudderingly into local space, leaving Blake and Pointer retching.

"You sort of get used to it," said Hawkins. "Or better at pretending you can ignore it, even when you still feel like crap." There was a note of accusation in her voice.

Blake coughed violently. "Get me through to Fleet Admiral Duggan," he managed.

Pointer had recovered enough to look embarrassed. "Shouldn't I go for a common-or-garden Admiral first, sir?"

"Normally I would agree. On this mission, Fleet Admiral Duggan is our direct contact."

"I don't think I've spoken to an Admiral before," said Quinn. "Let alone the top man himself."

"Got him," said Pointer.

Blake put a finger over his lips to tell the others it was time for quiet. He plugged in his earpiece.

"Captain Blake," said Duggan. "What can I do for you?"

"There's a weapon onboard, sir. I'm denied access to it."

Duggan's laughter was unexpected. "Secrets, eh? I used to hate them myself, but as I get older I find they have their uses."

"Will this secret weapon improve our chances of success?"

"If you stick to the guidelines of the mission there should be no need for you to use any weaponry."

It was obvious which way the conversation was going. "Is there any point in me keeping you on the comms, sir?"

More laughter. "I won't change my mind quite yet. I can remote-activate your access if it ever becomes necessary. If you handle things correctly, I won't need to."

Blake was disappointed, though he had no right to be. "I understand, sir. We're nineteen hours out from Cheops-A. I'll update you when we get there."

"You absolutely cannot allow the Vraxar to detect you. We don't know what the result will be – they might have rules of war which are completely at odds with anything we understand."

"If the *Blackbird* is as good as the spec sheets, we'll be fine."

"It's not just about the spec sheets, damnit! It's about what you do as a captain – how hard you can push things to get a result. You've got to know when to back off and when take a chance. None of this comes up in the design manuals!"

"I know that, sir. I'm not here to piss about."

"Good. Return to lightspeed and keep me informed when you arrive."

"He's gone, sir," said Pointer helpfully.

"Thank you, Lieutenant." Blake gritted his teeth. "Sorry, folks, it's time for us to be on our way again. I've learned my lesson."

A few seconds later, he was once again regretting his decision to initiate what had turned out to be a fruitless conversation with Fleet Admiral Duggan. His body was starting to adapt to the violent launches to lightspeed – if he tensed his muscles just right and kept his head lowered, it wasn't quite so bad, though not something to be experienced any more than strictly necessary.

The journey was a comparatively short one in terms of duration. Nevertheless, there was sufficient time for the crew to get enough sleep to ensure they'd be in good shape to manage whatever there was to come. Blake spoke to Quinn and Hawkins – it was no surprise to find they were amongst the most experienced officers in the Space Corps. Pointer was something of the exception and her inclusion spoke volumes about how much Duggan valued personnel with first-hand knowledge of combat. The short time on the ES Lucid had pushed her to the front of the queue and ahead of comms personnel who'd served for fifteen or twenty years.

"What happened to Sergeant McKinney?" asked Pointer, cutting into his reverie. "I haven't been able to find out."

"Lieutenant McKinney, you mean? I don't know exactly what happened to him other than the fact he got promoted. It was well-deserved."

"And that nice Lieutenant Cruz? Where's she?"

Blake thought himself a good judge of character. "She'd have hated to be called *nice*. I bet she's been plagued by that label her whole life."

"Some people *are* just nice, sir. That's who they are."

"To answer your question, Lieutenant Cruz is still on the *Juniper* – she's been excused from duty while her ankle is reconstructed and fused. Her file didn't go into greater detail on her health. She put in a request for a transfer onto a warship. If she gets accepted, it'll be another year of additional training."

"Shame," said Pointer. "I liked her."

"She was one of those people. If she toughens up, there's a good chance she'll go far. If humanity isn't annihilated first."

"Aren't senior officers meant to put a positive swing on things, no matter the circumstances?" said Hawkins. "I'm sure I read that somewhere."

"The Space Corps values its personnel, however they choose to interpret the guidelines," Blake replied.

Hawkins laughed. "If I may be permitted to speak my mind, I think I'm going to enjoy serving on your ship a lot better than the last one."

"Which ship were you on last time?"

"You might remember it, sir. The Galactic class New Beginning."

Blake started. "You weren't in Response Fleet Alpha, else you'd have known about the Vraxar."

"Lieutenant Quinn and I were both on leave. We weren't close enough to be recalled."

"Captain Kang was a coward," said Blake simply. "He caused many deaths."

"I'm not surprised, sir," said Hawkins. "The man was a complete bastard."

"I'm glad they kicked him out," said Quinn.

"It's hard to keep things quiet for long in the Corps," said Blake. "Anyway, let's not talk about him any longer. Just the mention of his name pisses me off." He took a deep breath. "When do we reach Cheops-A?"

"Two hours and five minutes."

Blake spent the remaining time studying the known data on the Cheops-A solar system. It was a rarity in that it had been visited by the Space Corps' scouts and prospectors on several occasions. Most planets in Confederation Space were treated to a perfunctory scan if a prospector vessel's captain thought there was a chance of unearthing valuable minerals. That was generally as far as it went – the Confederation had an abundance of everything it needed apart from Obsidiar and, to a much lesser degree, Gallenium.

"A massive red star, with twelve orbiting planets and a total of ninety-eight moons."

"I assume the monitoring station was able to narrow it down?" said Pointer. "You mentioned it was a fleeting glimpse, but they must have analysed it to death."

"They did analyse it and the results show a 99% likelihood of the target planet being the fifth one out. It's called Ranver."

"After the mathematician?"

"I have no idea. Anyway, we're going to exit lightspeed as close to Ranver as possible. Usually, we'd need to be a few hours away to reduce the chance of our fission signature being detected. Luckily, the *Blackbird* is fitted with..." he looked at Lieutenant Quinn. "What did you call it?"

"Fission suppression, sir. It's like a net that pulls in the stray particles and throws them out the back. Sort of how an old exhaust system worked, only completely different. In theory, it should allow us to safely arrive within ten minutes gravity drive travel from our destination, though the recommendation is to push that out to thirty."

"And this requires Obsidiar to work, I assume?" asked Pointer.

"It's the way forward, Lieutenant," said Quinn. "If we ever find a way to make enough of this Obsidiar stuff, you can be sure that one day it'll be powering your toothbrush."

"Let's concentrate on the mission," said Blake. "When we enter local space, I want the stealth modules online immediately and I need a comprehensive in-depth scan of the area. Sixteen Obsidiar processing units should be fast enough to keep the sensor feeds clean. On top of that, provide status updates to the *Juniper* at regular intervals. If anything goes wrong, I want there to be a record of what we found."

The crew didn't need telling twice and they got on with the final preparations. It was beginning to sink in that this wasn't one of the Space Corps' training exercises – this was a vital reconnaissance mission and whatever they found here could well determine the path of the war.

With five minutes to go, Lieutenant Quinn began a countdown. When he announced ten seconds remaining, Blake braced himself for the intense discomfort of the *ES Blackbird*'s entry into the Cheops-A system. When it came, it was bad, but no worse than the others.

"Status update," he grunted through the pain.

"Stealth modules active," said Quinn.

"Beginning local area scan," said Pointer.

It didn't take long to discover the news.

CHAPTER FIVE

ADMIRAL HENRY TALLEY'S destination was a few kilometres outside Roban's planetary capital city of Miklon. The building he'd seen on the sensors was in a walled compound and protected by covert surveillance, along with an array of automated lethal and non-lethal systems to repulse unwanted guests. Andrews paused to check in with Miklon's main civilian airfield. Once he was certain they had clearance to land he brought the shuttle onto the compound's dedicated pad, which was a raised concrete slab set a hundred metres away from the place Talley was expected.

"They've sent a welcome party, sir," said Andrews.

Talley watched a group of five dressed in red uniforms as they walked smartly along a wide path which led from the main building to the landing pad.

"Unarmed?" he said, squinting at the feed.

"Looks like. They're security men, though, except that one at the front. I know the type."

"I agree," said Talley. "Nothing to be alarmed about, I'm sure."

He left the cockpit and entered the passenger bay, to find his escort already at attention.

"Sir, I recommend we accompany you," said Richards.

"That's fine. Open the door," said Talley.

The man closest to the side iris activated the door. It spun open and a set of concertinaed metal steps extended to the ground. Talley looked out. The group of five were standing twenty metres away, with the lead man tall and impassive. This man had an additional insignia on his chest which the others lacked.

"You four, follow me," said Talley, indicating three of the soldiers and Lieutenant Richards. "That's Councillor Edmonds at the front."

Talley descended the steps. It was early evening on Roban and the sky was pure blue. It was warm, though not excessively so – the sort of day to be savoured in other circumstances. There was a faint breeze, cool and welcome. Trees of a type local to the planet rustled quietly.

When he reached the bottom of the steps, Talley strode over to Edmonds with his hand extended. Edmonds was lean and with a neutral face which indicated the man was good at keeping his cards hidden.

"Councillor Zachary Edmonds," Talley greeted him.

Edmonds took the hand in a firm grip and nodded once. "Admiral Henry Talley."

"We have much to discuss, Councillor."

"Straight to the point, I see, Admiral."

"Always."

Edmonds looked at the accompanying soldiers, as though seeing them for the first time. "Firearms are not permitted within the building."

Talley hesitated – his rank meant he was permitted an armed guard wherever he went. It wasn't the time for stubbornness.

"Leave the guns here," he said.

Richards looked as though he wanted to protest. Instead, he put his plasma repeater on the ground and unslung his rifle which he also laid down. The others did the same.

With that, Talley and Edmonds turned and walked towards the main building. The two groups of four escorts fell in behind, eyeing each other suspiciously.

The building had been designed to look like a large house, with wood-framed windows and a sloping, tiled roof with three chimneys. Talley wasn't fooled by the homely appearance – vital business would be conducted within the walls of this place.

The grounds were magnificently manicured, reminding him of gardens he'd seen only in pictures. A variety of delicate scents reached his nostrils from the colourful flowers and shrubs, most of which he didn't recognize. The Space Corps' aesthetics were non-existent and the military bases on which Talley spent most of his time were enormously drab. There was beauty in the lines of its spacecraft, though not of a type directly comparable to the exquisiteness of carefully-tended nature.

As he walked, Talley noticed how much thought had gone into the design of the gardens, such that it was nearly impossible to see the perimeter walls as he walked. Movement caught his eye and he saw a distant shuttle trace a line across the sky, its silver hull spoiling the illusion of the party's isolation from technology.

Talley wasn't forced to endure small talk for long. The party ascended a wide set of white stone steps to a pair of hard wood doors, which were already open to reveal a marble-floored hallway within. There were two robot attendants – old models which were little more than floating cylinders with arms and a screen showing an androgynous face.

"Look after these men," instructed Edmonds.

"Sir?" asked Richards, looking for confirmation he was to follow the robots.

"It's fine," said Talley.

Richards didn't look happy but did as he was asked.

Once his escort was gone, Talley followed Edmonds into the house. It was cool within and when his eyes adjusted, Talley was able to pick out details which indicated how much this place had cost to build. There was a stone staircase leading up, with carved wooden bannisters, a magnificent chandelier and a series of paintings along the walls. Talley could appreciate the workman-ship, though part of him couldn't get past the idea that it was wasteful – a notion he admitted was absurd given the cost of building even a single, small warship.

"This way," said Edmonds, indicating an open doorway a few metres along.

Talley glanced left and right as he went and saw that the side rooms were packed with screens and expensive consoles. There was evidently more to this place than met the eye. He was directed into a waiting room, which was carpeted and with several leather chairs. It was as though there was a concerted effort to divide the house such that there was either no tech-nology present at all, or the best the ruling council could obtain.

"Have a seat," offered Edmonds.

"I prefer to stand," said Talley, crossing to look out of a window. Someone had parked a gravity-engined car outside – it was a boxy affair made up to look like a vintage model with wheels. "I don't like to be kept waiting, Councillor. The situation is too serious for us to dance around it."

"Councillors Alexander and Lacy are on their way. We three can speak for the others."

The next five minutes would have been uncomfortable were Talley not such a seasoned officer. As it was, he kept his mind focused until the others arrived. Councillor Nicholas Alexander was in his fifties - broad, short and bald, with piercing blue eyes. Councillor Kyla Lacy was also in her fifties, slim and with greying hair. They both had the look of lifetime politicians. Not long after their arrival, one of the robot servants floated into the room to announce in its soothing tones that dinner was served.

Talley made his way to a large dining room, as lavishly-appointed as the other rooms. There was seating for twelve, though only four places were set. Soon enough, he found himself in discussion with the members of the Robani Council. Talking was a distraction from the food – the meal was probably excellent, but Talley hardly noticed it.

"Why have you been sent here?" asked Lacy. "In one of the Space Corps' few battleships, no less."

Talley knew he had to tread carefully. "Do you need to ask?"

She smiled. "No, but I'd like to hear it from you."

"The Confederation Council does not accept your secession. If their stance doesn't change, they will send the fleet wherever they choose."

"They seem in no hurry," said Alexander. "Is our Gallenium not important to them?"

"News reaches us of other problems," said Edmonds. "Perhaps we are now a low priority mission for you and one from which you will soon be recalled."

Talley put down his fork. "Have I been brought here for interrogation? I am a military man – you must surely be aware I have no influence."

"The Space Corps has a far greater sway over the Confederation Council than most people care to acknowledge," said Lacy. "And with the *ES Devastator* in orbit, you personally have the ability to put great pressure upon us should you choose it."

"In this matter I will be led by others, Councillor. There is nothing personal involved." Talley looked at her. "Why now?" he asked. "Your citizens are not exactly poor. Why the need to rush? The Confederation has always been about serving the common good."

"The common good no longer serves *us*, Admiral," said Edmonds. "We are treated as little more than a mining outpost. Every day we receive new instructions telling us what we must do and how we must do it. We do not grow rich from our Gallenium reserves – our resources are taken from us in the name of this *common good*. Roban and Liventor are treated with contempt! It is ironic to think if we had no such resources we would be given much greater respect! We could not permit this to continue indefinitely! We do not even have representation on the Confederation Council, in spite of promises it would happen!"

As he spoke, Edmonds' voice rose in volume with his passion and Talley saw nothing that made him think it was an act. A politician he was, but Edmonds truly believed in his cause.

"The Confederation Council will meet shortly, Councillor. There is much for them to deal with."

"There you have it!" said Lacy in angry triumph. "Roban and Liventor are so unimportant, we do not even merit an emergency convention! Instead, we have a battleship in orbit as a scarcely-veiled threat to show what will happen if we do not fall into line!"

"We know about the Vraxar, in spite of the efforts to keep this tragedy under wraps," said Alexander.

Talley took a sip from a glass of fine local wine to give himself a chance to think. He'd expected to be subjected to such an onslaught and accepted it was something he had to endure. He'd told the Councillors he had no influence, which was only partially correct. There weren't many Admirals in the Space Corps and each was there on merit. When they spoke, the Confederation Council listened – as far as military matters went. That didn't mean the Corps could dictate policy, but it was best to have the military onside.

It was already apparent the declaration of independence was badly thought out and Talley felt a momentary sympathy. This dinner was clearly being used as an opportunity to try and gain his support in the hope he'd have a word in the right ear once he returned to the *Devastator*.

"What do you hope to achieve with all this?" he asked. "And what of the Ghasts? Their treaty is with the Confederation."

"They won't return to war," said Edmonds.

"No, probably not. You realise the Council is unlikely to permit you selling Gallenium to the Ghasts?"

There was silence for a moment – they'd evidently considered this already. There was no way the Confederation would allow such a rare commodity as Gallenium to fall out of their grasp. The use of force to prevent it was inevitable. It was unlikely the Ghasts would get involved, but even so, it was an unacceptable risk.

"We want better terms with the Confederation," said Councillor Lacy bluntly. "A partnership of equals, in which the fruits of our labour benefit the citizens of Roban and Liventor."

"You have this now," said Talley. "You are part of a much larger whole. If you continue on your current path you will be alone with your stockpiles of Gallenium. There are other sources within Confederation Space."

"Exhaustible sources, Admiral."

"As are yours, Councillor." Talley wondered if he should let them know about several new Gallenium discoveries elsewhere in Confederation Space, since they appeared to be ignorant of the fact. He made up his mind. "The Confederation will always find more. In fact, we already have."

The disclosure had less effect than Talley anticipated.

"It's a shame no one has managed to figure out how to obtain more Obsidiar," said Edmonds, clearly hinting at something.

"As close associates of the Confederation Council, you are aware it remains a high priority goal. If the Estral experienced shortages even with all of their destructive capabilities and technology, it is understandable we have experienced only limited success."

"How does a military man such as yourself feel about the removal of the Obsidiar cores from fleet warships? A vessel with an energy shield is a much more imposing proposition than one relying on armour alone, is it not? The Confederation is at war with the Vraxar and will need its warships to be at their most capable."

Talley looked at Councillor Lacy, feeling as if this was building to something. He shrugged as though it was of little importance. "The cores are being replaced."

"The Confederation's stocks are insufficient to equip more than a handful of warships," said Alexander.

"Tell me, Admiral – how much Obsidiar does it take to create one of the processing cores on a fleet warship?"

"I'm sure you know the answer, Councillor. A fragment and no more."

"One fragment for one core. Thousands of tonnes to equip a single spaceship for war. How much better would the Confederation's chances be against the Vraxar if every ship in the fleet had backup Obsidiar power?"

The answer was evident and Talley didn't see the need to spell it out. Obsidiar was the single known substance which could generate more power than Gallenium. The difference between the two wasn't marginal – there was a phenomenal increase. Decades ago, the Estral had come through a wormhole seeking it and their methods were blunt in the extreme, involving the destruction of entire planets. Obsidiar was only created when the core of a shattered world expanded, fusing an exceptionally rare mineral with Gallenium in its purest form. The Confederation had tried for decades to mimic the reaction in a lab and had failed, in spite of limitless financial backing for the project.

Now, humanity was left with a little more than two million

tonnes of Obsidiar, taken in the brief war against the Estral. These precious supplies didn't come close to fulfilling the countless demands.

"I am told the major stumbling block on the development of augmentation technology is lack of a suitable power source for the implants," said Alexander.

"The Confederation Council will never permit augmentations," said Talley.

"A time will come when the tide of public opinion shifts."

"Perhaps. Why the sudden interest, Councillor?"

Councillor Edmonds reached into one of his pockets and drew out a plain metal box, a few centimetres along each side. He placed it onto the wooden surface of the table, the sound indicating the box was heavier than it looked. With a careless motion of his hand, Edmonds slid the box over.

"Open it."

There was tiny clasp and a hinge. Talley slid the clasp aside with a fingernail and opened the box. A smooth cube of black stone rested within. He lowered his palm until it was over the cube, being careful not to touch it. Talley felt the cold radiating outwards. He closed the box and returned it to Edmonds.

"Where did you get it?"

"A place nearby."

Talley recognized he wasn't going to be given specifics on the location of the find and didn't press the matter. "How much is there?"

"We don't know," said Councillor Lacy.

"It's a significant quantity," added Edmonds. "Certainly far more than the Confederation's existing stocks."

"We have thousands of people dedicated to finding or making this substance," said Talley. "Not one of them believes it's possible to create without monumental levels of heat, pressure and destruction."

"That may be true," said Edmonds simply. "Nevertheless, we already have many thousands of tonnes stored in a safe place and we are extracting more every day."

"I'm not going to mince my words, Councillor. How do I know this single piece of Obsidiar wasn't obtained elsewhere and brought here?"

"I'm sure the Confederation's reserves are exceptionally well audited. However, I understand your suspicion that we somehow managed to procure an illicit supply and had it shipped in. Such an accusation would achieve little."

"I'm sure," Talley replied. "Why are you telling me about this, instead of the Council?"

"Because you are here, Admiral. Because we have little time. The Vraxar have come and soon, inevitably, the *Devastator* will be asked to return. You are the man here and now."

"The Vraxar will find you," said Talley softly. "This is not the time for humanity to divide."

"We have something the Confederation needs. Now is precisely the time for us to drive home our claim for independence," said Alexander.

Edmonds leaned forward. "We need you to understand what it at stake, Admiral. We would prefer a mutually beneficial relationship with the Confederation, with whom we might trade exclusively. If we don't get what we want, we could simply withhold our supplies."

"Ensuring the destruction of both parties," said Talley.

"The biggest risks invariably grant the biggest rewards."

"If we can't reach an agreement with the Confederation, I'm sure the Ghasts would make reliable trading partners. Our Obsidiar in return for their protection."

"The Council won't permit that to happen."

"They will have no alternative, Admiral," said Alexander. "The Obsidiar isn't here – it is elsewhere and I must assure you there is no chance you will find where it is. The choice is clear – negotiate with us for exclusive access to our Obsidiar, or have it divided between the Confederation and the Ghasts."

With their pre-planned message delivered, the three Councillors changed tack and the remainder of the meal was spent engaged in small talk, during which Talley learned about the local food and wines and a smattering of detail on Robani politics. It might have been captivating, except he was unable to take his mind away from the cube of Obsidiar he'd been shown earlier. If Roban or Liventor had indeed located a source of the material, it would strengthen their hand immeasurably. It would also make things considerably more complicated than they otherwise might be.

The meal finished. Admiral Henry Talley thanked his hosts and rose to leave. There was no attempt to kidnap him, nor otherwise obstruct his departure. One of the robot butlers led him from the house, where he met with Lieutenant Richards and the rest of his escort. Richards was too much a professional to fish for details and the five of them returned to the waiting shuttle. The blue of the sky was so deep as to be almost black and the gardens were subtly lit. Glowing insects hovered in the air and the perfume of the flowers was accentuated by the darkness

Minutes later they were in flight, heading towards the *ES Devastator*. Talley sat in the cockpit, his eyes open but his brain registering nothing of what was in front of him. The difficulties he'd foreseen were soon to become infinitely more involved.

CHAPTER SIX

FLEET ADMIRAL DUGGAN stared impassively at the dead body. It wasn't a pretty sight – the remains of the Vraxar had been subjected to an extensive and highly intrusive examination. There were signs of blood and sticky, clear fluid, accompanying the stench of decomposing flesh and the equally harsh odour of preservatives.

A medical terminal floated next to the oversized bed, with numerous wires and sensors strung across to the Vraxar's arms and torso. There was another machine nearby – this one was a brute force processing cluster. A cable extended from this second machine and through the now empty left eye socket of the alien.

Dr Faith Clarke waited nearby with the impatience of a person who could see her duties building up while she had her hands tied. In fact, there was nothing more important than what could be gleaned from the corpse in this white-walled room in the New Earth Command Station medical lab.

"Tell me," said Duggan.

"It is beyond belief," she said. "Everything about it is an affront to life."

"What is it? Why does it exist?"

"I can't answer your second question, Admiral. As to the first? It's part metal and part flesh as you can see. The metal is crudely interfaced with the flesh and a mesh of nanofibres carries the signals to and from a processing unit implanted in the brain stem."

"You said the external metal isn't needed?"

"An early conclusion," Clarke admitted. "And one we're still running with." She threw her hands up in a display of pent-up frustration. "There's no need for these alloys to be part of its body. There's no need for it to possess a processing unit. Its body is riddled with a dozen different cancers, each of them suppressed by a hundred different drugs. It should have died long ago."

"One of my warship captains spoke to a different Vraxar. It told him they were old."

"I was getting to that part. This particular specimen is biologically near-identical to a Ghast, but it was two-hundred and sixty years old at the time of its death. The Ghasts don't live any longer than humans, yet this one..."

The magnitude of the Estral-Vraxar conflict made Duggan shiver and he wondered if this soldier had died in the early stages of the war or if the conflict had raged for a thousand years before. He experienced a strange feeling – an emotion close to sympathy for the Estral to have perished to such a sickening foe as the Vraxar.

"This one was an Estral – the parent race of the Ghasts. Do you have any idea what killed it originally, before the Vraxar got hold of its body?"

"I don't even know if it ever *was* killed before these three gauss injuries finished it off on the Tillos base." Clarke was flustered – she was the sort of person who hated being asked a professional question to which she lacked an answer.

"It's probably not important. We know they do conversions on living subjects. My curiosity wants to know how they choose who to convert and who to kill."

"We might not find the answer to that without speaking directly to a living Vraxar."

"They're in short supply at the moment. What have you learned from this processing box?" He waved a hand towards the second machine in the vicinity of the body.

"It's still plugged in, but it's been idle for hours, sir. The Vraxar's built-in processor is a fairly primitive unit. We pulled the code from it, but it's going to take the coding team a while to interpret the data, since the Vraxar use an entirely different numbering system to ours."

"I put our best language experts on it," said Duggan.

"This is getting outside my field, sir," said Clarke. "The way I understand it is that there's a lot to do."

"I know."

As it happened, Duggan had already spoken to the coding and alien language teams. Both departments were reluctant to serve up guesses, though Duggan's insistence was enough to overcome the reticence. In summary, there were surely major advantages to be gained from studying the Vraxar coding, except it would take time. In addition, there was as yet no way to cobble together an understanding of their spoken tongue.

"Will there be anything else, Admiral?" asked Clarke.

"No, thank you," said Duggan.

He left the room. A small team of his staff was waiting and they followed as he made his way from the medical lab. Duggan didn't speak. His brain retained the image of the dead Vraxar, the edges and details as sharp as they were in the lab. He wasn't sure why it was so important for him to see one with his own eyes instead of through an image feed. There was a need within him that required a first-hand view of the enemy. Since his duties made him effectively office-bound he knew this may well be his last opportunity to do so.

With a heavy heart Duggan returned to his office and prepared to deal with the onslaught of business.

"LIEUTENANT MERCER - GET me Fleet Admiral Duggan," said Admiral Talley.

"It's two in the morning on New Earth, sir," said Ensign Callie Sykes.

Talley held back the reprimand. *She's just trying to be helpful,* he thought, not convincing himself for a moment. "Go about your business, Ensign."

"It doesn't look like he was asleep, sir," said Mercer, wise enough to get on with it. "And he doesn't sound like he's in a good mood."

"Let me worry about that, Lieutenant."

Talley hooked his earpiece in place. "Sir. There is good and bad news."

"In equal measures?"

Movement caught Talley's eye. "One moment, sir. My engine man requires my attention."

"There's a fission signature," said Lieutenant Johnson.

Talley frowned and made an urgent signal for Mercer to shut off the open comms channel.

"Are there any Corps ships due?" he asked.

"No, sir. There's nothing on the flight plan for weeks. I've checked the list of rebel-held assets and they're all accounted for."

If the incoming vessel wasn't from the Space Corps, the alternative was unlikely to be something they should welcome with open arms. "Battle stations!" shouted Admiral Talley.

He watched the sensor feeds anxiously. He had no idea what was approaching and he hated being in the dark.

"Everything we've got is loaded into its chamber," said Commander Adams. "I recommend a pre-emptive launch of shock drones and activation of our energy shield."

"Hold the drones, Commander - that might look like a hostile act." Talley made a snap decision. "Power up the energy shield."

The shield came online with a hum and a protective sphere surrounded the *Devastator*, as close as a thousand metres from the vessel's nose and tail. The shield was near-invisible, though the sensors showed an occasional spark of pure energy crackling across the surface. On Talley's left-hand screen, a series of gauges climbed several million percent and the ship's AI cores frantically re-routed to keep the other critical systems fully powered up.

"The energy shield is active," said Lieutenant Johnson.

"Prepare for evasive manoeuvres."

"Yes, sir. I'm loading us up for fission jumps across eight of our twenty-four cores. If it's something we don't like, we'll be able to dance around them."

"The *Juniper* is aware we have inbound." Mercer was terrified – the fear evident in her voice.

"Keep it steady, Lieutenant. We're no sitting duck. What do our friends in escort make of what's happening?"

Mercer blinked uncertainly. "They don't seem to be doing very much at all, sir."

Talley nodded in response. "They already know what's inbound."

What emerged from lightspeed was unexpected, though Talley wasn't excessively surprised. A warship appeared, a quarter of a million kilometres away and closer to Roban's single red-dust moon than it was to the planet itself.

"The Ghasts?" said Mercer. "What are they doing here?"

Talley had a sinking feeling he exactly knew what the Ghasts were doing so close to a Confederation planet they weren't meant to know the location of.

"An Oblivion. They sent a whole damned Oblivion," said Adams.

The Ghost battleship was almost as large as the *Devastator* – it was an uneven mixture of angles and curves, with missile clusters, Shatterer launch tubes, particle beams and whatever else the aliens managed to squeeze inside its hull.

"They're shielded, sir," said Adams. "They must be Obsidiar-equipped."

"The stupid idiots!" shouted Talley, his temper snapping. "The Robanis have told the damned Ghosts the coordinates of their planet! This is really going to screw things up!"

He took a deep breath. Under the Human-Ghost peace treaty, the Ghosts were only permitted to know the location of eight Confederation worlds. Now the Robanis had thrown caution to the wind and told the aliens how to find them. The only explanation was the unrecognized Frontier League wished to play the Ghosts and the Confederation off against each other in the hope it would allow them to get what they wanted.

"The rebels must have told the Ghosts before they declared independence," said Adams. "It's a long journey to get here."

Talley cast his mind back to the recent meeting he'd had with the councillors. How they'd smiled at him and put on a show. In reality, they were playing him for a fool while they schemed. He put the matter to one side, too worldly-wise to take it personally.

"Do we know the name of the Oblivion?"

"No, sir. It's not on our databanks."

"Hail them, Lieutenant Mercer. Ask what they are doing here in Confederation Space, so close to one of our planets."

"They've provided a standard greeting, sir. It's the *Gallatrin-9*. Their captain wants to speak to you."

"I'm sure he does," said Talley. "What's his name?"

"Tarjos Rioq-Tor," said Mercer, struggling with the pronunciation.

"*Tarjos* is the Ghast title for a senior officer – he's their captain. Get him on. Open channel."

The Ghasts had harsh-edged voices, which made them sound perpetually angry even when they were probably not. Language modules installed on all fleet warships did their best to interpret the emotions behind the sounds and add a humanness to them. After decades of fine-tuning it still wasn't perfect and the Ghast captain sounded vexed when for all Talley knew the alien was in a joyous mood.

"Admiral Henry Talley," growled the Ghast.

"Tarjos Rioq-Tor. What are you doing here?"

"We have been invited by the council which governs this place. They wish to speak with us."

"The Confederation does not recognize the Frontier League. The Ghast Subjocracy cannot grant legitimacy by holding talks with the rebels."

"We do not wish to involve ourselves in the Confederation's squabbles, Admiral. We are here in friendship."

"In which case, you will return the *Gallatrin-9* to its usual place and provide proof to the Confederation that all records of Roban's location have been removed from your databanks."

"This is not something you have the authority to order, Admiral. Our races are at peace and I am here - at a location the details of which were freely provided by an elected representative of your planet Roban. I must stress, we do not recognize the Frontier League. Roban is a Confederation planet and we are here to speak with its council."

Talley had dealt with the Ghasts before and knew the aliens found it difficult to lie directly – it was either inherent or a part of their society and there were dozens of research teams being paid to argue over the matter. Rioq-Tor, unlike the others of his species, appeared to have the smooth tongue of a lifelong diplomat.

"We will provide you with an escort until I have conferred with my superiors," said Talley.

"Of course," replied the Ghast.

"Obtain the details of their trajectory and follow them at a distance of thirty thousand klicks," said Talley once the connection went dead. "Keep our shields up and remain on full alert. I don't give a damn whether or not they like it."

"Yes, sir," Lieutenant Johnson acknowledged.

"Every time I think this situation couldn't get any worse, I'm proven wrong," muttered Talley, returning to his seat.

The arrival of the Ghasts was entirely unwelcome, not least of which because an Oblivion battleship would make an exceptionally powerful opponent. He wondered if the Robanis had mentioned the discovery of Obsidiar.

The *Gallatrin-9* approached Roban at an unthreatening speed and established an orbit with an altitude of forty thousand kilometres. The *ES Devastator* followed and behind it came the six rebel-held warships.

Once he was sure things had settled as much as they were likely to, Talley got hold of Duggan on the comms for the second time.

"I take it the scales of good and bad have tilted?" Duggan asked at once.

"That they have. There's an Oblivion here, John, with an Obsidiar core."

Duggan swore loudly and repeatedly – he didn't need to have the ramifications spelled out to him. With an effort that was obvious even without a visual link, he got a grip on himself.

"I think I'd like to hear the good news."

"Obsidiar, sir. These damned rebels tell me they've located a major source of it."

"We both know that's impossible. What proof have they given?"

"No proof. The thing is, I believe them."

The channel was silent for a long, drawn-out moment. Then, Duggan sighed. "If they're telling the truth, everything changes – our relationship with the Ghasts and our relationship with the frontier worlds. I assume they didn't give away the location of the source?"

"Naturally not."

"They have us over a barrel and we have no time to tiptoe around in search of a diplomatic solution."

"What is the plan?"

"I don't know yet. Is the situation stable?"

"For the moment."

"Keep it that way. I'll get back to you soon."

The channel went dead, leaving Talley with his thoughts.

CHAPTER SEVEN

"THERE'S NOTHING HERE, SIR," said Lieutenant Caz Pointer.

Such was the inescapable conclusion after three cautious circuits of the planet. Ranver was cold and barren, with high, jagged mountains, deep canyons and plenty of windborne dust – the sort of place the Space Corps would choose for training exercises if it ever wanted to test the morale and resolve of its soldiers.

"Do those canyons check out?" asked Blake.

"I've run a scan over every geographical feature which might possibly hide a Vraxar warship greater than two thousand metres in length, sir," said Pointer with a hint of disapproval at the implied lack of trust.

"Fine. We'll need to widen the search."

"I've already started," she replied. "These Hynus sensor arrays have a much wider arc of visibility than the old arrays."

"We'll still need to loop around each of these other eleven planets at least once, right? Plus a whole lot of moons?"

"Yes, sir."

"We'd better get on with it," said Blake. "It strikes me that the

Vraxar have moved elsewhere. On the other hand, we're here and there's no need to leave until we've reached a state of certainty."

"All the planets are pretty big," said Quinn. "We could be here for days."

"Is there anything in the monitoring station's scan that suggests if we should start further out or closer in?" asked Blake.

"Nothing, sir," said Pointer. "They didn't get much more than a shadow."

"We'll head inwards towards Cheops-A," said Blake.

"The fourth planet is Auvial," said Pointer. "It's another upper mid-sized one, with a circumference of four hundred thousand klicks."

"I'm setting a course towards it," said Blake. "We'll do it on the gravity engines, rather than chancing a short-range transit."

With that, he took hold of the *Blackbird*'s control bars and altered their course towards the new planet. The warship's AI generated a couple of advisory notices that it could do the piloting more efficiently. Blake ignored the messages. *I didn't spend years in training to let a damned computer do all the work.*

With its combination of Obsidiar drive and standard Gallenium gravity engines, the *Blackbird* was blisteringly quick, even operating under the additional load of the stealth modules. Within thirty minutes, they'd covered half of the distance, giving Pointer enough time to complete a detailed scan of most of the exposed surface.

"Much the same as Ranver, except it's warmer and a bit smaller," she concluded.

"I'll bring us around the planet at a distance of a million klicks – think you can get what you need from there?"

"As long as you don't go too fast."

In normal circumstances, the scanning work would have been merely boring. As it was, Blake found himself sweating more than usual. The Space Corps had little to go on when it came to planning how to counter the Vraxar threat and the lack of intel ensured the potential significance of every lead was enormous.

An hour passed until Pointer professed herself satisfied. "The surface was exceptionally uneven on the dark side of Auvial. There was room to hide a dozen smaller warships."

"It's definitely clear?"

"There are no small ships and certainly nothing Neutraliser-sized."

"This feels like it's turning into a waste of time," said Blake. "What's the third planet?"

Pointer called up the details. "This one's called Saird."

"Where do they pull this crap from?" he muttered.

"There are only twenty-six letters to name an effectively infinite number of planets..." Quinn began.

Blake was aware of the facts but wasn't interested in hearing them spelled out to him. He waved for silence. "What about the sun?" he asked. "That would make a pretty good place to park a war fleet, wouldn't it?"

"Depends on your definition of *good*," said Quinn.

"We don't know how the Vraxar got here," said Blake. "If they flew directly here, their system of coordinates should still function. If they did what the Estral did before and came through a wormhole we don't know about, maybe they have no working system of navigation."

"A sun would make a good point of reference," said Pointer. "There again, so would a planet – any planet."

"Are you thinking of taking a closer look at Cheops-A?" asked Hawkins. "I hope you realise precisely how massive it is."

"A circumference of three hundred million klicks," said Blake. "Yes, it's a big old star. Bring it up on the main viewscreen for me."

The image on the bulkhead changed from a one of image-intensified darkness to a series of sensor-attenuated reds and oranges. Light filled the bridge and the crew were forced to shield their eyes.

"Turn it down a bit," said Blake.

"Sorry. Here you go."

Without a side-by-side comparison against a smaller sun, Cheops-A looked like any other red supergiant. Its surface roiled and burned, each millisecond generating an incomprehensible quantity of energy and hurling it out into the unlimited reaches of space.

"Three hundred million klicks around," repeated Blake.

He shivered at the magnitude of the number. No matter how far any living species advanced, their greatest creations would be nothing compared to this.

"I don't think we have the capability to scan it," said Pointer. "There's too much interference for the sensors to produce a reliable reading."

"Our prospectors didn't even bother trying," said Hawkins. "They recorded the size and a few unusual features and that's about it."

"This one will supernova in less than ninety thousand years," said Quinn. "I don't have to be reminded we'll be gone before it happens."

"The Vraxar shouldn't need to hide from us, sir. There's no reason for them to be anywhere other than sitting patiently in deep space or orbiting around a planet somewhere."

"How do the Vraxar know they don't need to hide from us?" Blake asked. "They attacked one of our planets and overcame it easily enough. However, we did manage to shoot down three of their warships. They have no idea how many other *ES Lucid*s we have in our fleet. The Confederation could span a hundred thousand worlds and have a fleet of twenty thousand."

"They probably got the idea that we're a lot smaller than that," said Pointer.

"I'm sure, but think about it Lieutenant – the Vraxar must have been fighting for centuries. Maybe even longer. Perhaps they've learned to act cautiously in the opening stages. They shut down Atlantis easily enough, that's true. It was still a lightning raid – in and out once they had what they came for."

Pointer nodded. "As soon as they find out how few we are, they'll have no need to hide."

"Could be."

"That still doesn't mean they're here," said Quinn.

"It suggests we shouldn't expect the Vraxar to be sitting brazenly out in the open, waiting for us to find them," said Hawkins. "Maybe the Captain's right and they're sitting close to Cheops-A."

"Let's hope I'm wrong," said Blake. "A single circuit will take weeks, even at the *Blackbird*'s highest speed."

"Want me to speak to the *Juniper* and see if they'll send out a team?" asked Pointer.

"They aren't going to commit anything on the basis of our guesswork, Lieutenant. The monitoring station saw a ghost and we're here to check it out. There'll be no fleet to help us."

"Does that mean we're going to Saird?"

"It does. Fleet Admiral Duggan would hang me by the neck from the back of the *Maximilian* at high lightspeed if he learned I'd chosen to scan an entire red supergiant before finishing up with the smaller stuff around it."

"It's really not feasible for one vessel to scan Cheops-A," said Pointer quietly. "I need to make sure you're aware of that, sir."

"Consider me informed, Lieutenant. I'll take us in towards Saird."

"This is a hot one. There's plenty of gas and plenty of radiation. We won't be able to make the same quick flyover as we did for the other planets," said Pointer.

"I have every confidence in you, Lieutenant." *I actually mean it*, he thought in surprise. He chuckled inwardly. *What's the world coming to?*

They didn't make it as far as planet Saird.

"Sir?" asked Pointer with rather more timidity than usual.

Blake detected something in the question and was instantly alert. "What is it, Lieutenant?"

"I mentioned the wide scanning arc on these Hynus sensor arrays. With the old kit, you point an array at something you want to examine and then try to interpret the data. These Hynus sensors can take in a lot more. Even with a load of Obsidiar processors to back things up, they take in far more data than we can handle."

"You've found something," he stated.

"Yes, sir." She brought up a chart on one of her screens and showed Blake the accompanying image.

"What is it?" he asked.

"I can't be certain, sir. This double-peak on the chart shows there are two objects near to Cheops-A."

"Transfer the data to Lieutenant Quinn."

"She already did, sir," said Quinn. "That's a good spot, Lieutenant."

"You can shake hands afterwards," said Blake. "What is it?"

There was uncertainty in Quinn's voice. "There isn't a hope in hell of giving you an accurate assessment, sir. We're too far away."

"It's not a natural fluctuation, is it? Something fooling the sensors?"

"Absolutely not."

"We'll need to take a look. Are you sending everything on to the *Juniper*, Lieutenant Pointer?"

"Yes, sir. I'm updating them every few minutes."

"These objects you found are too far away for the tactical

system to register them as targets," said Blake. "The navigational system won't accept them either."

"I'm not surprised," said Pointer. "Whatever we've found, it's too close to Cheops-A for the sensors to get a solid lock. There's a lot of interference."

"Let's go and find them," Blake replied.

With a surge of acceleration, the ES Blackbird reached its maximum gravity drive velocity of three thousand two hundred kilometres per second. Blake was sure no other vessel in the Space Corps could match it.

"It'll be seven hours until intercept," said Quinn.

Blake wasn't happy. "That's too long."

"There's a chance we might lose them as well, sir. The target objects are moving at speed and interference from Cheops-A is making it hard to keep track."

"Are you telling me there's a chance you might lose them?"

"Yes, sir. Or they might go to lightspeed."

"The presence of these objects is significant enough," said Blake. He rubbed his chin in thought. "It's imperative we gather more information. How far away from the sun are they?"

"Sixty million klicks, give or take," said Pointer.

"Hot enough to make us sweat, not enough to melt the hull," said Hawkins.

"If we perform a short range lightspeed transit, will the stealth modules function amongst all the interference?" asked Blake.

The question was met with silence. He looked at Pointer and Hawkins and they averted their eyes. It wasn't really their field.

"Lieutenant Quinn?"

Quinn shifted uncomfortably at the question. "I don't know, sir."

"Are you able to put together a halfway reliable guess?"

"We don't need to land on their doorstep, do we?"

"If we come to within half a million klicks it'll give us a better chance of getting a thorough scan."

"We could try going to seventy million klicks from Cheops and see how the stealth modules hold up. I'd be confident at seventy million."

"Whatever you decide, you need to make your mind up quickly, sir," said Pointer. "They're entering an area of heavier interference. It might be that I lose them entirely."

Sometimes you gotta take risks.

"Fire us towards Cheops. Aim to arrive half a million klicks away from the target objects."

Quinn didn't question it further. "Yes, sir. Half a million klicks it is."

The *ES Blackbird*'s immensely powerful cluster of processors didn't take long to do the lightspeed calculations. They churned away for a few seconds and then hurled the spy ship towards Cheops-A. Blake did his best to prepare for the double transition. It made him feel like crap but this time he managed to put on the same outward show of indifference as Quinn and Hawkins. Pointer appeared to be adapting and she spared a second to look up from her console in order to grin defiantly when he glanced across.

"Where are those spaceships?" Blake asked. "And what's the status on the stealth modules?"

"The stealth modules are active and they appear to be holding up," said Quinn, not trying to disguise his relief.

"I'm having difficulty finding the targets," said Pointer.

"Are we definitely in the right place?"

"Bang on target," confirmed Quinn.

Blake chewed on his lower lip as Pointer did her thing. While he waited, he cast his eyes over the various status displays on his console. Sixty million kilometres was a good distance but given how much energy was pouring out of Cheops-A, it wasn't as far as he'd have liked.

"We've got a few amber warnings," he said. "Good job we're shielded from solar radiation."

"Heavily shielded," said Hawkins.

"I've found them!"

"Something tells me I'm not going to like what you're about to say."

"No, you're not. You're really not going to like it."

"Pass the details to my console."

"Over to you and Lieutenant Quinn."

"Holy crap," said Quinn.

Blake remained silent for a moment, unsure what to say. "There's no possibility of a misread?"

"No, sir. What you're seeing is an accurate representation of what there is."

It wasn't two objects as they'd first thought. In fact, there were four vessels, moving in a close formation and following a trajectory that kept them sixty million kilometres above the surface of Cheops-A. Blake grabbed the control bars and swung the *Blackbird* on a course that would shadow them. The enemy warships were moving at two thousand klicks per second, so it was no effort to keep up.

"Forty thousand metres long," he said.

"Forty-one thousand, sir."

"Plus two Neutralisers and a battleship."

Blake's statement of what everyone could already see was met with dumbfounded silence.

"What the hell is it?" asked Hawkins.

"Damned if I know. Any signs we've been detected?"

"I doubt it, sir. They'll suffer the same effects from the interference as we are. The difference is, we know there's something to search for."

"I'm reading a simultaneous surge across each of the four enemy vessels," said Quinn. "They're warming up fission engines."

Blake swore.

Seconds later, the Vraxar were gone into high lightspeed, leaving the Cheops-A system far behind.

"Can you get a reading from that fission signature?" asked Blake at once. "It's vital we discover where they're going."

"Our sensors captured plenty of information," said Pointer.

"I'm holding the details in our data arrays," said Quinn. "I'll start off the predictive flight modelling process. It's going to slow everything else down for a while."

"Can you predict how long until you'll have a result?"

"Not yet. As the analysis progresses I'll have a greater chance of narrowing it down."

"Keep me informed," said Blake. "And get me Fleet Admiral Duggan. He needs to hear this directly."

Several hours later, the ES *Blackbird* was still in the Cheops-A system, skimming far above the sun's corona at the same altitude of sixty million kilometres. It was hot enough to trigger alarms, but not enough to melt the external plating of the spy craft. The intense radiation was causing sporadic movement on a few of the gauges which monitored a variety of critical systems.

The waiting was painful and Blake drummed his fingers until they ached. Duggan's orders were for them to continue the hunt for Vraxar around the sun. In reality, there was so much area to search they were doing nothing more than killing time until the *Blackbird*'s sixteen processing cores could produce a meaningful guess as to where the Vraxar had gone.

"It's been thirty hours," said Blake. "My patience is running low."

"I think it's because there were four big ships in one go, sir," Quinn replied. "Their jump into lightspeed produced vastly more energy than a single ship and there's a lot more to analyse." He paused. "I think it's about finished."

Blake was caught unawares by the suddenness. "What are the findings?"

"One moment," said Quinn. "I've got a list of three possible destinations, ranked in order of likelihood."

"Anywhere we know about?"

Quinn's eyes widened and his face went pale. "Sir? The flight modelling software has placed the moon Nesta T-3 at the top of the list."

"Get me a comms channel," snapped Blake. "They're going after the *Juniper*!"

CHAPTER EIGHT

THE *JUNIPER* NEVER REALLY SLEPT. Many of the orbital's personnel had worked there for so long, they'd developed their own shift patterns. The Space Corps scheduling computers produced countless rotas and tallied up endless hours clocked. As long as targets and milestones were met, a degree of flexibility was permitted.

There were quieter periods, times during which eighty percent or more of the *Juniper*'s staff were either off duty or asleep. It was during one of these periods it happened.

Seventy thousand kilometres from the orbital, a fission cloud formed in the nothingness of space. The *Juniper*'s sensors detected the anomaly immediately. There were no additional Space Corps warships due here for another three days, so the orbital's AI cores sent Priority 1 messages to dozens of different people across half a dozen locations both within the *Juniper* and on distant planets.

The Imposition class cruiser *ES Impact Crater*, stationed nearby, was halfway around the moon Nesta-T3. Its battle computer received a warning to go on full alert and the warship's

AI fired up the gravity drives before the human captain had the time to comprehend the urgency of the situation. The *Impact Crater* reached its peak velocity and flew across the cold surface of the moon at an altitude of only a few hundred kilometres.

Within the *Juniper*'s main command and control room, personnel scrambled to assess the risks. The woman in charge on this particular shift – Captain Marta Drake – found the decision taken out of her hands. The orbital's immense array of Obsidiar processors had seen enough and they initiated the warm-up routines for the fission engines.

The *Juniper*'s lightspeed engines were kept running at tick over. Unfortunately, the huge orbital wasn't a spaceship and it wasn't designed to travel at the drop of a hat. Time and preparations were needed.

Twelve seconds after the incoming fission signature was detected, four Vraxar warships entered local space. In the three additional seconds before the *Juniper*'s vast Gallenium engines were shut down, Captain Drake was granted sight of what had come.

There was a Vraxar battleship. It was six thousand metres of black metal, shaped like an ungainly, elongated cuboid, with blocky outcroppings and thousands of slender pillar-like arrays of unknown purpose.

Along with the battleship there were two Vraxar Neutralisers. They looked similar to the file pictures of the old Estral ship *Excoliar* – at eighteen thousand metres in length, they had a trapezoidal central section with cylindrical beams jutting from two opposite faces. At the end of each beam was a sphere, crackling with a sickly green of barely-restrained energy.

The last vessel was something else entirely. It was more than forty thousand metres in length and bulky with it. This vessel's shape was similar to that of the Vraxar battleship, except there were additional turrets dotted about its surface. Barrels protruded from these turrets, with enormous bores and an obvious threat that the weapons could punch a hole clean through anything smaller than a light cruiser.

The spaceship had colossal hangar doors, clearly visible beneath. These doors were already opening, revealing tantalising glimpses of a cargo bay that stretched for much of the vessel's length. There was room inside to contain four or more Neutralisers. Or a single, larger object.

———

LIEUTENANT ERIC MCKINNEY was fighting boredom. After years of the same old patrols around the same old Tillos base, he'd finally had a taste of the action and now he wanted more. The *Juniper* orbital was technically impressive and given its size, there was plenty of interior space. Somehow it still felt confining.

"When will the Vraxar come back, Lieutenant?" asked Corporal Johnny Li. "I can see you want to shoot something."

"Word is, they might take years to crack the encryption on that data array they stole on Tillos," said Rank 1 Trooper Huey Roldan. "Imagine that, Lieutenant? Years."

"A man could get old and die before it happens," said Corporal Nitro Bannerman.

McKinney could tell when the baited hook was being dangled in front of him and he steadfastly ignored the temptation to bite. He leaned back in his chair and stared at the metal ceiling of the level 128 break out area. He did his best to imagine blue sky with clouds. It was no good. McKinney couldn't put words to it, but the *Juniper* felt like a tightly closed metal coffin.

Unwilling to succumb to the tedium, McKinney had developed the twice daily habit of running a few laps around some of the more remote areas of the orbital. There were plenty of gyms and the troops had access to personal trainers. Somehow it didn't appeal.

So, before and after every duty period, McKinney would put on a spacesuit and run six kilometres through the *Juniper's* interior. It garnered him more than his fair share of curious looks and the occasional expression of outright hostility, usually from one of the more short-tempered scientists or researchers. He didn't care and gradually some of his companions-in-arms from the Tillos base joined him in his routine. Tonight's run had been more popular than usual.

"The next ten days are twelve-hour shifts," said Li, too carefree to actually grumble about the vagaries of the schedule. He cast his eyes around the near-empty room. "Where is everyone?"

"It's late," said R1T Zack Chance. "They'll be in bed."

"Or drinking illicit liquor," said Dexter Webb, with a faraway expression.

"It's only us poor soldiers that aren't allowed to get pissed, you know that don't you?" asked R1T Martin Garcia. "Everyone else is trusted they won't try to steal important hardware."

"Like heavy cruisers."

"Yeah. Lock 'em up or lose 'em," said Darell Causey.

The destruction of the Tillos base hadn't been too long back. McKinney and his men had been out hunting AWOLs, rumoured to have got themselves drunk by extracting alcohol from a malfunctioning replicator. They never did find out what happened to the missing soldiers, but the story that they'd been attempting to steal the Galactic class *ES Lucid* was already well through the process of entering folklore amongst some of the troops.

"I think I'm going to catch an airlift back to the barracks," said McKinney, climbing from the meagre padding of the break out area chair.

At that moment, he heard the sound of an alarm somewhere

within the depths of the orbital. High up on the nearest wall, a
red light pulsed softly.

"What the hell?" asked Roldan.

"We need to check in and find out what's happening," said
McKinney. "All of you – up!"

In moments, the other six men were on their feet and looking
along the four exits from the room, in the hope they might
find clues.

McKinney was rather more practical. He dropped his spacesuit visor into place and patched into one of the local comms
nodes. There was plenty of noise, but as yet no indication what
the matter was. He left his visor in place.

"Something's wrong. Get your visors down – and connect to
the Squad A comms group I've just created."

"I think we're about to lose power," said Li with remarkable
prescience.

"What makes you say..."

A few metres away, the row of free access public terminals
went blank. A couple of seconds later, the lights went out, not
only in the break out area, but in the adjoining corridors. The
sensor in McKinney's visor adapted almost at once, projecting an
image of green shapes and lines onto his HUD. Then, the lights
flickered and returned, soon joined once again by the noise of the
siren. The bank of consoles remained offline.

"It can't be, can it?" asked Garcia. "We just got away from
that shit."

"Shhh!" McKinney urged. "Listen!"

"What for?" asked Webb. "I can't hear anything."

"The *Juniper*'s engines are gone," said Roldan.

He was right – the ever-present, comforting vibration of the
Juniper's dual drives was missing. McKinney crouched down and
pressed one of his palms to the bare floor. The material of the

spacesuit was an excellent insulator, but it still allowed a muted sense of touch.

"They've found us," he said.

McKinney checked through the lists of security personnel and found out who was in charge. He attempted to open a channel to Captain Marta Drake and wasn't surprised when he couldn't get through. There were another thirty soldiers of lieutenant rank on the *Juniper* and not one of them was available on the comms. McKinney swore. There were other senior personnel on the orbital, many of them in the science and research arm of the Space Corps. In addition, there were fifteen of captain rank aside from Captain Drake. Captain Gary Nagy appeared briefly online and McKinney requested a channel.

"Who is this?" asked Nagy.

"Lieutenant McKinney, sir."

"Get the hell out of my channel, Lieutenant McKinney. I've got to speak to Admiral Murray."

"Sir, the Vraxar have..."

It was too late – Nagy was gone. In truth, McKinney wasn't sure exactly what he'd expected. He cursed himself. *Already looking to others. Stop pissing about and do something.*

A name he recognized came onto the comms network. In a flash, McKinney connected to it.

"Corporal Evans?"

"Sir? What's going on?"

"Vraxar. Round up who you can. Get them suited, kitted and await orders. There're seven of us on level 128 – we're going to make for the armoury on 197. Bring who you can and meet us there."

"Shouldn't there be someone taking charge, sir?"

"You'd think. It's only been five minutes – I'm sure they're working on a response."

"I'll listen out for updates."

McKinney ended the connection and addressed those with him.

"We can't stand around here. Our first stop is the armoury – while we're running for it, I'm going to see if I can prepare some sort of organised response until a senior officer steps in. There are three thousand ground troops onboard and as far as I can see, not one of them is doing anything useful."

With that, he oriented himself and started towards one of the exit corridors.

"The closest armoury is on level 197," said Corporal Li. "You're going the wrong way."

McKinney paused mid-step. "The airlifts," he said.

"Maybe not working," confirmed Li.

"There might be some residual power. We'll check it out before running up nearly seventy flights of steps."

The *Juniper* was big and although much of it was taken up by engines, hangars and monitoring arrays, the internal levels were widely-spaced within its hull. Seventy flights would be a hard run if the airlifts weren't powered up.

The squad reached a bank of airlifts after a hard run along one of the wide corridors. There was no housing in this part of the *Juniper* so there were few other personnel in evidence. Those they passed looked confused and alarmed. McKinney didn't want to get bogged down speaking to everyone they met, so he ignored the questions shouted in his wake.

There was a power light on the airlift. McKinney hammered on one of the buttons with the flat of his hand.

"Come on," he muttered.

The airlift took longer than expected and he pressed the side of his head to the doors to allow the visor microphone to pick up any sound from the other side. The airlifts were silent in operation and even quieter when they weren't functioning. It didn't take long for McKinney to accept the inevitable and he kicked the door in frustration.

"The steps are along here, Lieutenant," said Webb. "It's one of the main stairwells and should take us up as far as level 175."

McKinney waved them onwards and jogged after, doing his best to make sense of the jumbled noise on the *Juniper's* internal comms. Contrary to his prior belief, promotion to the rank of lieutenant didn't give him any greater level of access than he'd been granted as a sergeant. Everything in the Space Corps was placed into its own compartment, outside of which you weren't permitted to wander. The fact of the matter was, ground troops were expected to stay within their unit and to mostly communicate within that same group of men and women. McKinney was able to speak to any of the warship captains currently on the *Juniper*, but he could only request a channel rather than forcing one open. As a consequence, he discovered he was side-lined and any attempts to discover specifics about the current situation were quickly rebuffed.

Ahead, his squad were getting away from him, their feet pounding along the gradually-curving corridor.

McKinney picked up the pace, doing his best to ignore the distant siren, the strobing reds of the alarm and the dull thud of his own feet on the alloy floor. Ahead, Corporal Bannerman was the first to reach the stairwell. The man broke left and vanished from sight, with the others following.

"Keep moving," McKinney urged.

The squad didn't need encouragement and it was a struggle to keep up with them. The steps were solid, like they were hacked from the insides of a huge block of metal. They climbed for twenty metres and then switched back on themselves. From experience McKinney knew they were hardly used, which was unusual given the high fitness demands the Space Corps placed on its personnel. There were a few people hurrying in both directions. He pushed past them, giving only the briefest of responses to those who spoke.

After the first four or five flights, McKinney found himself slowing - his reserves of energy were already drained from two hard runs and a day of patrol duty. The loudness of his breathing prevented him from fully registering the first of the explosions.

"Crap, what was that?" asked Li, stopping abruptly to listen.

"Wait up!" shouted McKinney.

There was another explosion and then another. The sounds were muted by the density of the *Juniper*'s walls.

"Are they going to blow us to pieces?" asked Webb.

"I don't know," said McKinney.

He remained in place, listening intently. More explosions came, their direction impossible to pin down. Then, for a time, there was silence and McKinney directed the men to continue climbing. He wasn't used to getting hunches, but he had a feeling something terrible was coming.

"Can you hear that?" asked Garcia.

"My suit's registering a ten-klick wind," said Bannerman in puzzlement. "Now it's fifteen."

"That's what the noise is," said Garcia. "It sounds like wind blowing through a narrow space."

McKinney could hear it too, though he had no idea what was causing it. The movement speed of the air had increased to twenty kilometres per hour. It wasn't sufficient to knock anyone over, though it was enough to push someone off balance if they weren't careful.

"Comms noise on levels 20 through 35 is dying off," said Bannerman.

"Same on 36 through 50," said McKinney.

"Levels 226 to 275 are showing reduced comms activity now, sir."

"Are they shutting the comms down?" asked McKinney.

Bannerman was a comms man and knew his stuff. "No, sir, I don't believe they're shutting anything down. If you look at the list of receptors, you can see they're still active."

"That can't be right. If the receptors are open and there's no one on the comms, that must mean they're...?"

"...dead," said Bannerman. "Or unconscious. It's the Vraxar, sir. I know which my money is on."

McKinney watched the *Juniper*'s sensor network as, section by section, the noise cut off. A couple of senior officers on the topmost levels attempted to assert some degree of control and there were sporadic requests for assistance elsewhere. It was too late.

"My suit's picking up something in the air," said Causey.

"Toxins," said McKinney. "My suit doesn't recognize them."

"Nope."

The voice of Corporal Evans intruded. "Sir? It's all going to shit around here. Me and some of the guys got suited up and were coming towards the 197 armoury, then everyone just started dying." There was a note of panic in the man's voice.

"Steady, Corporal. How many are you and what weapons have you got?"

"There's me and another ten. We've got a few gauss pistols and most of us have rifles. Nothing else."

"What have you seen? Are there any hostiles?"

"No, sir, there's nothing. Just lots and lots of dead people."

"Keep your visors down – they're pumping some kind of toxin into the air circulation system. Get to the armoury on the double and if you find anyone else alive, bring them with you. The *Juniper*'s been attacked and we need to find out what the hell is going on and put a stop to it."

Even as he said the words, he realised how feeble they sounded. If they managed to meet up with Evans and his men, that would only make a total of eighteen. The *Juniper* was massive and it didn't seem likely the Vraxar would be especially troubled by such a tiny amount of resistance.

The quantity of the unknown toxin in the air increased, though the spacesuit's computer was still unable to offer a suggestion as to what it might be. At the moment it was irrelevant – the substance was deadly and McKinney had no intention of exposing himself to it by lifting his visor.

With his squad gathered around, he dropped to his haunches on one of the stairwell landings. The action he thought he craved had come to him and now he found it wasn't worth the price. It was certain that thousands of the *Juniper*'s personnel were dead. The Vraxar had come for something and once again McKinney found himself having to conjure up a way to stop them. Except this time there was no *ES Lucid* waiting in the hangar bay to shoot the alien bastards out of the skies.

CHAPTER NINE

FLEET ADMIRAL DUGGAN sat forward in his chair and stared intently at his desktop communicator. A connection was open to Captain Charlie Blake on the *ES Blackbird*.

"The warning was too late," said Fleet Admiral Duggan. "We've lost contact with the *Juniper*."

The response took a fraction of a second to come – a sign of the distances between New Earth and the Cheops-A solar system. "Is there anything available to mount an assault, sir?" asked Blake.

"The *Maximilian* will be ready in two days. The technicians are running the final connections to its Obsidiar drive. It would take an additional eight days to reach the *Juniper*. After that, the *ES Abyss* will land and work will commence fitting an Obsidiar core to that one. Even with efficiency improvements, the shipyard estimates a further sixteen days. There are more warships lined up after the *Abyss* and we'll fit them out, one at a time."

"Does that mean the *Maximilian* isn't coming?"

"That is yet to be decided. I won't throw it at the Vraxar just for the sake of doing something. The *Juniper* is precious, but..."

"We're working on the assumption it's already lost?"

Blake talked fast and with the eagerness of the young. In spite of his efforts to be accommodating, Duggan found it irritating.

"Don't interrupt me when I'm talking," he snapped.

His wife Lucy was in the room with him. She moved to stand behind him and placed her hands on his shoulders. He felt the tension ease and he was able to speak calmly.

"You're not correct, Captain Blake – we have to assume the *Juniper* is going to be *difficult* to recover and that there may be extensive casualties. I will not give up on our men and women, but without further intelligence, we are not going to cast our battleships into those turbulent waters."

"Let me and my crew bring the ES *Blackbird* to Nesta-T3, sir. If there are any Vraxar remaining at Cheops-A we stand little chance of finding them."

Duggan heard the sound of a young female voice in the background, before Blake resumed speaking.

"My comms lieutenant estimates that with an entire *year* of searching, there's only a thirty percent chance of locating any Vraxar ships in orbit around a sun of this size, sir."

Duggan smiled, remembering the days when he, too, had valued the illusionary solidity of putting a number to everything - the chance of life or death, success or failure calculated to twenty decimal places by a computer and spat onto a screen to be digested like the protein paste from a Ghast replicator.

"I want you to return to Nesta-T3," he said. "Keep an eye on the situation and report in with anything you learn."

"Will do, sir. Any chance of you telling me what this weapon is? We might need it."

"I'll let you know if the situation arises. Now get yourself into lightspeed."

Duggan ended the connection.

"John, why won't you tell him?" asked his wife when the communicator light winked out.

He turned in his chair and looked into her face. The lines in her skin were fine, but her hair was as dark as ever and the glittering eyes had lost nothing of what first drew him to her. "He doesn't need to know. We used one before and you know what the consequences might be."

"We used two," she corrected him. "You're not telling him because he keeps asking."

"An Obsidiar bomb...it's a lot of responsibility."

"You don't think he's ready for it?"

Duggan shook his head. "I'm not sure he has the maturity to make the right call."

"Maybe he'll learn."

"I have hopes."

"What next?"

"I'm waiting for an update from the Council. If they give me the go-ahead I'll speak to the Ghasts. Subjos Kion-Tur offered the services of three Oblivions in exchange for twenty percent of our Obsidiar. That's if the price hasn't gone up."

His wife had never been one to miss an observation. "They may regret their generosity once they see what they're up against."

At any other time, Duggan might have laughed. "The Ghasts have never feared war, have they? I've spoken to a few of them over the last week and there's a definite shift. You know what? I think they want revenge on the Vraxar for what they did to the Estral."

"The Ghasts hated the Estral!"

"In a funny way, I think they coveted them as *their* enemy. Or maybe I'm reading it wrong and time had started to heal the old wounds. Whatever the answer, I'm sure the Ghasts are looking for an excuse to get involved. The only sticking point is pride –

they can't offer their assistance freely since I've already turned down an offer of paid help."

"The Obsidiar will overcome that obstacle."

"It has to. I'd hoped the Vraxar would go away for a while. In my head I had plans – organisation, construction, preparation. I envisaged a fleet of warships. And this news of Obsidiar on the frontier worlds. I told myself if we could take the opportunity – grasp it and pay a fair price, we might just have a chance."

"And now?"

"Now I can see the Vraxar are here to stay. They aren't going to give us the time to prepare for their return. Why should they fight fair? This is something they've been doing for a lot longer than we have and it's going to take every ounce of ingenuity to hold them off."

"Do you think we can do it?" she asked softly.

The set of his jaw told of his determination. "If I allowed myself to give into doubt, I might as well tender my resignation to the Council."

"Have you come up with any new theories about how the Vraxar got here? Is there another new wormhole out there some-where that we don't know about?"

"The numbers don't add up, Lucy. There are other worm-holes, the closest being five years high lightspeed from here. The *Valpian*'s databanks told us there were other wormholes in Estral space. The trouble is, the chance of them being linked is infinites-imally small. In other words, that isn't how the Vraxar reached Confederation Space."

"And the analysts figured out that it's ninety years high light-speed between here and Estral territory?"

"Give or take. So even if the Vraxar found out about us from stolen Estral data, they would have taken a lot longer than forty years to get here."

"Unless their warships are a lot faster than ours and

equipped with something similar to an Obsidiar drive. As fast as the *ES Blackbird*, perhaps."

"That doesn't work either. Those smaller warships which Captain Blake shot down in the *ES Lucid* – there was nothing about them which suggests they could travel so fast."

"They were equipped with energy shields."

"Which didn't hold up to much punishment, suggesting they weren't backed up by a lot of Obsidiar."

"Maybe they came in the hold of something else. You remember how the Estral mothership brought a fleet in its main bay."

"I remember."

"You're determined that it's something else, aren't you?"

"Yes. I just don't know what it is."

"There are people waiting to speak with you."

Seven lights flashed on Duggan's desktop communicator, appearing with a suddenness that suggested a coordinated effort. Behind each light waited a high-priority caller of the type able to bypass his personal assistant Cerys in order to reach him directly.

"The Council are holding an emergency meeting," he said.

"Do you think they've reached a decision already? It's been less than two hours since you told them about the *Juniper*."

"That third flashing light is Councillor Stahl."

"I should go."

Duggan didn't answer. He reached out with a forefinger and stabbed at the communicator.

"Councillor Stahl," he said in greeting.

Moments later, he was lost in conversation. His wife kissed him on top of his head and quietly left the room.

———

LIEUTENANT ERIC MCKINNEY found the journey to the

level 197 armoury a test of his mental strength. He and his squad were able to keep to one of the main stairwells for much of the route, but at level 175, this particular stairwell ended and they were required to travel through a series of passages and corridors in order to reach another stairwell that went as far up as level 200.

"Shit, how many did they kill?" asked Huey Roldan.

Level 175 was the first floor of one of the housing modules on the *Juniper* and there were bodies everywhere. The hundreds of corpses were stiff, as though rigor mortis had set in with exceptional speed, leaving the orbital's men and women frozen in parodies of photographic poses. Alarms continued to sound, adding a sense of tragic urgency to a situation which had already reached its conclusion.

"Looks like they didn't even know the gas was coming," said Webb, pointing at a long cabinet on the wall of one corridor. The cabinet was open and rows of civilian spacesuits dangled from a rack, along with a hundred over-face visors. None of the men were trained in chemical warfare and didn't know if the Vraxar toxins killed when they were breathed in or if they simply needed to make contact with skin.

"Poor bastards weren't even trying to protect themselves."

"What happened to the fail safes?" asked Bannerman. "The *Juniper* is made up from thousands of compartments. A gas attack shouldn't be able to kill everyone."

"We saw how much control the Vraxar had over the secure base on Tillos," said McKinney. "See how all the doors are open? This is how they wage war and it seems as if they're good at it."

"How many personnel were there on the *Juniper*, sir?"

McKinney closed his eyes briefly. "More than ninety thousand."

"Damn."

They walked along a corridor of numbered rooms. Every

door was open, revealing the horrific secrets within. McKinney looked into a few of the rooms and found each one decorated with the personal touches that the Space Corps eschewed. The occupants were dead on the floor – they'd been woken by the alarms but had been given no guidance on what to do, so here they'd fallen.

"What's going to happen next, Lieutenant?" asked Zack Chance. "I mean, what are the Vraxar going to do? They've killed everyone and since we haven't been sucked out into the vacuum, I assume most of the *Juniper* is still intact."

McKinney had asked himself the same question. Surrounded by so much death, he found it difficult to focus and hadn't yet come up with an answer.

"I don't know," he said. "Maybe they came for the same thing as they wanted from Atlantis – intel showing them where to locate the other Confederation worlds. Could be they don't want to keep an entire war fleet waiting while they try to break into the ES *Determinant*'s memory arrays."

"How did they find the *Juniper*, then?"

"Like I said – this is their kind of war. You don't wipe out a hundred civilisations without figuring out how to find them first."

They reached the next stairwell, each man burdened with sights he'd never forget.

"Up," said McKinney. "And let's hope there're a few people alive and they just haven't been able to reach the comms."

The lights flickered on and off at sporadic intervals on the stairwell. Adapting to such rapid changes of contrast was a weakness of the visor sensors and McKinney's eyes felt the strain of watching the colours shift from grey to green and back again. Mercifully, the alarm siren was muted here and McKinney realised how much it was starting to grate on his already frayed nerves.

"Level 197," said Garcia, reading the sign above the exit doorway from the stairwell.

"What if the armoury door is closed?" asked Webb.

"All these other doors are open," Garcia replied.

"There's no door on the level 197 armoury," said McKinney. "It's behind a guard station and there are a couple of mini-turrets. The *Juniper*'s AI decides who gets in and out."

"What if it chooses to shoot us?" persisted Webb.

"Any more questions and I'll send you in first, soldier."

The corridors of level 197 were nearly empty. This was one of the maintenance levels, where small-scale repairs and refurbishments were done on minor, non-critical equipment. There was no need for anyone to be working here at night, though in a place the size of the *Juniper* nowhere was completely empty.

The exit passage from the stairwell went to the left and right, curving slightly as it did so. To McKinney's relief, the lights were working properly here, though the alarms were back up to full volume.

"I wish someone would shut them off," remarked Corporal Li, evidently thinking the same thing.

"We're probably stuck with them, Corporal. I'm going to use my suit." McKinney ordered his suit visor to attenuate the sound and was immediately grateful. He didn't like to reduce any type of input from his senses, no matter how annoying it might be. This time he made an exception.

"Which way?" asked Webb.

McKinney was denied the opportunity to answer. The floor lurched beneath his feet and he experienced a brief feeling of weightlessness. He put out a hand towards the wall in order to steady himself. The sensation passed quickly, but through his palms he noticed a heavy, low vibration. A sound rose to accompany it, increasing in volume until it became louder than the plaintive wailing of the alarms, overwhelming them with the deluge of its power.

Several of the men staggered and Chance fell to one knee. A chorus of questions flew across the comms, each demanding answers McKinney didn't have. Something thumped against the exterior of the *Juniper*'s hull, many levels above. Another followed, this one lower and nearer. There was a third and a fourth, each increasing in intensity as it came closer to level 197.

The fifth noise was more like a thunderous clang and it felt to McKinney as though someone had put a steel barrel over his head and struck it with a sledgehammer. With the sound came a shockwave. It pitched him hard against the wall, his shoulder taking the force of the impact. The wind was knocked from him and he struggled to remain on his feet.

As McKinney and his squad gathered their wits, the shuddering thumps continued on the levels below until eventually they either stopped or were too far away to be heard or felt.

"Whatever the hell that was, I don't think I'm going to like it," said Bannerman.

"The alarms have stopped," said Webb. "Do you think the Space Corps got a rescue ship here already?"

"Yeah, the cavalry has come and they've brought a sackful of medals and bottles of neat gin to say thank you to everyone who managed to live through this terrible attack."

"Piss off, Garcia."

"Quiet," McKinney ordered. "I can't think with you two bitching."

"Sorry, Lieutenant."

"We need to find a porthole."

"This stairwell is just off central," said Bannerman. "From memory, if we go left along here, we can cut a right and after that there's a main route leading to the outer wall."

"It doesn't take us too far off our route to the armoury either," said McKinney. "We'll go the way you've suggested."

The squad had recovered and they waited for him to give the order to move. He didn't delay and they set off along the left-hand corridor, running two abreast. They turned right after fifty metres, entering a new corridor as featureless as the others. Signs hung from the ceiling every so often, announcing new areas. There were doors to offices and consoles fitted into alcoves every thirty metres or so.

After a short distance, a long window appeared in the left-hand wall. McKinney looked into the room beyond and saw one of the clean rooms leading to the *Juniper's* tertiary fabrication area. The place was lit in stark white and he guessed it must have its own dedicated power supply separate from that which provided the emergency lighting.

"The doors are working, Lieutenant," said Roldan. "This facility must be isolated from everything else. Must run on batteries or something."

"There might be someone alive in there," said Chance.

"I don't think so," said Bannerman. "The fabs have their own comms section. I've just checked and there's no one making a call."

"I don't want to interfere with it either," said McKinney. "There's still a crapload of this toxin in the air and anyone inside should be safe from it. I don't know enough about clean rooms to risk breaking anything by sticking my head inside for a look."

"There's the outer wall ahead," said Bannerman, drawing McKinney's attention away from the fab area.

The corridor ended at another T-junction. There were five bodies in a pile – men and women dressed in the white uniforms of the fab workers.

"A porthole," said Webb.

"Yeah."

The porthole was on the opposite wall - it was a clear lens, about a metre in diameter. Though some kind of trickery McKinney didn't understand, these portholes allowed a clear view through a hundred metres of the *Juniper*'s external plating and into the depths of space. He'd spent more than his fair share of time looking through those near to the barracks area. Depending on the position of the *Juniper*, the views could be breathtaking.

The now-dead personnel had evidently gathered here for a look at whatever it was triggered the *Juniper*'s alarms and McKinney stepped gingerly across the bodies in order to get close enough to the porthole for its view to snap into focus.

He pressed his face close and stared for a long time in silence.

"Lieutenant? What is it?" asked Corporal Li.

"We're not in orbit anymore," McKinney said at last. "There's all sorts of stuff out of this porthole I don't recognize, but one there's one thing for sure – we're inside another vessel."

"But the *Juniper* is..."

"I know. The Vraxar have something bigger. Those heavy noises we heard must have been gravity clamps attaching to the hull."

"What now?" asked Roldan. "I doubt they're going to stick us into a specimen jar and feed us worms."

"We get to the armoury," said McKinney firmly. "We group up and we think. I don't know about you, but I don't want to die just yet. If it's inevitable, I'm going to do as much damage to the Vraxar as I can."

Confronted with McKinney's suggestion of inevitability, the squad stirred uneasily. Without another word spoken between them, the seven men resumed their journey to the armoury.

CHAPTER TEN

"CORPORAL EVANS," said McKinney, eyeing up the eleven suited figures standing nervously at the armoury entrance. "Glad you could make it."

"We got kitted up while we waited, sir. There didn't seem like any point in waiting."

"Good. No plasma repeaters?"

"No, sir. Still, the ones we found are newer models than those we had on Tillos. Higher rate of fire and a bigger magazine."

"The ones we had did the business."

McKinney ordered the men with him to take what they needed from the armoury. It was the good stuff – presumably the *Juniper* saw the advanced weaponry before end-of-the-road places like Atlantis. It hadn't done the guards much good and there were a dozen of them within their station. They were dressed in military-issue spacesuits, but not one of them wore a visor. It wasn't the best time to judge, but McKinney couldn't help thinking this was another example of ingrained incompetence resulting from the troops and their commanding officers becoming too comfortable. It made them easy targets.

"Get what you need. Corporal Bannerman - the comms packs are in that corner. Webb, pick up a plasma launcher. Everyone else, rifles, grenades and repeaters."

Minutes later, they emerged, with McKinney feeling considerably more enabled than he had before reaching the armoury. He rested his hand on the barrel of the repeater and felt the comforting weight of its power cell. These new models were slung across a soldier's back, making them easier to handle even though their weight was increased.

What made these repeaters even better was how they interacted with the gauss rifles. If you wanted to swap weapons quickly, you could simply press the rifle to the side of the repeater pack. It would stick and wouldn't come loose until it detected a grip-and-pull motion from a soldier's hand.

"Like magnets, only different," said Corporal Li, familiarising himself with the method.

"What now, sir?" asked Bannerman. His comms pack was active and positioned at his feet.

"Find out who's alive. The suits can't access as many receptors as that pack, right?"

"Yes, sir. I'll see what we have."

The news wasn't good. "There's no one alive below us, sir. Or at least no one who's got a communicator. It's mostly personnel quarters down there – they have intercoms but I don't think they can patch into the main comms system."

"What about command and control? On what level is Admiral Murray stationed?"

"His personal communicator is located on level 283. Command and control fills a few levels above and below."

"And you're getting nothing from there?"

"No, sir."

"I can't believe we're the only ones alive."

Bannerman raised a hand for silence and listened intently to something. "We're not. I've got Sergeant Rod Woods on, sir."

"Where is he? What's his status?"

"He's way up on level 372. He's got eight soldiers with him, as well as non-combat personnel."

"How many non-coms?"

"Ten. Sergeant Woods reports they lack weaponry and they are heading towards the level 320 armoury. After that they were going to try their luck finding a shuttle."

"Tell him to stick with that plan unless I tell him otherwise."

"Sergeant Woods wants to know what the hell we're going to do about this current situation, sir."

"I'm working on it."

Bit by bit, Corporal Bannerman managed to contact the scattered groups remaining on the *Juniper*. His earlier assertion that there was no one alive on the lower levels turned out to be incorrect – there were three other groups, all on level 95 in an area which housed the *Juniper*'s primary fabrication facilities. The associated clean rooms had evidently been proof against the airborne toxins and given the scientists and technicians enough time to get into their spacesuits.

There was another group of survivors on one of the upper floors, in addition to those with Sergeant Woods. This group was based in Hangar Bay One on level 300. It was commonplace for the personnel working there to wear a spacesuit owing to the high risk of exposure to vacuum. The lead technician was a woman called Hattie Rhodes.

"Tech Officer Rhodes is in charge of a team of twenty, sir. They're all accounted for, though she says there have been a few *brown suit moments* amongst them."

"I'll bet. Ask her to confirm if the docked spaceships are powered up."

"Nothing's working, sir. Everything with a missile tube is offline."

McKinney caught something in the words. "Does that mean there's something that isn't offline?"

"Checking. There's nothing which she describes as *official*, but there's an ancient shuttle which doesn't run on Gallenium. Its engines are still online."

"What the hell is it doing on the *Juniper*?"

"TO Rhodes tells me she and some of her guys were fixing it up. It's a hobby they have. It doesn't matter – the external bay doors are closed and powered off. She says there's no way to get them open unless you have a lorry jack which can lift a billion tonnes. Besides, the shuttle is definitely not lightspeed capable and will take approximately ten years to reach Atlantis."

"Instruct TO Rhodes to keep her head down until I say otherwise."

"Roger."

McKinney was confronted with the uncomfortable truth – he was the highest-ranking officer left onboard with access to the *Juniper*'s internal comms and quite possibly the highest-ranking officer alive.

"What now, Lieutenant?" asked Corporal Li. "The men are getting itchy feet."

"Keep them in line," he growled. "This is a complex situation."

He prowled around the open area outside the armoury, doing his best to form a coherent strategy on how to proceed. They were trapped inside the *Juniper*, which was in turn stuck inside the hangar of what he felt certain was some kind of Vraxar mothership. Almost everyone was dead and there was no realistic hope of an immediate rescue. On top of that, he didn't know exactly what the Vraxar had in mind for the orbital. Maybe they just wanted it for spares. For some reason, the idea didn't fit.

"Corporal Bannerman, can you get a distress signal out with that comms pack?"

"I already tried, Lieutenant. The signal report shows a significant degradation when it passes through the walls of the *Juniper*. After that, it gets lost somewhere in the hull of this Vraxar ship. It might be that something is getting out into space – it won't be going anywhere very fast."

"The *Juniper* is running on its own backup comms. Can you tap into them and use them as a booster?"

"That would be a good idea, sir. Even the *Juniper*'s backup comms are way better than what this pack can do. The problem is, I don't have the authority to piggyback onto the central comms."

"Would I have the authority?"

"No, sir. If I understand it correctly, everything routes through the main comms room – that's on level 285 - and then, in normal cases, out into space via the comms arrays."

"Could you plug in directly or something?"

Bannerman did his best to smother a sigh at the question. "No, sir. I still wouldn't have authority. Does it even matter if we get a signal out? The command and control guys would have had more than enough time to send out a distress call before the Vraxar pumped in the toxins."

McKinney lifted his hands in frustration. "We're stuck here, Corporal – waiting to die. Do you want to sit back until it happens, or would you prefer to operate under the pretence that you can make a difference to your fate?"

"If you're asking me do I want to go down shooting, or die on the toilet with a triple cheeseburger in my hand, I think on balance I'd prefer go down shooting, sir. Just point me in the direction of whatever you want me to kill."

"I've got a feeling that'll come soon enough."

"We still don't have any way of using the main comms."

"What about the *Juniper's* weapons systems?" McKinney knew he was clutching at straws. He forged on regardless. "If we could trigger those, we might be able to blow a hole in the enemy's hull."

"I think we'd have fired those already if we were able, sir."

"We don't know it didn't happen, Corporal. For all we know, the *Juniper* might have shot down half a dozen Vraxar warships before it got taken."

"Why did we stop firing, then?"

"I'm just talking aloud, Corporal. Hoping that if I say enough words, some sense might come from them."

"Yeah."

"Get in touch with the other survivors again. Find out if there's anyone amongst them who knows about the *Juniper's* weapons systems. Ideally someone who knows how to activate them."

It was a long shot and McKinney knew it. In the end he got a result, though not the one he was expecting. After a couple of minutes, Bannerman raised his visor-covered face.

"There's no weapons officer, sir. There is, however a comms lieutenant in with Sergeant Woods' group."

"I thought I was the highest-ranked left?"

"A miscommunication, sir. The comms lieutenant in question is currently excused from all duties, owing to an injury she suffered in service on Tillos."

"You're shitting me?"

"No, sir. Lieutenant Maria Cruz is on level 370, along with the others accompanying Sergeant Woods."

McKinney tried to ignore the clenched feeling in his stomach. "The main comms room is right between our two groups. Tell Sergeant Woods to meet us there. We're going to try and get a message out to the Space Corps and see if they have any idea how we can escape from this steaming pile of crap."

While Bannerman passed on the message, McKinney began giving orders across the squad's open channel. He felt galvanised, though he wasn't foolish enough to think the eventual outcome would be any different. In his mind, action without hope of success was far better than taking no action at all.

It didn't take long to prepare. Bannerman closed up his comms pack and shrugged it onto his shoulders. The others formed into a line two abreast and waited while McKinney filled them in.

"We're going to meet up with another group of survivors. Our destination is the main command and control area up on level 285. There are a lot of stairs to climb and no doubt a lot of dead bodies. Once we reach our destination, we're going to send a distress signal to the Space Corps. There's a chance they might think of a way to get us out of here."

"Do they care enough about us, sir?" asked Rubin Musser, the tube of a plasma launcher balanced over one shoulder.

"I hope so, soldier. As far as I'm concerned, that's something we can't influence. Let's focus on the things we *can* do."

"Yes, sir."

McKinney opened his mouth to give the order to move out when he was distracted by a flurry of movement from Corporal Bannerman.

"Someone wants to speak to us, sir," he said, attaching a cable from the comms pack into an interface port on his visor.

"Who is it?" asked McKinney, sensing at once something was wrong.

"It's one of the guys in the level 95 primary fab." Bannerman swore. "It's the Vraxar, sir. They've boarded the *Juniper*."

"Tell them to stay hidden."

"It sounds like it's too late for that. I can hear gunfire in the background."

"Shit. Is the line still open?"

"The line is open, but there's no one on the other end of it. He's either run off or dead, sir."

McKinney gritted his teeth. The men and women on level 95 weren't his immediate priority and he'd expected them to remain safe while he got on with things elsewhere. The eventual plan had been to send someone down for them – now it didn't look as if that was going to happen. Furthermore, it appeared as though the task of reaching the command and control area had just got a whole lot harder with the arrival of the Vraxar.

"It looks like the Vraxar have decided to act," he said. "That's going to make things difficult. I'm damned if I'm going to give up. Corporal Bannerman – fill Sergeant Woods in and tell him to proceed as planned. If we hear from any more groups of non-coms, they'll need to hole up wherever they think is safe. It's not like there'll be a shortage of places to hide on the *Juniper*."

The tension amongst the squad was palpable. McKinney had fought alongside many of them on Tillos. There were a few new faces and he hoped they'd take strength from the others. *Another fight against the odds,* he told himself grimly.

"Come on!" he said. "Let's move out!"

CHAPTER ELEVEN

CRACKS WERE BEGINNING to show in Admiral Henry Talley's usually calm exterior. His primary, overriding emotion was one of frustration. The Vraxar had attacked the *Juniper* and here he was, way out on the fringes in what was currently the Space Corps' most capable warship. He ached to be recalled, or preferably, to be confronted by a Vraxar fleet so that he could unleash the *Devastator*'s arsenal of high-yield weaponry upon them.

"That would certainly get the Ghasts involved, whether they wanted to or not," he muttered sourly.

The Oblivion class *Gallatrin-9* was still out there, maintaining a lazy orbit above Roban. The entire rebel fleet was comprehensively outgunned by each of the battleships but they stayed close, as if the Robanis needed to feel they were equal partners. The *ES Rampage* was due in a few hours and the heavy cruiser had the potential to tip the scales one way or another. *For good or ill,* he thought.

Talley had spoken to the Ghast captain Rioq-Tor on more than one occasion. The alien seemed to be in no particular hurry, either to leave or to move things forward. There again, the Ghasts weren't currently under attack from the Vraxar.

"They're here to dissuade us from using force against the rebels," said Commander George Adams.

"Indeed," said Talley. "If the Robanis have told them about the Obsidiar, the Ghasts will want to get their foot in the door."

"I wonder if they'd actually fire upon us."

"It's a question I've asked myself ever since they showed up, Commander. We don't need a war on one front, let alone two. Let's see what transpires."

"Why won't the Robanis speak to you again, sir?" asked Mercer. "I thought dialogue was meant to be the way forward in disagreements like this."

"It is. However, there are times when stalling can ramp up the pressure on the other side. The Robanis must be aware of our situation with the Vraxar and they're hoping that by ignoring us we'll eventually come to them with favourable terms."

"The Ghasts don't seem to be getting the same cold shoulder," said Lieutenant Poole. "They've made two shuttle visits to the surface in the last twelve hours."

"It's just another lever for the Robanis to pull," said Talley. "I don't need to be a politician to see what they're doing."

"It would really screw things up for them if we figured out where their Obsidiar was," said Sykes. "They've effectively stolen it from the rest of the Confederation anyway, so it would only be right if we stole it back."

Something in Sykes's words generated a thought in Talley's head. His brain raced after the thought and turned it into an idea.

"You might be on to something, Ensign," he said.

"Yeah, you can rely on me, sir." She looked puzzled. "What was I on to?"

Talley didn't answer and sat down to think. The Robanis had told him they'd found a source of Obsidiar and that he would never locate it. Like a fool, he'd believed them and hadn't spent any time trying to figure out how an outlying planet might have pulled off something the rest of the Confederation had failed at so comprehensively.

He pulled up a few pages of information from the *Devastator*'s databanks and studied them. There was definitely no Obsidiar on either Roban or Liventor – both planets had been comprehensively scoured by fleet prospectors. That meant they'd found it elsewhere.

Talley checked the inventory of spacecraft available to the frontier planets. The warships he knew about already, but aside from that there were a dozen scouts and a few prospectors. It was hardly even two weeks since the declaration of independence and he had to assume it was the discovery of Obsidiar which had emboldened them to act.

"Lieutenant Mercer? I would like you and your team to check through the flight logs of every lightspeed-capable spaceship available to the frontier rebels. More specifically, I would like you to concentrate your efforts on any vessels that returned from their scheduled missions early."

"Yes, sir. We'll get onto that right away."

"Need any extra muscle on that one, sir?" asked Commander Adams.

"Thank you, I'll let you know."

It wasn't too long until Talley received his first update.

"Everything checks out, sir. There are only two reported changes to scheduled missions over the entirety of the last year and neither of those resulted in an early return or an extension for the craft involved. Once we get to the date where they declared independence, they started deleting their flight plans as well as the backups."

Talley thought about it some more. Physically stealing a spaceship from the Space Corps was one thing but cutting off its myriad of automated processes was entirely another. It required a great deal of knowledge and expertise to completely sever the ties. So, while the rebels might have control of the vessels, they needed to constantly delete logs and backups and jump through all manner of hoops to keep their activities hidden from the Space Corps.

"Did you audit the time stamps on the flight data?" he asked.

"No, sir. What does that mean?"

"It's possible the rebels attempted to cover their path by injecting some new data into the navigational system of one of their vessels after the event. Any new information would have a time stamp added automatically and this time stamp would be more recent than the actual flight time. It's difficult to hide."

The second search took longer and once again came up negative. Talley wasn't to be dissuaded. The frontier rebels had located Obsidiar using a Space Corps craft. One way or another there'd be a record of it, or some kind of anomaly to highlight an alteration to the logs.

"We need to see the backups," he said. "The rebels don't have the resources or the know-how to have interfered with every single one of those."

"The backups are on the *Juniper*, sir."

"There will be others on Roban – I doubt there's anyone in the rebellion with the authority to make high-level deletions from their main data store."

"We're unable to access them," said Adams. "They've created some new protection gates - I had a tiny little look a few minutes ago."

"We've got enough Obsidiar processors to crack any home-made walls they've programmed in around their surface data storage facilities," said Lieutenant Johnson.

"I'm sure they're monitoring for intrusions," said Talley. "And it might take us days to manage what you're suggesting. Once they figure out what we're up to, the situation becomes even more volatile and unpredictable."

"Can't an Admiral just send off a, you know, high priority *give me what I want* command to these data arrays and get stuff back?" asked Sykes.

Ensign Callie Sykes was having a good day, in her own inimitably annoying fashion.

"No..." mused Talley. "I don't have the authority to circumvent our security protocols. However, there are times the hand of friendship works where force will not."

Commander Adams made the logical leap. "A fleet warship such as the *ES Furnace* will offer up its own backups under certain circumstances. We might find what we need in there."

"They've put a block on our access, sir," said Mercer.

"They have indeed, Lieutenant. However, if the ship were to be told it was about to undergo routine repairs, we might find it more willing to give up its data."

"I don't understand," said Lieutenant Poole.

"Whenever a fleet warship is brought in for repairs, the shipyard technicians need to be able to gain access to all of the onboard systems in order to perform their diagnostics. They can't actually read the contents of sensitive data, but they can move it around if they need to. In order to facilitate this, the ship needs to be placed into maintenance mode."

"Which needs an authorisation code from the *Juniper*," said Mercer.

"Or, failing that, codes from an officer of Admiral rank or greater," said Adams.

"Won't they know we've done it?" asked Lieutenant Johnson doubtfully.

"Yes."

"Won't they see it as a hostile act?"

"Let me handle that," said Talley.

It was easy enough to put the plan into action. Talley simply had the ES *Devastator* transmit a code to the *Furnace*. It took a moment for the rebel warship's AI to acknowledge the command and then it was done.

"Extract their backups," said Talley. "I want everything."

"Sir, I've got Captain Mills on the comms," said Mercer. "He doesn't sound too happy."

"Wait ten seconds and then pass him through."

Ten seconds went by.

"What the hell are you playing at?" asked Mills.

An anger had been building within Talley ever since he'd arrived at Roban. Piece by piece it had increased until he realised how powerful were its currents and now it was too much for him to resist. The Confederation was under attack by an alien species whose sole aim was to kill every single living creature in the universe. And here he was, tiptoeing around, acting the diplomat, while the so-called Frontier League played their own games for their own ends. He was sick of waiting, cap-in-hand, to see what scraps might be thrown his way.

"Since you have prevented my usual access to the ES *Furnace*'s data arrays, I have placed the warship into maintenance mode so that I can take the information I require from your backups."

"You can't do this!"

"I can and I am. There are bigger issues at stake than your rebellion and I will not wait here at the beck and call of your council while the damned Vraxar murder our people!"

"This is an act of war, Admiral!"

"No, it is an act designed to ensure our survival, Captain."

The extraction of data from the *Furnace* completed.

"They've locked onto us with their weapons, sir," said Adams.

"Captain Mills, I didn't think the Space Corps allowed

foolish people to pilot their warships. I suggest you speak to your superiors before you do anything rash."

Mills swore, the petulant response of a man out of his depth.

"He's gone," said Mercer.

"They're maintaining the weapons lock," said Adams.

"It's his only way of saving face," said Talley. "Ignore it." He felt invigorated by taking action and he stalked around the bridge. "Lieutenant Mercer, get to it. I need you to cross-check every one of those backups against every flight record for all of the rebel ships. If there's a discrepancy in the time stamps, I want to know about it immediately!"

The comms team got on with it. There was a lot of collation to do and Talley would have liked to assign others of the crew to the task as well. With so many other warships in the area, it seemed better if they didn't have the distraction.

This time, they got lucky and found the answer quickly.

"Sir, look at this!" said Ensign Banks, waving his hand.

Talley crossed to stand at his shoulder. "What have you found?"

"A difference in the stamps, sir. Look at the details for this flight log – the current file looks normal, as do these four backup copies of the log. However, there's this other file here where the time stamp number has an additional decimal place."

"This must be the original record," Talley urged. "Let's see what happened."

It was all there, plain to see. Three weeks ago, one of the Robani prospectors had been surveying planets nearby. It was standard stuff – check to see if there was anything worth having and then record the findings. On this particular occasion, the vessel had aborted its mission twelve hours early and come home. The Robanis had subsequently tried to cover it up by replacing the original flight plan logs with a log showing the prospector at a different place entirely. It must have taken a lot of effort to fake the time stamps of the data, but their efforts were wasted because of a single decimal place which had allowed Ensign Banks to identify the altered record.

"Why didn't they just delete it?" asked Mercer. "Like they've been doing for everything else since they declared independence?"

"I don't know," said Talley. "I can only assume they thought they'd covered their tracks sufficiently. Maybe we found the only backup in existence that they hadn't managed to overwrite with falsified data."

Mercer looked like she wanted to say more. She was distracted by an incoming message on her comms panel.

"It's Councillor Alexander, sir."

"He took longer than I expected. Deny his request for a channel."

"Cut him off?"

"Exactly."

"That was empowering. He's gone, sir."

"It's likely to get interesting here in the very near future. Fortunately, we won't be around to witness it. Lieutenant Mercer, send a brief message to Fleet Admiral Duggan, advising him we're off to find the pirates' treasure."

"Pirates' treasure?"

"He'll know what it means. Lieutenant Johnson – we're going to lightspeed. The target location is planet Vontaren."

"Yes, sir. Ready on your word."

Talley waited for Mercer to send her message. Once she was done, he gave the order for the launch into high lightspeed. The *Devastator* burst away from its orbit of Roban and Talley had never been so relieved to see the back of a place as he was then.

CHAPTER TWELVE

REACHING the *Juniper*'s command and control levels was easier
said than done. The orbital was too large for all but the most long-
served personnel to have intimate knowledge of every passage
and McKinney was having to rely on a 3D overlay on his HUD
for directions. So far, it had given them enough of an edge that
the squad had been able to avoid an engagement with the alien
troops. McKinney wasn't usually shy when it came to shooting
aliens, but he didn't want to give the game away early. Once the
Vraxar knew about the human soldiers, they'd hunt them with
purpose.

The squad reached the top of a long flight of steps, which
ended at a wide landing. There was an opening to the left, which
the lead man looked through before announcing the all clear.
The squad cautiously entered what was the large reception area
of level 214. The walls were clad in a pristine white ceramic and
a number of reception desks were arrayed in a semi-circle in front
of the stairwell and the nearby bank of six non-operational
airlifts. During normal operation, these desks would have

presented a formidable barrier to any unauthorised attempt to access what lay beyond.

The emergency lighting was in effect, adding a sombreness to the area and it was silent, barring the noises made by the squad. Whatever was happening elsewhere on the *Juniper*, the sound of it didn't reach this far.

The soldiers spread out with their gauss rifles in hand, checking along the three exit passages which led from the opposite wall. Huey Roldan and Rudy Munoz hung back to watch back the way they'd come.

McKinney glanced at the sign overhead – *Level 214: Laboratory Areas 21-30, Augmentation Research Facility 1.*

"I thought augmentations were banned," said Corporal Bannerman, looking at the same sign.

"Maybe they're allowed to do the research and just can't make the final implants."

"Yeah, maybe."

According to the time on McKinney's HUD, ten hours had passed since the alarms first went off on the *Juniper. Or is it twelve?* he asked himself. Time was already losing meaning and he put it down to the extended time without sleep. It was no time for pride and he ordered his suit to give him a shot of something to keep him awake. He felt a sharp jab in his thigh and moments later, it was as though a veil was lifted from his brain and the creeping fog dissipated.

"Sergeant Woods is ahead of us, sir," said Bannerman. "He's just leaving level 352."

"It'll take him a few minutes to stock up at the armoury." McKinney grinned inside his visor. "That'll give us a chance to gain a few levels."

An unspoken game was in progress to see who could reach level 285 first. It was a game McKinney didn't want to lose, though he didn't want to die participating.

"Sergeant Woods hasn't come across any Vraxar yet. Maybe they're working their way outwards from the middle section of the *Juniper*."

"I don't think so. I'm sure they've got multiple access points. If Sergeant Woods hasn't seen the bastards, he's just got lucky."

There was a shortcut to one of the main stairwells. It involved crossing from the outer edge of level 214 to the centre. Even though the *Juniper* was narrower here than in other places, there were nine hundred metres of corridors to negotiate before they reached this mini-objective.

The relative calmness of the journey so far was about to be shattered.

"Sir, there's something coming up the stairs," said Roldan, the edge in his voice clear across the open channel. "Two flights down – I can hear footsteps."

"How many?"

"Hard to tell. Sounds like eight or more."

"Right, move!" said McKinney.

"There's no time, Lieutenant. They'll see us if we try to run."

"Belay that order," McKinney barked. "Squad A, cover the stairwell exit. Squads B and C cover those other three corridors! I don't want anything catching us by surprise."

The squad was already in positions of cover, watching the exits. In seconds they'd adapted, with the men of Squad A training their weapons on the landing at the top of the steps. Roldan and Munoz fell back and pressed themselves against the wall a few metres to the right of the entrance. McKinney and Bannerman took the left side.

"Wait. Let them come into the room. We can't allow any to escape."

As he stared along the barrel of his gauss rifle at the opening, McKinney found he was holding his breath. He blew out gently and forced his breathing into a steady rhythm. The heavy sound of the approaching enemy's footsteps was clear now. *What if it's a bunch of human survivors, trying to get to safety?* he thought suddenly.

"Make damn sure it's not friendlies before you start shooting," he said.

It wasn't friendlies.

"Vraxar confirmed," said Corporal Li, with a much better vantage onto the stairwell landing.

The first pair of alien soldiers walked into the room. They were hulking lumps of reclaimed Estral flesh, patched up with metal and stinking like red meat left in the sun. The size of them was intimidating the first time - McKinney remembered them well and wasn't frightened. He released the air from his lungs and put a slug through the metal-wrapped skull of the closest one.

McKinney's shot was the trigger and the other men followed, sending a hail of gauss rounds into the front two Vraxar. The aliens toppled without a sound, exposing the group behind. McKinney took a step to the side and fired in short bursts, the bullets from his gun raking into the alien soldiers.

The Vraxar reacted quickly, as if surprise was no impediment to them. McKinney heard the crack of a hand cannon and was dimly aware of something ricocheting off the floor at his feet. He pressed himself against the wall to let the rest of Squad A finish things off.

It didn't turn out to be quite so easy.

"More coming up," said Garcia.

"Sounds like dozens of them," said Webb.

"Squad B, assist," said McKinney, suddenly feeling exposed away from the cover of the metal reception desks. He waved Bannerman to move away from the door and followed, keeping his gun trained on the doorway. On the opposite side, Roldan and Munoz got the message and did likewise.

The intensity of fire increased and the droning hum of warm gauss coils became a constant background noise. McKinney's view into the stairwell landing was limited by the tightness of the angle and he craned out to see what was coming. There was a chaos of movement and shapes – a tantalising sight that failed to provide him with a clear idea of what was coming.

Something metallic sailed into the room. It bounced once and then came to a stop in the middle of the reception area. The warning shout left McKinney's mouth even while his brain was asking why a grenade would be more of a cube than a cylinder.

"Get down!" he yelled.

The Vraxar grenade detonated with a solid thumping percussion and an explosion of pitch black flames. The grenade was poorly-thrown and the fires licked at one of the desks without harming the men behind it.

A second object followed the first. It clattered across the floor, skipped twice and came to rest a metre away from McKinney's feet. The grenade was size of his fist and he looked at it with anger. He lifted one leg, intending to kick it away, knowing it would be far too late.

Before it could explode, the grenade skittered away to the side at high speed. It struck the wall at an angle and bounced away without detonating.

"You owe me one, Lieutenant," said Corporal Li.

McKinney didn't have time to offer thanks, nor to wonder at Corporal Li's superhuman reactions and perfect aim. A couple of doses of the spacesuit battlefield adrenaline could give a trained soldier the ability to shoot the balls off a rat at two hundred paces.

"Webb, get a damned rocket in there!" he yelled.

"I thought you'd never ask, sir."

The missile was flying before the words were finished. It streaked into the opening and erupted into white hot plasma. The landing and stairwell weren't enough to contain the blast and the explosion spilled into the reception area, washing to either side. McKinney ducked and turned away. He felt the heat lick against his side and then it receded.

"Hold fire!"

He was moving at once towards the doorway. As he ran, he snapped out a grenade, priming it with a flick of his thumb. He threw it with a sideways action across the landing and down the stairs. A second grenade followed a moment later, just as the first one exploded. He threw a third and this time his aim was better – it arced with precision towards another switchback landing at the bottom.

The light from the third grenade blast had hardly receded when McKinney stepped onto the landing, the barrel of his repeater in hand. He heard footsteps as some of the men rushed to join him. Before anyone could get to him, McKinney saw movement below. Amongst the carnage, one of the Vraxar was struggling to stand. Its flesh was blackened and split and one arm had been torn clean away. McKinney squeezed the activation trigger for the briefest of moments and the alien was thrown backwards by a dozen repeater rounds.

"Clear," he said, panting for breath as if he'd finished a hard-run thousand metres.

"We'd better get out of here, Lieutenant," said Corporal Evans.

"How many did we kill?" asked Garcia.

"Roldan reckoned there were eight," said Clay Reeves with the light tones of a man coming to terms with his first engagement.

"*Twenty*-eight, maybe," said Garcia. "Look at these rotting bastards. I hate them even when they're dead." He kicked out at a piece of metal plating. Whatever it had been originally attached to was no longer recognizable and it clanked away to the bottom of the stairs.

"I think we finished off this party of Vraxar," said McKinney. "We need to move – there'll be more once they realise what's happened."

"It might be a little harder to dodge them from now on," said Corporal Li.

"We'll kill the ones that get too curious."

McKinney set off, heading for the middle of the three exit corridors. He stopped for a moment to examine the floor where the Vraxar grenade had blown up. The dark flames had done something to the metal, leaving it pitted and uneven. He scuffed at a patch with the toe of his boot and the alloy crumbled into dust. Whatever tech the Vraxar filled their grenades with it was something new, though seemingly no more effective than the plasma used by the Space Corps.

With the first engagement over, McKinney felt a calm descend upon him. He kept the squad moving at a good pace, whilst at the same time ensuring they didn't leave themselves too exposed to a surprise attack. His suit comms received the occasional update from Sergeant Woods, which he listened to without providing detailed responses. There wasn't enough intel for him to spend much time planning out tactics with this second group. It seemed best to simply get a move on and reach the meeting point as efficiently as possible. To McKinney, this meant getting there without anyone dying.

They continued through the corridors, their guns at the ready and with more than an occasional glance over their shoulders. The previously-muffled sounds coming from other areas of the orbital were now louder, and they echoed through the structure. It was impossible to pinpoint the direction from which the noises came and the added uncertainty set the squad on edge. A few of the men muttered amongst themselves, conjecturing that the Vraxar were now actively seeking to find whoever had killed one of their patrols. McKinney thought the same and he broke into a jog.

They reached the central stairwell without further incident. For the ascent, McKinney set up a routine whereby the three squads would advance one at a time. The front squad would hold every landing and the other two squads would move up to claim the next. It wasn't too slow and it was reassuring to McKinney that he was taking a careful approach that didn't risk his men any more than necessary.

The stairwell ended and deposited them onto level 250. An overhead sign bore the words *Main recreation area.*

"This is more like it," said R1T Ricky Vega. "Look – we've got a gym to the left and get this – a *massage* area over this way."

"Hey, there're video games along this corridor according to my overlay," said Mills. "Why don't we get this treatment in the barracks?"

"Because the Space Corps hates you," said Garcia.

"Everyone shut up for a minute, or take it out of the channel," said McKinney. "I'm thinking."

He studied the HUD overlay again. The *Juniper* was logically laid out, but it was still hard for him to plan more than two steps in advance, simply because there was so much information to take in. He extended his left arm and moved it in a curving gesture.

"If we follow this corridor to the outer wall, there's another flight of steps to level 251. From there we can access one of the secondary stairwells which will take us up to the level 280 entrance foyer."

"My overlay shows nothing when I try to look at levels 281 through to 289," said Corporal Evans.

"Maybe it's rank locked," said McKinney. "Those levels show up on my HUD."

"Try not to get lost, huh?" said Corporal Li, pushing his knuckles into Evans' upper arm.

"I'll do my best," muttered Evans.

"I can hear movement on the stairwell, sir," said Roldan.

"Coming our way?"

"I don't know. I think it's a few flights down. Or up."

"The place must be crawling with them," said Bannerman. "It's like we're finding more resistance the higher we go."

McKinney didn't like the idea of being the prey in a Vraxar pursuit. Part of him wanted to wait here and see what turned up, so he could fill it with bullets. He knew it was a bad idea – there were surely thousands of the aliens onboard and there was no hope of winning an extended shootout.

"Let's pick up the pace – we're heading left."

The corridor was wide and had regular distance markings to suggest personnel were encouraged to use it as part of a training circuit. After a fast-marched fifty metres, a long window appeared in the right-hand wall. McKinney peered into the room before committing his men to showing themselves.

"Must have been peak time when the toxin reached this gym," he said. He swore and punched the wall twice.

Without further word, he strode off, struggling to keep his anger in check. He squeezed the barrel of his repeater. The metal was solid and with no flex at all. He took comfort from it and wished there were Vraxar for him to shoot. *Can't think like that. If we reach the C&C without bloodshed it'll be a victory.*

He clung to the idea even though it didn't clear his anger. The window turned into solid wall and McKinney experienced a kind of relief at knowing the dead were hidden from his gaze. It didn't change the truth, but it saved him from having to stare at it directly.

A little way ahead the passage offered a right-hand turn, whilst also continuing on straight. According to the overlay, this new passage continued for a few metres and then opened out into the second of level 250's four gyms. More than anything McKinney wanted to go a different way, to avoid looking into the accusing eyes of the dead. Unfortunately, the next best alternative added another five hundred metres onto the route and he couldn't allow his weakness to result in such a waste of time.

He raised a hand and the squad stopped, maintaining their two-abreast column. With great care, McKinney leaned out just far enough for his visor sensor to see along the corridor. The doorway was wide and afforded him a good view beyond. There were Vraxar in the room and though McKinney couldn't make out the specifics, he didn't like what he saw.

"They're in there," he said across the open channel. "I can see seven or eight. It's some new type – these ones are smaller and I don't think they're armed. They're dragging bodies somewhere."

"Maybe we should skip past, sir," said Corporal Evans. "It'll add time but avoid conflict."

"We can't get by without them seeing us and I don't want to wait it out. There's no way to tell whether or not they'll end up coming along here and then they'll find us anyway."

"We shouldn't wait here," said Corporal Li. "It's too exposed if we get unlucky and the Vraxar come from in front or behind."

The words were prophetic.

"There's something coming into the room we just left, sir," shouted last man Jeb Whitlock.

McKinney made his mind up. "We're going in there. Squad A first and take the left, Squad B, right. Squad C, deal with it as it comes."

"Want me and Musser to clear it out first, sir?" asked Webb.

"No, we're not waiting. Get in."

Without checking to see if everyone understood, McKinney broke cover and charged along the short corridor. He sensed the others of Squad A at his back and heard the muted contact of their boots on the floor.

Five Vraxar were visible ahead – they were six feet tall and spindly, with the dry, yellowing skin of a corpse left in the desert for a century. They had dark metal bars and plates fastened to their limbs and shoulders. Two of them were crouched over the body of a man, poking at it with long fingers. McKinney was in the lead and without breaking stride he sprayed the aliens with a roaring burst from his repeater. Gobbets of dry flesh flew into the air and the Vraxar fell soundlessly.

He entered the room and his brain took in the details – plain metal walls thirty metres long, with a high ceiling. Gym equipment of all types was arranged in neat rows, some of the display screens still running from whatever power source they were plugged into. There were lots of Vraxar here – maybe thirty or forty in total, most of them the smaller types. In the far corner, a group of larger soldiers were already lifting their guns in preparation.

McKinney took aim into the corner and sprayed it with slugs from his gun. Garcia and Roldan stood to either side, the thunder from their own repeaters joining with his. McKinney heard the pings and clangs of ricochets, and debris from a row of treadbikes flew into the air.

Then came the sound of heavy-duty plasma tube coils charging up and a rocket screamed over his shoulder, detonating amongst the larger Vraxar and turning their flesh into charcoal.

"Reeves, Munoz, cover our backs! Roldan, get that bastard! Webb, hold fire!"

The sound of gunfire reached a deafening crescendo. McKinney knew the tales of soldiers who revelled in it – who gave themselves over to the madness of chaos. He felt the seductive pull as he poured the hatred of his bullets into the enemy.

The Vraxar fell – there were dozens of them in here, far more than McKinney had expected. Wherever he saw movement, he swung his repeater towards it, the muscles on his forearms straining against the kick. Pieces of flesh – alien and from the *Juniper*'s dead personnel – joined the pieces of metal and plastic from the shattered gym equipment, clouding the vision of the squad and making it hard to pick up the few remaining Vraxar as they dashed for the exits. Even the jerky, bobbing stride of the aliens was repulsive and reminded McKinney of long-limbed insects. His anger rose again and he didn't lift his finger from the repeater's trigger.

For the first few seconds of the engagement, McKinney dared to hope these smaller aliens were unarmed. Then he saw a dark shape in the hand of one. The Vraxar fired its pistol only once before it was killed in a converging barrage of gauss slugs. That single shot was enough and it took Chance right between the eyes, smashing through the man's reflective visor and sending him straight to the floor.

McKinney spat in fury and fired again and again wherever he saw movement.

The Vraxar weren't done yet.

"Behind!" shouted Munoz. "Lots of them!"

"Squad C reinforce!"

The sound of two thumping grenade explosions reached McKinney. He didn't dare turn until he was sure the left side of the room was clear. There was another blast and then another.

"Left side clear," he called.

"Right side clear," Corporal Li confirmed.

The passage along which they'd entered the gym wasn't clear and Squad C continued to roll grenades through the open doorway to keep the Vraxar from approaching. The Vraxar threw their own grenades in response and the dark energy mixed and swirled amongst the plasma fires. Luckily, the alien soldiers had no angle to land a throw close to the squad and it was already looking like a standoff.

"Squad B, cover these two exits," barked McKinney, indicating the passages leading from the opposite wall of the gym. "Corporal Evans, how many are they?"

"Shitloads, sir."

It was as good an estimate as any.

"Fall back slowly. Squad A provide cover – keep up the pressure on that opening. Musser, rockets."

Step by step they retreated over the floor of the gym. Musser fired rockets along the corridor to keep the enemy at bay and some of the men lobbed grenades during the recharge period of the plasma tube. The walls of the corridor glowed dull red and lumps of molten alloy dripped from the ceiling.

Twice, McKinney nearly tripped over the mangled body of a Vraxar as he walked backwards. He took final note of the tragedy in the room - there was a pile of human bodies against one wall and other, uncollected, bodies were scattered amongst the broken equipment.

He reached the exit passageway – Squads B and C were already fifty metres ahead, having taken cover around a corner.

"Webb, Musser, we're going to make a run for that next turning."

The men knew what to do and they fired in turn. As soon as the first rocket exploded, McKinney shouted out the order to retreat. He turned and joined the soldiers in a frantic sprint towards the safety of the turning ahead.

They made it. McKinney had no intention of stopping and he carried on at a run, barging his way through to take the lead. The stairwell was some way ahead, though there was no guarantee it would offer any kind of safety.

"Sir?" said Bannerman urgently. With the expertise of a born pack man, he was able to operate his comms unit under almost any circumstances.

"What is it?" grunted McKinney.

"It's TO Hattie Rhodes, sir. You need to hear this."

McKinney reached a T-junction and stopped to look both ways. "This isn't a good time." He set off again to the right.

"You need to hear."

Bannerman didn't wait for the go-ahead and simply patched Rhodes directly through to McKinney's suit comms.

"What?" he asked.

"I thought I'd better let you know, Lieutenant. We just saw something running across the hangar floor here on level 300."

"Tell me something new."

"You need to listen to me. These were big – really big. Ten feet tall big, with lots of armour and carrying some kind of guns."

That got McKinney's attention.

"How many?"

"I saw four. There could be more. Lieutenant McKinney – they entered the stairwell. They're coming down. I don't think you want to meet them."

"Thanks for the warning."

He cut off the comms and kept running. Most of the Vraxar he'd encountered up until now were originally Estral. If the aliens had conquered hundreds of other species, it made sense there'd be plenty of other types. Whatever these new ones were, he didn't like the sound of them and hoped he wouldn't meet them soon. Deep inside, he knew the Vraxar had deployed these new creatures for the specific purpose of locating and killing his squad. He ground his teeth together and ran on.

CHAPTER THIRTEEN

"HOW LONG UNTIL WE REACH NESTA-T3?" asked Captain Charlie Blake.

"Six hours, sir."

"Still plenty of time to figure out what Fleet Admiral Duggan is keeping hidden from us."

"We have no right to know," said Lieutenant Hawkins.

"I disagree with your assertion, but don't worry – I'm not about to go against the Fleet Admiral's wishes and try to circumvent whatever locks he's put in place," said Blake. "As tempting as it is to try."

He put the matter from his mind and directed his energies towards other priorities. The *Juniper* was a vital asset to the Space Corps and it was protected by numerous advanced missile batteries. What it lacked was an Obsidiar energy source. Therefore, it was easy enough to guess the Vraxar had managed to disable or destroy it without a problem. The records showed the cruiser *ES Impact Crater* was assigned to the orbital's protection – an Imposition class was a powerful warship, though not something that would stop the Vraxar. In addition, there was a Crimson class destroyer in one of the hangars, along with a scout and a prospector in for scheduled maintenance. Again, nothing of a threat to the four Vraxar warships.

"Why would they attack?" he muttered to himself. "What is there to gain?"

"Do you want a list?" asked Lieutenant Pointer.

Blake was curious to hear her thoughts. "Go on, then."

"I've been told the *Juniper* has seventy-two Obsidiar processing clusters." said Pointer. "That's *clusters,* rather than individual processors."

"You heard that?"

"I told you I have my sources." She smiled primly. "It strikes me that they're not going to break through the *Juniper*'s encryption if it has so much processing power. The enemy could steal the physical data array again – I'm sure it holds plenty more secrets than what was on the *ES Determinant*. That might benefit them long term, but in reality, they'll still need to break it down for analysis, however long that will take."

"So, what do they want it for? They may have simply destroyed it."

Pointer shook her head. "Some of the Space Corps' best minds work on the *Juniper*. If you were an alien race which used the bodies of your opponents, would you pick a man from the gutter or would you choose someone working in a tech lab?"

Blake understood what she was suggesting. "If the Vraxar converted everyone on every planet, they would number in the trillions."

"Maybe that's not what they want," she said. "Maybe they pick the best from every race. What if the conversion to Vraxar allows them to utilise the expertise of the subject?"

"The Vraxar we spoke to on Tillos told us the conversion process destroyed the mind of the individual. If I remember correctly, you were unconscious during that part of the conversation."

"You told me afterwards!" she said accusingly. "The Vraxar told you the conversion often destroys the mind, while sometimes they are able to extract memories afterwards."

"Yes, that's what it said," he admitted.

"The new subjects are still able to serve, sir. With or without conscious memories of what they once were, perhaps the new Vraxar retain the knowledge of what they did in life. It could be that a human scientist becomes a Vraxar scientist. A human soldier becomes a Vraxar soldier."

"It makes sense to me," said Hawkins.

"I can't really offer you an argument," said Blake. "Your idea makes as much sense as any other."

"It makes *more* sense, sir. Admit it."

He opened his mouth, without knowing quite how to respond to the teasing challenge. He gave up.

"Fine, I'll admit that as far as theories go, it's a decent one."

"Thank you."

"How does it help us?"

"I don't know."

"You've still got nearly six hours to come up with something, Lieutenant."

"I'll do my best, sir."

The flight continued until, with an hour to go, Blake gave the instruction for them to come out of lightspeed in order to find out the most recent information on the status of the *Juniper*. Once again, he found Admiral Duggan was available and the news was grim.

"We have little in the way of intel. In truth, we don't know a damn thing about what's going on. I am pulling a fleet together which I may or may not send to the *Juniper*'s location. I can tell you already, it won't be enough; furthermore, it's several days away and there won't be a single Obsidiar-cored ship amongst the numbers."

"There're still no comms from the orbital? I thought the backups worked in pretty much any situation?"

"A short while after we initially lost contact, one of our bases on Overtide started receiving low-speed distress signals from the *Juniper*. Much of the information was scrambled, consistent with interference from somewhere close to the source. A jammer, perhaps."

"I take it from your voice there is no longer a distress signal, sir?"

"No there is not. The signal stopped without warning."

"Have they destroyed the *Juniper*?"

"We don't know. We've got an old monitoring station on Atlantis focused on Nesta-T3. An hour ago, it located the two Neutralisers and the mothership. We've had no sighting of the Vraxar battleship or the *Juniper*."

"What aren't you telling me, sir?"

"There's a chance the Vraxar mothership has picked up the *Juniper* – brought the whole damned lot into their bay. The alternative is, they've destroyed the orbital and are scavenging whatever pieces they think might be of use. The monitoring station isn't sophisticated enough to perform a quick sweep of the area to find evidence of wreckage. The technicians are recalibrating it and we should have an idea soon."

"My comms lieutenant thinks the Vraxar might value the personnel onboard, sir. Based on our experiences on Tillos, she believes the enemy may try to make use of their expertise through conversion."

Duggan was silent for a moment. "It's a strong theory and similar to an idea one of my own teams came up with."

"If it's true, the personnel on the *Juniper* may already be lost to us, sir."

"I know." Duggan swore, revealing the depths of his anger. "Some of our leading scientists are working on the *Juniper* – in the field of weapons, defence and propulsion. In death they might become our enemies. It's a terrible thought and one which makes me despise these Vraxar more than I thought possible. They're our men and women. Until I'm certain, I won't give up. I will *never* give them up."

"We will be there within the hour, sir. Once the ES *Blackbird* is in position, we should be able to give you something to work with."

Duggan answered, his voice strong with the certainty of a man who'd made up his mind about something he wasn't going to divulge. "Your primary mission is to discover if there's anyone left alive on the *Juniper*, Captain Blake. Learn what you can about the Vraxar and send the details to the Space Corps' main command and control. Mostly, I want you to find out what's happened and then I can decide."

"Decide on what, sir?"

"Too many questions, Captain Blake. I'm glad you didn't ask me how to accomplish your mission. It gives me hope you have the ability to pull it off."

Blake was nonplussed. "It's what I signed up for, sir. Basic training tells us there's no such thing as a suicide mission – there's always a way."

"Is that what they tell you these days?"

"Was the lesson lacking in accuracy, sir?"

"Ask me the same question when we've beaten the Vraxar, Captain Blake."

"I will definitely do so."

"Good. Now stop wasting time and get on your way to Nesta-T3."

"We're on it, sir."

The comms went dead abruptly. Blake was quickly learning

that Duggan wasn't a man who partook of extended goodbyes.

"I think he likes you," said Lieutenant Hawkins.

"You reckon?"

"Absolutely, sir. You're the most experienced captain in his fleet."

"That only means he's going to throw the most crap my – our - way."

"Don't you know anything about the Fleet Admiral?" asked Pointer with surprising heat.

"No, I don't suppose I do, now you mention it," said Blake.

"Maybe you should do some more reading, sir."

"I will."

"And thank you for telling him it was my idea, sir. About the Vraxar wanting to convert our best personnel."

Blake studied her for a moment. Perhaps in the world of Caz Pointer, everyone stabbed everyone else in the back whenever the opportunity arose. He scrubbed the uncharitable thought. The old Caz Pointer was either gone or somewhere in hiding, leaving behind a much more appealing example of humanity. He caught himself staring and averted his eyes before it became obvious.

"No problem," he said.

He twisted in his seat and made a familiar gesture towards Lieutenant Quinn. Quinn acknowledged with a nod.

"Fission engines coming online, sir."

It was another rough transition. Blake kidded himself he was getting used to them, when in reality they were distinctly unpleasant to endure. Nevertheless, he smiled and pretended it was little more uncomfortable than finding a stone in his shoe.

"Do you understand what we're doing, Lieutenant Quinn?"

"Yes, sir. Admiral Duggan sent through the trajectory and speed of the Vraxar warships. We're going to arrive low to Nesta-T3 and on the far side of the moon, to reduce the chance they see our fission signature."

"With the additional protection from the fission suppression system, we should be safe," said Blake.

"It's riskier than dropping out of lightspeed ten million klicks out and coming in on the gravity engines, sir."

"In technology we trust."

At the precise moment predicted by its navigational system, the ES *Blackbird* arrived. The fission engine shut off, ejecting the vessel into local space seven thousand kilometres above the ice-clad surface of Nesta-T3. On the bridge, a series of proximity warnings chimed their gentle notes. Seven thousand kilometres was a wide enough buffer and Blake ignored the alarms.

"Activate the stealth modules," he ordered.

"Stealth online, sir," said Quinn. "The power contribution from our Gallenium blocks has dropped to zero and we're running solely off our Obsidiar core."

"The Vraxar are close," said Blake.

Lieutenant Pointer was looking hard at her console. "Scanning the vicinity."

"Remember there's a battleship unaccounted for."

"I've got my eyes wide open. You'll learn the moment I see anything, sir."

"We're searching for wreckage as well," said Blake.

"There'll be no wreckage," Pointer replied.

"What makes you so sure?"

"Firstly, because I am. Secondly, if the Atlantis monitoring station was capable of locating the Vraxar warships, it will certainly be able to find pieces of something as large as the *Juniper,* whatever Fleet Admiral Duggan says."

"I'll accept your assertion, Lieutenant."

"I could be wrong, so I'm still checking out every possibility, sir."

"Thank you."

Blake glanced at the navigational and guidance systems. So

far, everything was as he'd hoped and the *Blackbird* was on the exact opposite side of Nesta-T3 to the predicted position of the Vraxar warships. As moons went, Nesta-T3 was fairly large, with a circumference of fifteen thousand kilometres. It was the sole moon of the planet Elude, which it orbited at a distance of more than a million kilometres. Both the planet and its moon were what many in the Space Corps would fondly refer to as *shitholes.* They were bleak, barren and with nothing of interest unless you were an excessively keen geologist specialising in cold, grey stone buried beneath layers of ice.

"Let's go find that mothership," said Blake.

Flying on manual was frowned upon in the Corps, but the control bars were already becoming familiar friends to Blake. The navigation system plotted a vector and all he had to do was guide the ship along it. *If anyone wanted to complain, they had the opportunity when they audited the ES Lucid.*

He recognised when he was becoming distracted and snapped his attention to keeping the *Blackbird* on course.

"There's no sign of the battleship so far, sir," said Pointer, finishing the medium-range scan. "The other three ships should be visible to sensor sight shortly."

"It's got to be close," he muttered. "Why else would they have brought it?"

"Unless we're exceptionally unlucky, they won't see us with the stealth modules running," said Quinn.

"I don't like unknowns, Lieutenant."

The navigation system had plotted a textbook trajectory that took them far higher above Nesta-T3 than Blake judged was necessary. He deviated, bringing them lower and lower until they were within fifty kilometres of the icy peaks and frozen lakes which covered much of the surface. The underside sensor feed showed a blur of white alternating with grey.

Gradually, the moon fell away as he once again adjusted their heading onto a course intended to intercept with the predicted position of the three Vraxar spaceships.

"The shielding of the moon should end in less than a minute," said Pointer. "If they're at their expected location, I'll pick them up straight away."

In terms of their position, the Vraxar offered no surprises, being within a few metres of what turned out to be an exceptionally accurate prediction from the Atlantis monitoring station.

"Got them," said Pointer. "The forward sensor has a lock."

"At least they're not jumping around like those other ones," said Hawkins. "I've got the big one targeted with our Shatterer and Shimmer launchers."

"Two of each," said Blake.

"Even a needle can kill if you stick it in the right place, sir."

Blake didn't accept the invitation to respond. He watched the three enemy warships for a time. The mothership was thirty thousand kilometres above Nesta-T3 and orbiting slowly. It was flanked by the two Neutralisers at the comparatively short distance of five thousand kilometres. There was something repulsive about these ugly constructions of alloy. As he directed the *ES Blackbird* onto a following course, it struck him that everything about the Vraxar was so far from removed from what was natural, there was no way to appreciate anything about them in the way that the most sworn enemies might see something to admire in their opponents.

"If I could kill every last one of them with the press of a button, I'd do so without hesitation," he said.

"You'd have to fight me for the pleasure, sir," said Hawkins.

With his palms suddenly greasy from cold sweat, Blake positioned the *ES Blackbird* ten thousand kilometres from the rear of the mothership. The sensor feed on the main bulkhead screen somehow managed to convey the vastness of the enemy vessel and it was hard to tear his eyes away.

"How long do you think it'll take them to spot us?"

"At this distance, sir? I wouldn't like to guess. I can run you a simulation if you want, though there are a great number of unknowns," said Quinn.

Blake was about to agree. Then, he experienced an unexpected moment of enlightenment, which darted fleetingly across the front of his mind so quickly he couldn't properly form the words to describe it eloquently. "Don't bother," he said. "We'll live or we'll die whatever the simulation tells us."

"That's not how it works, sir," said Quinn. He saw Blake's face and didn't offer any further argument.

"Are you getting a detailed scan of their hull, Lieutenant Pointer? And what about broadcasts from the *Juniper*?"

"I'm getting plenty of scan data, sir. I've identified numerous areas that are consistent with weapons housings."

"Can you figure out what types of weapons they are?"

"Beam weapons, sir. Capabilities unknown. I'm streaming the details away to New Earth – I'll bet they've got teams of people checking it out already. I don't think it takes a genius to imagine what those massive turrets can do. They have dozens fitted."

"I hope I'm never on the receiving end of anything from those guns," Blake replied. "Anyway, once you've finished with the mothership, swap to the Neutralisers. It could well be they're an overall greater threat, since we don't have a damned clue how to combat them."

"Will do, sir."

"And what about comms from the *Juniper*?" he reminded her.

"Nothing. It's completely silent."

"Are there any sporadic comms? Maybe a signal that comes every few minutes?"

"I don't think so. I'll keep monitoring."

He saw his own expression reflected in her face. If there was no outbound comms from the *Juniper*, it almost certainly meant everyone onboard was dead.

"Maybe they brought the *Juniper* into their hangar and evacuated everyone," she said.

"Maybe. Keep listening out."

They shadowed the Vraxar for another few minutes, each member of the crew aware that the passing seconds increased the chance they'd be detected. The comms were utterly silent.

"Patch me through to Fleet Admiral Duggan." He had a thought. "We're still on main comms, aren't we?"

"Yes, sir. I think the Vraxar have to know we're here in order to disable our main communication systems."

"Get me the Admiral."

"I've got him, sir. I think he's forgotten how to sleep."

"Just bring him through."

It didn't take long for Blake to fill in the details and it appeared as though Duggan had already been monitoring the flow of information coming from the *Blackbird* to the New Earth Central Command station.

"Are you certain there's no one alive?" Duggan asked.

"Not absolutely certain, sir. I've given you the facts as we know them."

"Have you checked for ground packs? Maybe one of the soldiers is using one."

"My comms Lieutenant has checked every possibility, sir."

"Gone, then," said Duggan. A dangerous edge came to his voice – one which Blake had never heard before. "There will be a reckoning, Captain Blake. The Vraxar have murdered our people in a war we didn't ask for. However, they've made a mistake in keeping three of their most valuable assets clustered so tightly."

"It's ten thousand klicks from flank to flank," said Blake, wondering if Duggan had misread the data.

Duggan continued speaking. "We must strike before they take off to lightspeed again. They're in our grasp and they will soon learn that humanity will not give in easily."

"What is the plan, sir?"

"The weapon you're carrying on the *Blackbird* is known to only a few people in the Space Corps. It has not been deemed safe for the knowledge to be more widely disseminated."

"What is it, sir?"

"Something's lighting up on the weapons panel, sir," whispered Lieutenant Hawkins. "We've just received some access codes."

"You're carrying an Obsidiar bomb, Captain Blake. That particular example has enough explosive force to destroy all three of those Vraxar warships. Perhaps Nesta-T3 in the process. I want you to use it."

Blake's mind did the rough numbers. A blast sphere such as Duggan described was almost beyond imagination. *No wonder it's locked down.*

His eagerness to destroy the Vraxar was a strong as ever, yet he suddenly felt burdened by the enormity of the weapon he'd been given charge of.

"The access codes have been accepted by our battle computer, sir."

"It's a bomb with a fairly rudimentary propulsion system, so you'll need to get in close to use it and you'll need to get out of there fast," Duggan continued. "Act with purpose, Captain Blake. Kill those bastards."

"Yes, sir."

Then, Duggan was gone, leaving the crew of the ES *Blackbird* to contemplate the upcoming use of an Obsidiar bomb.

CHAPTER FOURTEEN

MCKINNEY and his squad spilled out into the foyer of level 280, having first made sure it was clear of Vraxar patrols. They spread out quickly to positions of cover, whilst taking the opportunity to catch their breaths from the long run up the stairwell.

There was nothing unusual here - a row of fixed metal desks and security scanners extended all the way across the lobby. In front of those were three reception booths, clad in a poor veneer of dark wood. Visible behind, numerous corridors headed off into the depths of the C&C area.

Bodies were strewn about as liberally as anywhere else on the space station. McKinney's eyes skated over them, his brain adding to the mental tab of payback the Vraxar were accruing.

"Level 280," said Corporal Li, spelling out the obvious.

"First floor of command and control," panted Corporal Evans.

"All clear this way, Lieutenant," shouted Vega.

"And clear this side," said Clifton.

McKinney paused on the landing at the top of the steps and cocked his head to one side. There was lots of Vraxar activity in this area of the orbital and it was a miracle they'd made it up the stairwell without encountering any groups of the aliens. Fighting on stairs was a shitty job for those at the bottom.

"Where now, Lieutenant?" asked Li.

"Along that second corridor – the one with the *Projections and Research* sign hanging above it," said McKinney. "Sergeant Woods is on floor 302 and we're going to beat him to our target."

The game wasn't really important anymore. It served as a distraction and caused a few laughs amongst the squad. Against the backdrop of mass murder, it wasn't much.

They didn't wait and headed off in the direction McKinney indicated. The C&C area had definitely been in a state of high activity when the toxin came. There were bodies along every corridor, across thresholds of open doors and slumped face down over consoles as lifeless as their operators.

The contents of one room caused McKinney to perform a double-take. A large, square table was surrounded by the seated figures of men and women dressed in a variety of uniforms. At first glance, they appeared to be discussing plans and tactics to combat the Vraxar. In reality they were dead, with printed reports and coloured folders spread in front of them, the words unread.

They came upon a bank of airlifts, dedicated for the use of the C&C floors. The lifts were no more operational than any of the others, but there was a narrow set of steps off to one side. It was up these steps McKinney directed his squad. It was steep and the lighting was poor. Their footsteps and clattering weapons produced no echo whatsoever.

The steps ended at level 281, where they opened into a hub area twenty metres to each side and from which many exits were available. McKinney was momentarily lost and tried his best to combine the information from his HUD overlay with what his eyes were seeing.

"Over here," he said, pointing to a sign which read *Target and Analysis.*

"Can you hear that?" asked Roldan.

"No. What?"

"That's it, sir. It's quiet up here. Maybe we've lost them."

Roldan was right about the silence – there was much less sound on this level of the *Juniper*. McKinney wasn't convinced they'd lost the Vraxar, but he was grateful for any let-up in the pressure. He certainly didn't want to reach the main comms room with an army of Vraxar at their heels. In reality, he was aware the walls were closing in and it was only a matter of time before they were flushed out and killed by the enemy. He couldn't allow himself to dwell on such a future and called on his anger to sustain him.

With McKinney guiding the others they reached another set of steps, this one wider than the previous flight. Once again, the stairs only ascended a single floor, taking them to level 282.

"*Engineering,*" said Corporal Li, reading the sign at the top of the landing. "Could mean anything."

They entered a huge, square room, with three wide passages leading off. It was clearly a workshop of some kind and there were reinforced alloy benches arranged in long rows across the left and right sides of the floor. Along the centre, was a wide aisle. A couple of mini lifters had been grounded here, their gravity engines shut down by the appearance of the Vraxar Neutralisers. Overhead, there were runners for several winches and there were multi-jointed lifting arms protruding from each of the walls.

The benches were covered in components, most of them unrecognizable to McKinney's eye. He saw something which might have been the barrel of a light tank's main armament. There were parts of a repeater artillery piece and also what looked like a landing strut from a single-person shuttle. Other objects with unknown uses filled the available bench space.

"This must be where they fix the little stuff," said Munoz. "Seems a bit stupid having it in the middle of the command and control section."

"They had to split this level and the one above," said Sergeant Woods. "There are offices and planning areas on the far side from here."

"The real maintenance areas are way above us," said Reeves. "See that tall cabinet over there? That's a data cruncher. It analyses faults in metal so they can iron out the flaws in the manufacturing processes."

"You just made that up," said Garcia.

"I did a year of study on it. I had to drop out, but some things stuck."

"There's nothing we can use is there?" asked Corporal Evans.

"Doesn't look like it," said McKinney. "If there was something big enough to be of use, there's no way we'd get it up to level 285 anyway. The cargo lifts are just as dead as the passenger lifts."

He set off along the centre aisle and the others followed. The workshop personnel must have been off shift and there were no bodies in sight. The comfort was short-lived.

"What was that?" asked Mills.

The men were instantly on their guard.

"I didn't hear anything."

"There. Listen."

"Sounds like someone hitting the walls with a hammer."

"Sounds more like footsteps to me."

"It's coming from ahead," said McKinney, suddenly remembering the words of Technical Officer Hattie Rhodes.

He peered along the corridor. The emergency lighting was dimmer here than elsewhere, as though it was slowly failing. There was something further along – it was another of the mini lifters with an object resting on its bed. The lifter was four metres wide and its cab was over three metres tall. It didn't fill the passage and McKinney could see beyond it to a junction. It was along this way they needed to go to reach the next stairwell.

The sounds were clear now – metal upon metal with the regular cadence of footsteps.

"Get into cover," he said quietly. "Behind these benches."

The men detected the concern in McKinney's voice and moved quickly to comply. They crouched under the reassuring cover of the reinforced metal, with only their heads and weapons showing. McKinney joined them, hiding near to the central aisle.

"What is it, sir?" asked Bannerman.

"Vraxar."

A shadow appeared on the far wall at the end of the passage. It grew in size with each thudding footstep. A moment before it appeared, the creature paused out of sight, as if to allow the squad a period in which to contemplate their deaths.

Then, it stepped into view. This new Vraxar wasn't ten feet tall like Rhodes had reported. It was closer to twelve and it was a wonder it had managed to fit through some of the tighter spaces within the *Juniper*. The alien was humanoid, with arms as thick as McKinney's torso and legs that were much thicker again. Hardly a patch of its red skin was visible, since it was covered in jointed plates of thick alloy. Each plate was a different shape and size, but they were fitted together expertly. With the enhanced vision of his visor sensor, McKinney was able to see the armour across the Vraxar's chest flex as it moved.

Small eyes peered out through a metal faceplate – expressionless orbs which gave away nothing. McKinney wasn't interested in what it was thinking since it was definitely here to kill him and his squad. He was far more concerned with the huge multi-barrelled chaingun it held casually in one hand. The barrels rotated slowly, giving hints of what was to come.

"Kill the bastard," snarled McKinney.

The opening burst of the squad's repeater fire was shockingly loud. Bullets racketed against the Vraxar's armour and the flatbed lifter in front of it – a thousand rounds per second of high velocity hardened alloy. The creature staggered without falling and lifted its own weapon, aiming into the workshop.

Beneath the apparent harshness of the discord were patterns of order – a perfection only audible to a soldier in tune with the brutality of war. In those opening seconds, McKinney caught hints of it and he allowed it to embrace him. His repeater felt alive in his hands and he rode with it, directing it towards the few places he could see the Vraxar's bare flesh.

Rockets whooshed overhead, aimed high by Webb and Musser to reduce the chance the missiles would be shredded by the repeater fire. Webb was the more skilful of the two and his rocket detonated against the Vraxar's shoulder. Plasma erupted, spilling over its armour and filling the corridor for the shortest time with a heat to rival that of a sun. Musser's rocket exploded too, adding to the ferocity and the destruction.

The fire receded and incredibly, the Vraxar was still alive. It was on one knee and its head was bowed. Here and there, patches of its armour were alight and a thick, filthy smoke poured away from it.

The squad didn't let up and they continued firing. Most of the rounds deflected from its armour, but others found a way into to the skin beneath, tearing holes through its body. At last, it fell sideways into the wall before slumping forward and ending up partially hidden by the flatbed lifter.

"Hold!" ordered McKinney.

He stood from his crouch and looked around to check over the squad. The Vraxar hadn't managed to fire its evil-looking gun and none of the men were harmed.

"Sir?"

There was a second Vraxar at the end of the corridor. In the

moments it had taken McKinney to make sure his squad were
alive, it had come. This one didn't act the same as the first. With
appalling speed, it launched itself along the corridor. The Vraxar
trampled its dead fellow before smashing its way past the lifter,
knocking the vehicle aside as though it weighed nothing.

McKinney opened his mouth to give the order to fire. The
soldiers didn't need to hear the word and they opened up immediately. To McKinney's left, Webb rose smoothly, spinning his
plasma tube once and dropping it into position on his shoulder. It
hummed gently and fired, just as the Vraxar burst from the
tunnel, still thirty metres away from the squad.

The creature was met by a storm of gunfire and the blast from
Webb's rocket. It wasn't sufficient to finish it off and the alien
lifted its gun, the eight barrels already spinning up. McKinney
predicted the path of its opening burst and threw himself to the
floor behind the bench. The Vraxar chaingun thundered and its
rotating barrels glowed. The weapon was every bit as savage as it
looked. It sprayed out high-velocity death, throwing huge-calibre
bullets in a sweeping arc across the room, punching holes into
everything before it.

A few metres to McKinney's left, Elder and Rice were too
slow to get out of the way. The two men were smashed into
bloody lumps and hurled many metres away. As soon as the hail
of fire swept across the aisle to the opposite side of the room,
McKinney pushed his head over the top of the bench and hurled
a primed grenade at the Vraxar. To his horror, he saw a third of
the armoured creatures emerge into the room, armed with the
same type of chaingun.

He ducked again and heard his grenade detonate. A few of
the other men copied and threw their explosives in high arcs from
where they lay on the floor. McKinney crawled the short distance
until he was close to the aisle and looked around. He saw a
grenade explode right at the feet of the closest Vraxar, enveloping

it in the blast. It hardly even flinched and continued firing, keeping the men pinned down.

"Webb, Musser, can you get a shot off? We've got two of them now."

"I can get a shot off, sir," said Webb. "There'll be no time to aim it unless you're trying to get me killed."

"Do what you can, else they're going to wipe us out!"

Neither Webb nor Musser were visible from where McKinney was hiding. He saw one rocket race away, its trajectory clearly marking it as a miss.

"Damnit," said Musser.

"That third one is coming our way," shouted McKinney, flicking another grenade around the edge of the bench towards the two aliens. "Try harder!"

The ominous sound of heavy footsteps informed him that one of the Vraxar was advancing, doubtless with the intention of getting a clear shot at the squad. A few of the men rose up, trying to bring it down with repeaters. McKinney joined them, firing a short burst before a clattering of enemy fire drove him to the floor again.

Clay Reeves was killed, reduced to something unrecognizable when he remained in sight for too long. Ricky Vega screamed something across the open channel and the squad medic Armand Grover swarmed towards him, pulling a med-box behind him.

"Clifton, what have you got?" yelled McKinney to the squad's lone explosives man.

"You don't want to know, sir."

"I do want to know!" shouted McKinney furiously. "Why do you think I'm asking? Stop pissing around and throw something, you stupid bastard! We're getting murdered here!"

"Whatever you say, sir."

McKinney wasn't sure which bench Clifton was hiding behind. He looked frantically around and caught sight of a square, light-blue object sailing through the air overhead. He tried to predict where it was going to land – somewhere near the far exit he guessed.

"Everyone get down, that's on a really short..."

The explosion drowned out the end of the sentence. The entire, vast room was lit up in brilliant white-blue light, overloading the sensor in McKinney's visor. Static covered his vision and his earpiece emitted a high-pitched squeal of distress. Flames from the plasma charge washed outwards and upwards. They hit the ceiling with tremendous force and were diverted sideways and downwards, creating a hurricane of fiery wind. It swept over the bench in front of McKinney and engulfed his body. He shouted his defiance at the fire, commanding it to leave him alive.

The light faded, taking the worst of the heat with it. The sensor feed in McKinney's visor stabilised and the squealing in his ears disappeared. He raised his head cautiously over the top of the bench to see what damage the explosive charge had wrought.

One of the Vraxar was almost completely incinerated – its armoured body was slumped over one of the flatbed lifters and it burned fiercely and brightly. The second was upright and aflame. It was still alive and it struggled to lift its chain gun. McKinney opened up on it with his repeater and watched impassively as his bullets plunged through the heat-softened armour. In a moment it joined the other Vraxar in death.

"Up!" he ordered. "TO Rhodes said there were four of these things and it won't have escaped your attention that we've only killed three."

McKinney assessed the situation. Three soldiers had died in the engagement and Ricky Vega had lost a hand. His spacesuit had sealed over the wound and in combination with Grover's med-box, the man spoke as if he couldn't give a damn about the injury. If he lived through this, one of the Space Corp's medical facilities would happily grow him a new hand. For the moment, he couldn't fire a gun very well but he wouldn't slow them down.

If there was one positive to be taken, it was proof that the level of toxins had fallen far enough that the human skin's exposure to the air wasn't sufficient to cause death. Or at least McKinney hoped that was the case.

"My repeater's out of ammo," said Munoz. "Those bastards sucked up a lot of bullets."

A few of the other men were in a similar situation and they dropped their repeaters to the ground. The weapons could be reloaded easily enough, but here on the *Juniper* it was just as likely they'd be able to pick up a whole new replacement rather than finding a spare magazine. McKinney checked how much ammunition remained in his repeater. *Thirty percent.* It was lower than he wanted, but not so low that it was time to abandon the weapon.

"What if there's another of those things along there, Lieutenant?" asked Corporal Evans. "There's no way we could kill one if we ran into it in the corridor."

"The rockets took out the first one," said McKinney. "We'll need to take care we don't get surprised, so we can get the first shots away. More importantly, there's no choice for us – we have to keep moving or we're going to be overrun by the Vraxar behind us."

"Yeah."

McKinney rounded the men up and got them moving. He tried to convince himself there'd be time to mourn the fallen later, but he couldn't give himself that promise.

The workshop was a mess and the air was more than a hundred degrees hotter than it had been when they first entered it. McKinney's suit was blistered in patches but still intact. It now creaked when he walked, which he figured was an acceptable outcome given what the material had endured.

"Clifton, what the hell was that?" he asked, remembering the size of the blast. "Didn't you have anything smaller?"

"I didn't want to take any chances, sir."

"There's something wrong with you, Clifton," said Garcia.

After the struggles so far, it was a surprise to meet no further resistance on the way to level 285. The squad heard occasional sounds, without being to identify exactly where they were coming from. Other than that, it appeared as though they'd outpaced the Vraxar coming from behind and whatever enemy were on the upper levels, they hadn't yet reached this far. McKinney wasn't at all convinced it would be plain sailing from here – there was another one of those huge Vraxar out there, still looking for the survivors. *The Juniper is big. Maybe it got lost.*

They reached the *Juniper*'s primary comms hub room a full five minutes ahead of Sergeant Woods. The hub was another square room amongst the thousands of other square rooms that filled the orbital. It was accessed by a single doorway in a wall at least ten metres thick. The door was in its recess to one side – all the alloy in the world didn't make a difference if the enemy could disable your most sophisticated locks.

McKinney walked slowly into the room, his eyes taking in the three rows of comms consoles. There'd been a full shift working here by the looks of it – most of the chairs were occupied, whilst there were seven or eight bodies on the floor and another propped forehead-first against the replicator. A cup of dark fluid sat unclaimed in the serving slot.

"I worry that I'm getting used to all this," said Garcia. "Look, these two consoles are operational."

"Leave them, soldier. I don't want you breaking anything before Lieutenant Cruz gets here."

"Sergeant Woods and the others are coming, sir," said Mills. "I can see him outside."

"Give him a wave."

Moments later, several figures dressed in a mixture of military and civilian spacesuits entered the comms room. It wasn't exactly crowded, but they were too bunched up for McKinney's liking. He ordered most of the people out and instructed Corporals Li and Evans to find somewhere outside they could fortify.

There wasn't a lot of time for greetings, nor to find out how Sergeant Woods had made it so far without apparent difficulty. McKinney was sure he'd find out later.

His HUD overlay identified Lieutenant Cruz amongst the figures remaining in the room. McKinney stepped forward. "We're in deep trouble again."

"I'd laugh if it wasn't so awful," she said, holding her gauss rifle across her chest as if she were afraid to lower it for even a second.

"We need to get a message out to the Space Corps. In case they think we're all dead."

"They won't come for us, Lieutenant," said Woods. "Our fleet doesn't have the firepower to take out whatever it is that's captured the *Juniper*."

"We're going to do something – even if it fails."

"These look like the secondary comms consoles," said Cruz, taking a few steps across the floor. "They must run off an alternative power source."

"We haven't had a chance to pull the bodies away," said McKinney.

He joined Cruz at one of the consoles. The former operator's head was tipped back and his mouth was open, as if he'd fallen asleep at his station. McKinney put a hand under the man's shoulders and hauled him off his seat. The body was stiff and it retained its pose when he placed it reverently onto the floor.

Cruz took the dead man's place. She studied the console briefly, before reaching out with both hands. Her fingers darted here and there across the screens and the buttons.

"There," she said. "I've send out a distress signal, letting the Space Corps know we're still alive." She turned in her seat. "Do you want the bad news?"

"Go on."

"The signal will take a couple of hours to reach Atlantis and longer to get to Overtide."

"I can wait," said McKinney. "It's not so long to find out whether they're going to attempt a rescue or not."

A message appeared on one of the console screens. McKinney had been around this stuff long enough to realise it was a response code. Cruz was on it in a flash, sending an acknowledgement.

"There's a Space Corps warship shadowing us," she said. "A spy vessel."

"That's not going to get us out of here," said Woods.

A note of excitement appeared in Cruz's voice. "It's Captain Blake," she said. "He's asking details about our situation."

"Tell him we're in the crap."

"He wants specifics."

McKinney smiled behind his visor. "Give him a run-down."

It took a few minutes and Captain Blake asked a series of questions which Cruz answered concisely. It seemed as if Blake had something in mind, though McKinney couldn't for the life of him predict what it was. Shortly, he was to get an answer.

"He's got a plan, Lieutenant McKinney!" said Cruz. "He's sending over instructions about what we should do. You are not going to believe this."

McKinney listened and, as Cruz had promised, he didn't believe.

CHAPTER FIFTEEN

ON A SPACESHIP as fast as the *ES Devastator*, the journey to planet Vontaren took only a few short hours. The planet itself was nothing out of the ordinary. It had a diameter of fifty thousand kilometres and circled its sun at a distance which ensured its surface temperature rarely climbed much above freezing. The battleship arrived into the endless chill of the vacuum, dropped to an altitude of thirty thousand kilometres and established a course and speed which would complete a full circuit of the planet every forty minutes.

Admiral Henry Talley watched the sensor feed for a time, as if the strength of his intent could somehow pull answers from nothingness. They'd arrived here only a minute ago and already he was feeling impatient. Vontaren was a place like countless others, though its unusually jagged surface hinted at millennia of tectonic movement. It was a good place to hide something.

"I recommend we activate the stealth modules as a precaution, sir," said Commander Adams.

"I acknowledge your suggestion. We'll stay as we are – I'm not in the mood for subtlety."

"Our first scan covering the visible side of Vontaren has come back negative, sir," said Mercer. "We'll definitely need a second sweep if you want to be sure."

"Keep at it."

"What exactly are we looking for?" asked Ensign Banks.

"When the Robanis first told me they had found Obsidiar, I expected they'd discovered some kind of natural formation – a seam of it on the surface, waiting to be mined. Now, I think there's something else. You're looking for something made of metal, Ensign."

"A spaceship?" asked Lieutenant Johnson.

"It seems the most likely explanation."

"We have nothing out here."

"Which leads to the conclusion that it would not be one of ours," said Talley. "Let us have no more speculation for the moment."

For the next fifteen minutes, he kept his crew on edge by pacing around the bridge. He was convinced they were on the brink of something and he was desperate to find proof of it.

"Here!" said Mercer. "What the hell?"

Talley hurried over to her console. "What have you found?"

"This, sir. There's a Robani scout craft circling over an object. They're way lower than we are."

"Have they seen us yet?"

"I don't think so."

"Let me see the sensor feed."

The image appeared at once, cold and grey. It showed the small scout vessel at an altitude of only a few kilometres – just high enough to clear the peaks of a range of high mountains. There was something below, wedged between the walls of a wide canyon. Talley stared at it in wonder.

"How big is it?"

"Pushing thirty thousand metres long and ten thousand

across the beam, sir. It's hard to be certain, since a lot of it's hidden."

"Is there anything in our databanks?"

"Checking...no. That vessel type is unknown to us."

There was a spaceship on the surface – a vast, incredible construction of metal. Talley reached out a hand and traced an imaginary line across the sensor feed. There was no doubt the vessel had crashed. It had come in at an angle and it was easy to see the damage to the surrounding mountains where it had impacted. He guessed it had stuck the surface, skipped up, hit the ground again and then skidded along for a few hundred kilometres before coming to rest at an angle in the canyon.

The spacecraft itself was flat and from above it looked like the end of a trident, with squared-off tines making up the final ten thousand metres of its length. Its hull alloys were a lighter colour than those of the Vraxar spaceships. Talley supposed this could be a new type of Vraxar craft, but it didn't seem likely.

"There's something utilitarian about it," Talley said. "It's not a vessel of war, from its appearance."

"Their engines are offline," said Lieutenant Johnson. "I reckon there's a breach in their hull somewhere, since they're throwing a whole bunch of positrons into the sky."

"I can see weapons clusters," said Mercer. "Plus a few missile batteries and a particle beam dome near to what I assume is the front. I can see if the technology is a known type?"

"It's Estral," said Talley with certainty. "Has that scout still not detected us?"

"No, sir. They must be too busy looking beneath, rather than above."

Talley shook his head. "At least the Space Corps no longer has to put up with the incompetents piloting that particular scout. Bring us close above them – *really* close."

The battleship's autopilot did as it was asked. It put the

warship under maximum thrust and the *Devastator*'s engines grumbled for a little over eleven seconds. When the manoeuvre was complete, the huge battleship was less than two thousand metres higher than the scout craft and directly above it. The smaller vessel was only a few hundred metres long and utterly outclassed.

"We've got their attention now," said Mercer. "The ship's captain – Felicia Beck - wishes to speak with you as a matter of urgency, sir."

"I don't need to speak to her. Ask if she's carrying any Obsidiar. At the same time as you're asking, scan the scout's hull and find out if she's lying or not."

"She's playing dumb, sir – pretending she doesn't know what Obsidiar is. She also tried to sneak out a comms message to Roban, which I blocked."

"Let the message go to its destination, Lieutenant. It won't affect the outcome of what happens here."

"The scan of their hull is complete. They are not carrying any Obsidiar."

"Tell Captain Beck that now is the time to recover anyone she might have left on the surface."

"Their crew is all onboard."

"If she wishes to volunteer any information, tell her it will go in her favour when the reckoning for this nonsense comes."

"Captain Beck has nothing to say."

"In that case, tell her to piss off immediately or we'll blow her out of the sky."

Talley didn't swear often and this outburst raised a few eyebrows amongst the crew.

"Do you want me to use those exact words, sir?" asked Mercer.

"It'll get the message across."

Captain Beck showed no signs she wanted to test Talley's

resolve. The scout wound up its fission engine and skipped away into lightspeed. Lieutenant Johnson captured some details from the fission cloud and set the *Devastator*'s twenty-four cores working on a prediction. The scout was small and its destination wasn't far, so the result came back almost at once.

"I'm pretty sure they're going to Roban."

"No surprises there. I want drones launched as soon as possible. Set them to finding the hull breach in the vessel below. Next time I speak with Fleet Admiral Duggan, I would like to have some good news for him."

The *ES Devastator* was equipped with dozens of programmable drones. They were unremarkable to look at – two metre cylinders of smooth metal, with protruding arms, probes and sensors that could fold flat during flight. The drones could survive in the most hostile environments and it was generally a lot quicker to launch one instead of mobilising a unit of soldiers.

"I've launched ten drones," said Ensign Jay Lewis. "That's the recommended number based on the size of the target object."

The good old days when everything was by the book, thought Talley. It wasn't a criticism and he certainly wasn't going to mock any of his crew for following procedure to the letter.

"Contact with all ten is strong," said Ensign Harper. "I can divide the bulkhead screen to show a split of each drone's sensor feed if you wish, sir."

"That would be appreciated."

The drones were fast and agile. The feeds showed them darting this way and that as they separated around the stricken spaceship. The *Devastator*'s sensors had already established there was no breach in the upper side of the hull and the drones flew to the concealed edges where the spaceship was partway into the canyon.

"That gorge is about eight thousand metres deep and three

thousand across," said Mercer with a low whistle. "And it's still nowhere near big enough to fit that thing inside, whatever it is."

"It's an Interstellar," said Talley quietly.

Drone #3 found the breach and more besides. Where the left-hand side of the spaceship was wedged into the canyon, there were extensive markings on the thick metal plating of the hull. Several thousand square metres were blackened, pitted and heavily cratered.

"Particle beam," said Commander Adams. "And damage from other stuff I don't recognize."

"Those other areas nearby look like the result of impact with Vontaren's surface," said Talley.

The drone hovered for a few seconds and then it was off. It accelerated rapidly towards the front end of the vessel. There was a five-hundred-metre tear in the hull, where the metal plates were buckled and bent. Talley saw a duller metal which he recognized as Gallenium engines. The drone flew onwards, until it found a place where the rip was deeper still – there was a three-hundred-metre jagged-edged hole leading to the interior. Drone #3 wasn't programmed with fear of the unknown. It sped through the hole and into the spaceship.

The drone emerged into a huge, open area within the vessel. It was difficult to be sure of the dimensions – Talley guessed it was several thousand metres wide and with a far greater length. The floor was scratched grey metal and the ceiling was more than two hundred metres high. There were no lights but the drone's image intensifiers picked up a jumbled stack of objects a thousand metres to the left. The spaceship was tilted and the drone sped down the slope to investigate.

"What's all that stuff?" asked Mercer.

"Cargo," said Talley. "It must have been held in place by gravity clamps until they lost power."

There was an enormous quantity of equipment – ten billion

tonnes of excavation machinery, construction vehicles, pre-made factory units, compact smelters, cranes, engine modules. Everything necessary to start afresh was crushed together in the hold of the ship.

The drone didn't remain in place – it flew through the room until it located a wide exit doorway towards the front of the ship. Here, it entered a second storage area. This room was smaller, though still with a large enough footprint for a Galactic class heavy cruiser to have landed upon, were it open to the skies.

"Drone #3 has registered a catastrophic drop in temperature," said Harper. "I'm not sure what that's all about."

"Obsidiar," said Talley. "Chill exudes from it. Hold the drone there and rotate its camera slowly so we can get a better view."

This part of the hold was packed with shaped pieces of Obsidiar. Brackets were fitted to the walls and floors and each set of brackets held a block or a cylinder of Obsidiar. The pieces were many different sizes. Some were only as big as a four-seat transport shuttle, whilst others reached from the floor to the ceiling.

"Billions of tonnes," said Talley. "Enough to fulfil the Confederation's needs for a hundred years."

"And give us a fighting chance against the Vraxar?" asked Lieutenant Johnson.

Talley wasn't ready to commit an answer to that question and he simply shrugged to indicate he'd heard the words.

"Drone #5 is inside and has found a second exit from the rear cargo area," said Harper. "Maybe there'll be even more Obsidiar."

"Perhaps." Talley dragged his eyes away from the emperor's ransom in the forward storage bay and followed the progress of Drone #5. It entered a series of narrower corridors, turning left and right apparently at random.

"Another holding area," said Harper. "What's all this?"

The drone hovered patiently in the middle of a space much

smaller than either of the cargo bays. Its instrumentation measured the room to be ninety metres long, eight wide and ten high. There was no decoration, but there were alcoves in each wall. These alcoves were three metres long and a metre high. They were arranged in rows and columns, with absolute precision. This room contained exactly one hundred of these alcoves and in each recess was a grey-skinned humanoid. They lay flat on their backs, their eyes closed and their expressions unreadable.

"Are they Ghasts?" asked Mercer.

"Not Ghasts, Lieutenant. I think these are their parent race - Estral."

"The drone isn't picking up any life signs," said Harper. "They're all dead."

The drone had seen enough of this room. It located an exit on the opposite wall and it continued its flight deeper into the spaceship. The horror of it soon became apparent – there was a vast area of the vessel given over to identical rooms. They were linked together by a series of grid-patterned corridors, each one leading to another of the rooms.

"Endless rooms, endless dead," said Talley. The Estral had sought to destroy humanity, but there was something profoundly sad about all these bodies lying here, perfectly preserved.

"How many do you think there are?" whispered Ensign Chambers, her eyes wide. "And could any of them be alive?"

"They're all dead," said Talley. He didn't want to put a number to the catastrophe.

Lieutenant Poole wasn't so restrained. "If this pattern is replicated throughout the remainder of the ship, there could be upwards of eight hundred million bodies here."

"What were they doing?"

"Running," said Talley. "When the Estral realised their defeat by the Vraxar was inevitable, they sent their people as far away as they could with the resources they'd need to start again."

"A last throw of the dice," said Adams. "I wonder how many more of these Interstellars are out there."

"We'll probably never find out, Commander."

"Why did this one crash, sir?" asked Sykes.

"I don't know, Ensign."

Talley sat down to think. The Estral Interstellar had suffered damage to its hull, consistent with a beam weapon attack. On first glance it didn't appear to be that which had resulted in the hull breach – the impact with Vontaren was the more likely cause. The only thing he could think of was some kind of complete and utter failure of several critical onboard systems. *Consistent with a total loss of power,* he thought. Talley sat upright.

"Lieutenant Mercer, please analyse the marks on the surface of the planet produced by the Estral ship's landing."

"What do you want to know, sir?"

"I would like to know when this happened. Ensign Harper, I assume those drones gather enough information for us to ascertain when the ship was attacked?"

"Yes, sir. I'll run the data through one of the *Devastator's* cores and tell you what it comes back with."

Mercer answered first. "The marks on the surface were made sixteen days ago, sir."

"Is that a certainty?"

"Yes – sixteen days, nine hours and twenty minutes ago if you want it a little more precise."

"It took them a long time to get here," said Adams.

"They had a long way to travel."

Ensign Harper was looking nervous. He rubbed his face and muttered to himself.

"What's the matter, Ensign?" asked Talley.

"I can't get the results I was expecting."

"The results are what they are. You can't alter them to what you want them to be."

"I know that, sir."

"What's the problem, then?"

"The analysis shows that this vessel was attacked nineteen days ago, sir. In addition, I've accessed data from the *ES Lucid's* encounter with the Vraxar near Atlantis, which confirms the same weapons types were used in both places. It probably wasn't the exact same Vraxar, of course."

Talley went cold at the news. He had no reason to doubt these findings, but what it meant was that the Vraxar were also in the Confederation's Tallin Sector.

"How the hell did they get here?" he asked.

"Maybe they've got a way to follow through lightspeed, sir," said Lieutenant Johnson. "It could be that this Estral carrier thought it had reached safety, only to find a pack of Vraxar ships were after it."

"The Estral got away, though."

"It's a big ship, sir. It might have made a last-ditch effort to escape, but only managed a couple of days at lightspeed before its engines shut down and it crashed here."

"Why didn't the Vraxar follow?" mused Talley.

"Could be this Estral ship had an escort which took out the Vraxar, sir," said Adams.

In these moments of speculation, Talley had a thought of his own – one which he didn't like at all. "Maybe the Vraxar *did* follow. Maybe they arrived in time to watch the Robani prospector find this Obsidiar and then they realised they'd stumbled across another new race to conquer."

"The attack on Atlantis happened only a few days after this Estral carrier came down," said Adams. "Atlantis is a long way away, so how come they were able to attack at two ends of Confederation Space so quickly?"

Talley threw up his hands. "If only we knew more about them! What if there are a hundred independent Vraxar fleets, travelling in a hundred directions until they find something to kill? What if they are a single group, sweeping outwards in a pattern set out by a computer so powerful it can predict where other races are by the light from their stars?"

"And what if they've been waiting for the last two weeks in deep space somewhere close to Roban, watching until they decide it's time to attack?" asked Adams. "Or scanning comms traffic to see if they can find a link to other Confederation worlds?"

What if they followed the Devastator here to Vontaren? thought Talley suddenly. *To destroy us while we are away from the other warships at Roban?*

"I'm reading a fission signature, sir," said Lieutenant Johnson. "There's something big about to arrive."

"Get our shields up and activate the stealth modules!" shouted Talley, wondering if he'd learned to predict the future. "Get us moving but stay close to the crash site."

With the *ES Devastator* on full battle alert, the crew waited anxiously. Ten seconds later, the inbound vessel exited lightspeed forty thousand kilometres away.

"It's the *Gallatrin-9*, sir."

Talley thumped his clenched fist against the arm of his chair. "Those idiots!" he snarled. "Those stupid idiots!"

His fury wasn't directed towards the Ghasts - it was the Robanis. They'd evidently guessed where the *Devastator* was headed and, rather than allow the Confederation to take the Obsidiar away from them, they'd given the location to the Ghasts. What they hoped to achieve from their actions wasn't clear and Talley could only assume this was a last-ditch effort by the Frontier League to keep what they thought was their prize by stoking up conflict between humans and Ghasts.

The bad news kept piling up. Before Talley could order a

channel opened to Tarjos Rioq-Tor on the Ghast battleship, a highest-priority comms message reached the *Devastator*.

"Sir, we've received an automated signal from the *ES Furnace*, letting us know it's entered combat," said Mercer.

"Request more details, immediately!"

"I'm trying, sir," said Mercer. "Ensign Banks, try and contact one of the other rebel warships."

"And while you're at it, get me a channel to someone in the damned Robani Council," said Talley.

The *Devastator*'s comms teams tried to connect using every method available. Meanwhile, the Ghast battleship powered up its gravity drives and sailed with menacing, unhurried grace towards the Estral carrier's crash site.

"The *Gallatrin-9* has its shields up, sir, and there's a lot of power running through its beam turrets," said Adams. "Looks as though they're ready for anything."

"There's no answer from Roban or its fleet," said Mercer. "It's like they've had a complete shutdown."

There was only one conclusion to draw. "The Vraxar have decided to show up," said Talley. "With the *Devastator* and the *Gallatrin-9* out of the way, they've taken their chances and attacked Roban."

"It's only a matter of time until the *Gallatrin-9* sees through the stealth cloak, sir," said Adams. "They must already know we're here."

"I'm aware, Commander."

It was a difficult situation and Admiral Talley tried hard to think of the best way to proceed. He could only think of one thing and there was only one man who could authorise it.

"Get me Fleet Admiral Duggan," he said. "I don't care where he is, or what he's doing. Get me a channel to him *now*."

Talley sat and waited.

CHAPTER SIXTEEN

THERE WAS a palpable air of uncertainty on the bridge of the *ES Blackbird*, as there had been for the last forty-five minutes since they'd been in contact with Lieutenant McKinney and the other survivors on the *Juniper*. Blake's crew were shellshocked at the outline of the plan and they were clearly building up the courage to question him about it.

"Are you sure this is wise, sir?" asked Lieutenant Pointer, the first one to put words to what everyone was thinking.

"It is absolutely not wise," Blake confirmed. "We have no choice."

"You could hand off the decision to Fleet Admiral Duggan, sir," said Hawkins. "There's still time before we attempt a rendezvous."

"He does not want to micromanage every single one of my decisions. Besides, deep down, you know he's going to say the same thing. Admiral Duggan does not leave his people behind."

"But sir..." Hawkins began.

"Enough, Lieutenant. We're not abandoning Lieutenant McKinney to his fate. I made a commitment."

"Believe it or not, that isn't the suggestion I'm making, sir. I simply want to be sure we aren't throwing away a chance to destroy these three Vraxar warships. This might be the one and only time we find them clustered so conveniently."

"And what are the Vraxar going to do when they realise something's amiss?" asked Quinn. "Will they sit in one place, waiting to see what transpires?"

Blake remained silent, his eyes locked on the tactical display. The mothership was exactly ten thousand kilometres ahead and the accompanying Neutralisers continued flanking at a distance of five thousand. In his mind, Blake had an opinion about what the enemy vessels would do once he put his plan in to motion – he simply wasn't ready to share it with the others.

"There are fifteen minutes left," he said. "We're going for it."

None of the crew offered a further objection and Blake was pleased for it. He was sure they were as loyal to the Space Corps as he was and they would do their best to pull off the exceptionally risky plan they were embarking upon.

"I'm bringing us to within a thousand kilometres of the mothership. Activate the energy shield," he said.

"The shield is operational, sir."

"Please confirm the enemy vessels are still running without their own shields."

"The enemy shields are down, sir."

"How many of those cannons do they have on the underside?"

Pointer helpfully brought up a zoomed image of one of the brutal-looking turrets which the mothership bristled with. "Dozens," she said.

"Anyone want to hazard a guess how many rounds it'll take from one of those things before our shield gets knocked out?"

"Well, sir. The kinetic energy contained in a dense metal

object travelling at the anticipated speed from a gun with a bore the size of that would be..."

"Save the specifics for later, Lieutenant. I imagine the answer is in the approximate region of *not very many*."

"Yes sir, I'm sure you're correct."

The brightest minds in the Space Corps were of the opinion that sudden bursts of high acceleration were the best way to flag up the presence of a vessel running under the concealment of stealth modules. The second-best way was to load up for a jump into lightspeed. Consequently, any hopes of making either a quick approach or a fast escape were too big a risk for Blake to contemplate.

"Is there any way to see if we've been scanned?" he asked.

"These Hynus sensor arrays are able to detect that kind of activity," Pointer confirmed. "We've been subjected to a general wide-area sweep on more than two hundred occasions since Lieutenant McKinney made contact. That's standard stuff, which is why I haven't mentioned it."

"Will you get warning if they become suspicious?"

Pointer crinkled her nose. "There's a bit of guesswork involved in all of this, sir, since the Space Corps is distinctly rusty when it comes to on-the-edge engagements with vastly superior enemy warships. On the other hand, if they change their pattern of scanning, I'll pick it up straight away."

"That's when we start getting worried," said Quinn.

They reached a distance of a thousand kilometres from the enemy warship – in terms of space combat, it was a miniscule gap. Blake knew if the *ES Blackbird* was detected, there was an excellent chance they'd be destroyed before any of them were able to blink, with or without an energy shield.

"I'm going to close to within ten klicks of the enemy warship," he said. "Lieutenant Pointer, are you sure you can determine the thickness of those bay doors once I get close enough?"

"Assuming they aren't made of something totally new, then yes I can tell you how thick the metal is."

"Lieutenant Hawkins, you're the most familiar with these Shimmer missiles. They're as good as I've heard, right?"

"Possibly better, sir. I'm sure you know the rumours about what they cost."

Blake knew only too well what each missile cost to build. After his escape from Atlantis on the *ES Lucid* with its locked-down Shimmer tubes, he'd done some digging. When he eventually unearthed the information, he wasn't surprised the Space Corps didn't want the costs made public. Hawkins implied she knew specifics, but it was almost certain she was guessing or relying on hearsay.

"We're only carrying four Shimmers," Blake said. "If the first two fail, we're not going to get a second chance."

"Not with a thirty second reload interval."

At ten klicks, Blake was sweating. The mothership was close enough to see with the naked eye, had there been a way to do so from the *ES Blackbird*.

"Those cargo doors are something else," said Hawkins in wonder. "This probably isn't a mothership at all, you know? I reckon it's just a heavily-armed lifter."

"You might be right. Either way there's plenty of room for them to do all sorts of other crap onboard, as well as stealing our orbitals."

"I'm beginning an intrusive scan of their hull," said Pointer. "It might take a few minutes to interpret the data."

There was an instant reaction from the Vraxar vessels.

"Oh shit. They didn't like that."

"Have they found us?"

"Not exactly *found*, sir. They know something's up. They've replaced their wide-area scan with a series of narrower sweeps."

"They haven't altered course yet. It might be they are only acting cautiously."

"It could be, sir." Pointer didn't sound like she was persuaded.

"Keep on with the scan of their hull."

Blake clenched his fists and did his best to ignore the numerous warnings on his tactical console. The ES *Blackbird's* AI was well-aware the enemy vessel was hunting for them and it provided estimates of how far each narrow-beam sensor probe was from pinging off their hull. As well as that, it provided a moving average of the figures. The chart showed the enemy's search was becoming steadily more effective.

"Not long until they pinpoint our location, Lieutenant Pointer."

"I'm aware of the urgency, sir."

Another warning illuminated on of Blake's screens. There was no mistaking this one for anything other than extremely bad news.

"They've just taken a shot at us," confirmed Hawkins. "A new type of beam weapon went by at a distance of eighty kilometres."

"For a first try that's a little bit too close for comfort."

"They've had another go. They've fired from three different beam domes. The closest was sixty klicks away."

"We're running out of time, Lieutenant Pointer."

"You don't need to repeat yourself, sir. The scan is almost done and the analysis of the data so far is ongoing."

She was right and Blake knew he was pushing her too far. Pointer's work up until now had been exemplary and he had no reason to think she was dragging her heels. On the other hand, he hated being unable to influence events and sitting waiting to be blown up wasn't an experience he wanted to last any longer than necessary. He glanced at his tactical – the enemy narrow-band sweeps were averaging five kilometres distance, with the closest coming to within two. He hoped the Vraxar hadn't realised exactly how close the ES *Blackbird* was.

"The Neutralisers are changing course," he said. "The left-flank vessel is dropping away."

"They probably expect we're running off Gallenium," said Quinn. "They're trying to envelop us in their neutralisation field."

"The doors are just shy of three hundred metres thick," said Pointer.

"That's a lot of armour. Lieutenant Hawkins, do we have the firepower to punch a hole through them?"

"It'll be close, sir."

"Close won't be good enough. Let's hope the weapons labs have done the business." He swivelled in his seat. "Lieutenant Pointer, can you tell me whether they've got the *Juniper* clamped at the front or the rear?"

"No, sir. It's going to be tight in there wherever it's positioned."

"The mothership's energy shield has just gone up and we're trapped inside it," said Quinn. "They're getting jumpy."

"There's no escape for us now unless we jump through it at lightspeed," said Blake. "And we're not leaving without at least attempting to rescue Lieutenant McKinney."

As far as he was aware, there were no reports of a spaceship successfully hiding within the internal perimeter of an energy shield sphere. When it came to it, there weren't many spaceships out there with the power to project a shield as far as this Vraxar mothership.

"Let's get to within five klicks," he said. "Arm the Shimmers and target the centre of the bay doors."

"The Shimmers are armed," said Hawkins.

"Something tells me we don't have long."

Blake was right. Before he could reach the desired range of five kilometres, twenty of the wide-bore cannons flanking the bay doors rotated from their rest positions and started firing. They didn't operate like the Bulwark cannons, which relied on firing speed as well as the high velocity of their projectiles. The Vraxar guns fired in a constant thump-thump-thump, each activation launching a twelve-metre slug into space.

"Crap," said Blake when his tactical warned him one of the projectiles had passed within a whisker of the ES Blackbird's energy shield. "Load the Shimmers."

Before Lieutenant Hawkins was able to complete the request, one of the Vraxar slugs struck the ES Blackbird's energy shield. The projectile was flattened to a depth of only a few inches and it fell away into space. The Blackbird's Obsidiar power reserves plunged.

"Shimmers loading."

"That hit on our shield is going to give them a pretty good idea where we are," said Quinn.

Another blow struck the shield and then another. Each successful strike took a big chunk from the power source which sustained it.

"Fire when ready."

"Still loading."

"We'll be dead in about ten seconds."

"Loading complete. Firing Shimmers."

"Begin reload."

"Yes, sir. Beginning reload."

The gap between the two vessels was only a few thousand metres. It was insufficient for the Shimmers to reach maximum velocity. Nevertheless, they crossed the intervening space in less than a second and struck the Vraxar mothership within a hundred metres of each other.

The Shimmer missiles were equipped with armour-piercing

warheads and carried an enormous payload. They detonated simultaneously, creating a vast, joined crater in the hardened alloys of the bay doors. Twin plumes of plasma were ejected downwards, their heat and energy dissipating into space. The area surrounding the impact site glowed in a variety of blues, oranges and reds, concealing the extent of the damage.

"Did we get through their armour?" asked Blake. "Lieutenant Pointer, get me a scan of that area!"

"Sir, it's not clear. The sensors are struggling to make sense."

The explosions had not stopped the turret fire and the barrage directed towards the *Blackbird* continued unabated. Not every projectile hit the spaceship's shield, but the accuracy was increasing.

"We've got less than twenty percent left on our energy shield."

"No! We didn't get through!" said Pointer. "There is no breach through their hull. Damnit – we came so close! There must only be ten metres left."

Blake swore. "How long on Shimmer reload?"

"Fifteen seconds."

A series of successful strikes against their energy shield knocked it to below five percent. It didn't seem like they were going to get those fifteen seconds.

Blake pulled on the control rods, dragging the *Blackbird* sharply to the left and then pointing it nose-upwards towards the impact crater from the missiles.

"We're going in," he said.

In his mind, Blake saw no other option. He fed a huge amount of power through the spaceship's engines and it rocketed forward. The nose of the *Blackbird* smashed into the damaged area of the Vraxar mothership's hull. The cargo bays weren't breached but the metal of the doors was soft from the plasma heat. At the moment of impact, the *Blackbird* was travelling so quickly and with such impetus that it burst through the metal doors. The alloys of both vessels buckled and rippled under the immense forces and for a second, Blake felt sure they were going to get all the way through into the bay. In the end, the *Blackbird* became stuck, with its rear four hundred metres protruding into space.

There was the briefest of lulls in the bombardment from the Vraxar turrets and Blake dared to hope the weapons were not able to strike at objects so close. It wasn't to be – the firing resumed, reducing the *Blackbird*'s energy shield to the brink of failure.

Blake gritted his teeth. "I won't have this," he said. With that, he pushed the control bars as far along their runners as they would travel. The muted humming of the spaceship's gravity engines climbed to a shrieking howl, unlike anything he'd heard before. Bit-by-bit, the *Blackbird* ground its way through the gap, pushing aside the metal as it burrowed deeper into the Vraxar mothership.

"Not going to make it," said Hawkins.

"Yes. We. Are."

The energy reserves of the *Blackbird*'s Obsidiar core dropped to zero. The energy shield winked out and one of the Vraxar slugs struck the rear of the vessel with a glancing blow, sending a shockwave rolling through the walls of the bridge.

With no Obsidiar power remaining, the *Blackbird*'s engines went offline without a murmur. The lights on the bridge stuttered, flickered and then strengthened. Almost every screen on the bridge went blank.

It was enough. The bombardment from the external turrets stopped and all was silent. With a shudder, the *Blackbird* settled, coming to rest on its underside at the bottom of the cargo bay.

"We made it," said Pointer. "I didn't think it would happen, but we made it."

Whatever victory they'd accomplished, Blake had no idea how short-lived it might be. He'd banked on the Vraxar lacking the foresight to line their cargo bays with weaponry. Not that they could be expected to predict the sort of manoeuvre they'd just witnessed.

"Lieutenant Quinn, see if there's any residual power left while the Obsidiar core recharges."

"There's something, sir. Nothing significant."

The screens within the bridge illuminated again. The looks were for show and most of the functions were disabled or unavailable for use.

"I want a sensor view of what's in here with us. Can you get me a feed?"

"Bringing one up now, sir," said Pointer. "It's going to be grainy, but I don't think that'll be a problem given how close we are to whatever's in here."

The image appeared on the main viewscreen and Blake had to squint and turn his head before he could make sense of it. The *Juniper* was suspended from the roof of the cargo bay, held in place by immense cube-shaped gravity clamps which were just visible on the closest side wall. There were fewer than two thousand metres between the orbital and the floor of the bay and Blake realised how close they'd come to crashing into it when they'd burst through the hull.

"What now?" asked Pointer.

"Now you try and reach Lieutenant McKinney. Tell him we've come and we're waiting for him in the bay."

"Yes, sir. I'm looking for a channel. I don't know if we'll be able to reach their suit comms through the walls of the *Juniper*. Let's hope their pack man is checking his comms unit regularly."

"I'm picking something up," said Quinn.

The tone of the man's voice caused Blake to look across intently.

"What is it?"

"I'm not sure. The data I'm receiving isn't complete. I thought I detected a reading."

"Spit it out! What sort of a reading?"

Lieutenant Quinn wasn't given the time to respond. The crew on the *Blackbird* experienced a brief feeling of dislocation, accompanied by a harsh nausea. Blake tensed his muscles to try and alleviate some of the racking pains in his abdomen. A few moments later, the feeling subsided.

"We've gone to lightspeed," he said.

The crew looked at each other, as-yet uncertain what to make of this new development. Blake attempted to put a brave face on matters, when in reality he couldn't think of any positives. Wherever the Vraxar were taking them, it wasn't likely to be a stretch of empty space into which the Blackbird could make an easy escape. The others picked up on his unease and they sat in their seats, with nothing to say.

Blake closed his eyes and hoped he hadn't ruined his chance to destroy these three huge Vraxar spaceships.

CHAPTER SEVENTEEN

LIEUTENANT ERIC MCKINNEY cast his eye over the men and women lined up in front of him. There were thirty in total – he'd lost four from his own squad and Sergeant Woods had lost three in a firefight with the Vraxar. The survivors were made up from twenty armed soldiers, many with their spacesuits showing signs of combat damage, and ten non-combatant personnel. The latter were dressed in lower-grade suits which were designed for day-to-day functions onboard the orbital. A few of them carried gauss rifles.

Lieutenant Cruz was senior by rank time served, but she wasn't trained as a troop commander in the way McKinney was. She followed procedure without complaint and let him lead.

"We have to get up to level 300," he told the group. "I've spoken to one of the technical officers up there and she tells me the hangar bay is clear."

"The enemy were flooding into the upper levels as we came through," said Sergeant Woods. "I can't understand why none of them were in the hangar bay."

"We can't worry about it, Sergeant. TO Rhodes is certain her shuttle will get us out of here and in the absence of any conflicting information, I'm happy to accept her word."

"The hangar doors are shut," said one of the new soldiers.

"Yes, they are," said McKinney. "Captain Blake told me he'd deal with that problem."

The most obvious way of dealing with the matter of the *Juniper*'s closed hangar doors wasn't lost on anyone.

"Who gives a shit if it gets messy?" said Corporal Li. "The Space Corps isn't getting the *Juniper* back any time soon."

"Let's say we bust out of here and get onto this spy craft – what happens next?" asked Roldan.

"One step at a time, soldier. If we keep taking those single steps, we'll get home safe and sound."

"Yeah. I didn't think we'd make it this far, sir."

McKinney called for silence and arranged the new men and women into squads, so he could have at least some semblance of control over them. The non-coms had all been through basic training when they entered the Space Corps and he was pleased to find they knew what to do.

"Let's move out, people!" he shouted.

They set off, aiming for the closest stairwell. Sergeant Woods had experience of the command and control levels and he was able to offer more efficient guidance than that provided by the overlay on McKinney's HUD.

"They used to have minigun turrets installed in the ceilings here," said Woods. "Years ago, that was. One day they took them out and didn't replace them."

"I heard about those," said Bannerman. "Rumour has it one of the guns chewed up a big group of scientists it mistook for Ghasts. Or something like that."

"Here – these steps will take us up to level 300," said Woods. "We came down the stairwell on the opposite side of this level."

"Why didn't you use these stairs?"

Woods shrugged. "Six of one, half a dozen of the other, sir."

"You didn't find much resistance?"

"We had to kill a couple of Vraxar on the way. Other than that, we didn't come across anything significant."

McKinney wasn't happy. "You should have taken us to the place where there were no enemy, instead of here where we don't have a clue how many there are."

"You're right. I'm sorry, sir."

There was no choice other than to let it go. "I suppose everything could have changed in the last few minutes. It's guesswork as to which way is safer," said McKinney. "Did you see anything big on the last few levels?"

"They're all pretty big, sir."

"I don't mean as big as a Ghast, I mean something that was twelve feet tall."

"Those *armoured bastards* I heard one of your men talking about?"

"Yes, those ones. There hasn't been a lot of time to fill you in on every detail," said McKinney. "They're resistant to explosives and our repeaters didn't do a lot to their armour."

"We aren't carrying anything heavy," said Woods. "We haven't come up against many Vraxar, so we've got plenty of ammo left in our rifles. Other than that..."

Woods left it hanging. McKinney didn't need it spelling out for him – he'd already checked out what additional weaponry this new group of soldiers had brought with them. They had no plasma tubes and few grenades, but they all carried rifles. They'd stopped by on one of the upper floor armouries and hadn't bothered to tool up properly. A reprimand was due, but it would wait for the appropriate moment.

The stairwell was wide enough for six people to walk abreast and it climbed away from one of the rooms on the perimeter of level 285. McKinney peered inside – it was a larger version of the many other stairwells he'd already climbed to get this far. Each flight went upwards and then turned back upon itself at a square landing.

"I can hear something," he said.

A few of the others listened intently, trying to figure out if there was any cause for alarm.

"Same old noises we've heard up until now, Lieutenant," Corporal Li concluded.

Woods didn't seem unduly alarmed and McKinney was worried the sergeant might have found the going too easy up until now. On the other hand, he'd managed to lead a group of survivors this far, so McKinney realised the man must have something going for him. *Or he might simply be exceptionally lucky.*

"These take us out not far from the main entrance to the hangar bay," said Woods. "We didn't need to visit the bay on the way down."

"Fine, we advance by squad," said McKinney. "Secure, advance, overlap and secure again."

"Yes, sir," said Woods, evidently aware of the tactic.

McKinney took off in the lead with Squad A, the members of which were now bolstered by the addition of Casey McCoy to replace the dead Zack Chance. The new man didn't say much, not that McKinney found the trait objectionable.

The advance went smoothly until they reached the landing for level 295. McKinney found a group of six Vraxar in the reception room, heading away along one of the corridors. Luckily, he spotted them before he was detected. It gave him great pleasure to order Squad A to shoot the alien foot soldiers in their backs. So swift was the attack that the normally fast Vraxar weren't even given the opportunity to turn and find out who was killing them with such efficiency.

When the last of the enemy fell, McKinney stayed in place for a moment, his eyes hunting along the two other exit corridors from the room. The deaths of the aliens didn't bring any others running.

"Hands up who's disappointed there were only six of them," said Garcia, picking up on the mood. Shooting the Vraxar was enjoyable work.

A couple of the soldiers laughed, while the others kept focus on the job.

They climbed the last five floors at a fast pace. The interior levels of the *Juniper* weren't evenly spaced and it seemed to McKinney as though it was more than a hundred metres between each new floor. Given the quantity of hardware he was carrying in combination with the weight of the spacesuit, he wasn't surprised that the muscles in his legs complained loudly. His HUD recommended he accept a mixture of three different stimulants, as well as a moderate dose of battlefield adrenaline to top up the drugs he'd taken earlier.

A moment after he'd given his agreement, he felt a series of jabs from the suit's micro needles. The effect was near-instant. The pain in his legs vanished and he felt as if he could carry two hundred pounds over each shoulder. With renewed vigour, he pressed on past level 299.

On the second-last landing, McKinney brought Squad A up from one of the mid-landings, in order to be in the lead when it came to entering level 300. Sergeant Woods was on the landing, with Squad D. Everyone was anxious now that their destination was within reach and the soldiers stood nervously, their gauss rifles trained towards the landing above. They didn't want to get caught here if a Vraxar patrol decided to take a look into the stairwell.

"Give me another quick rundown of what we're going to find at the top," said McKinney.

"There's plenty of maintenance stuff up on level 300, sir. They keep a few spare tech modules in case they need to do a swap out on anything docked. Levels 300 through 310 are where the *Juniper* has the biggest diameter, so there'll be a little bit of running."

"We'll enter the secondary storage area, cross into the maintenance yard and there'll be an exit to the far right which will enter the hangar bay?" asked McKinney, tallying the directions from his HUD overlay with Woods' on-ground knowledge.

"That sums it up, sir. If we end up fighting in those areas it might get messy – there are lots of places to hide and it could be that we get pinned down if the enemy plays it right."

"We'll need to move fast."

"Speed is good. Level 300 takes up a lot of space."

"More room for us to avoid the enemy, Sergeant."

"I hope it works out that way, sir."

With the battlefield adrenaline burning in his veins, McKinney took the steps two at a time. He clutched the barrel of his repeater, taking comfort from the weapon. As eager as he was to kill more Vraxar, he knew it would be infinitely better if they didn't encounter any more of the aliens.

He paused on the exit landing and looked carefully into the secondary storage area. As promised, it was huge. The lights were failing – in some places there were patches of near-darkness, whilst in other areas it was merely dim. He tried to figure out the dimensions of the room - according to the pings from his visor sensor, the ceiling was more than three hundred metres above. The far walls were obscured by the quantity of equipment crammed into the space, but he could see enough to be sure they were a long way distant.

The storage area was arranged like a warehouse – metal crates and boxes were stacked high to the ceiling in some places, whilst in others they were only two or three boxes high. Wide aisles ran between the stacks, though from McKinney's position in the doorway he could only see to the left and right. Directly ahead was a lump of what he assumed was solid Gallenium. A flatbed lifter was off to his left, as dead as everything else on the orbital.

There were positrons in the storage room – not sufficient to kill, but enough to flout all manner of the Space Corps' own recommendations. Then, McKinney noticed there was a door separating the landing and the room – the door was currently hidden away in its recess. Presumably when the power was on it served as a barrier against unwanted emissions.

McKinney didn't wait for long. After assuring himself here were no sounds to indicate the presence of Vraxar, he brought the rest of the soldiers up - there was plenty of room for them on the landing. He provided a few brief instructions and then set out into the storage area with Squad A on point.

With a quick run, he reached the block of Gallenium opposite. He walked alongside it until he could look around into one of the main aisles which ran directly across the floor of the storage area. This entire area was neatly arranged and he could see all the way to the far wall which was their destination. The exit itself was concealed from view. The group was going to be exposed for long periods when they advanced. It wasn't perfect but there was no choice.

It was strangely eerie and McKinney couldn't shake the feeling that this part of the *Juniper* was as alien as the Vraxar ship which had captured the orbital. He couldn't quite put his finger on why – maybe it was the scale and the size of the containers which loomed above, not that the storage room was any more impressive than other places he'd seen within Space Corps installations.

He looked over his shoulder to gauge the readiness of Squad A and then beckoned them to follow. He stepped out into the fifteen-metre-wide aisle and walked quickly and silently towards the next intersecting lane, fifty metres away.

From the landing it had seemed quiet. Now that he was in the room, he heard distant noises – the clanking of metal on metal and unidentifiable creaking sounds of something under stress. The footsteps of his men were muffled by the immense solidity of the scarred metal floor.

"Squad B moving to follow," said Corporal Li, his voice hushed.

"Squad C holding," said Evans.

McKinney reached the intersecting aisle and checked both ways. The storage area was arranged in a grid, which meant every one of the lanes stretched for a few hundred metres. It gave the Vraxar plenty of opportunity to attack from the safety of distant corners. McKinney switched on both his movement sensors and image intensifiers. This gave a less comfortable view than an unmodified feed and most soldiers were reluctant to rely wholly on this *enhanced* sight.

"Squad C moving up," said Evans.

"Squad D waiting."

It took a few minutes, but they made it across the secondary storage area without incident. During the course of the transit, McKinney found his eyes distracted by some of the punched metal label plates fixed to some of the crates. *LS Module Drop-In QD. Height Adjusting LL Hinges. Unit Console Models X1.* It was a world of terminology he was unfamiliar with. The contents of one particular box were easily understood. The main label stated *Model 19R3-W Response Restock*, underneath which someone had written further words in black ink: *Bulwark ammo – yo!*

The exit into the maintenance area was predictably large, since it needed to allow the movement of items from the storage room. The doorway passed through an internal wall a few metres thick and then opened into what was a larger version of the room in which they'd fought the armoured Vraxar.

McKinney remained in the storage area while he waited for the other squads to catch up and spent these few moments trying to make sense of the items laid out on the low, solid metal work benches. There were artillery gun barrels, the turret from a Gunther V tank, an object which appeared to be the landing foot from a fleet destroyer, lenses from a sophisticated sensor array, along with many other pieces of kit he only partially recognized.

The creaking sound McKinney noticed earlier was louder here, though he was no closer to guessing what it was. From the doorway he couldn't see the entirety of the room and he wondered if there was something balanced precariously which was grinding against another object.

"Once we're inside, we head right," said McKinney. "A couple of hundred metres, I make it from my overlay."

"Close enough, sir," said Woods. "This maintenance area forms part of the outer perimeter of the *Juniper*. When we get inside, you'll see the left-hand wall has a curve to it. The hangar bay makes all these other rooms look like small stuff in comparison."

"I'll do a check of the area with Squad A. We haven't seen a Vraxar in too long and I'm getting worried."

The others of Squad A gathered nearby without waiting to be called. McKinney stepped into the short tunnel formed by the *Juniper*'s thick internal walls. It wasn't far to walk and each additional footstep revealed more of the maintenance room. His eyes picked out bodies of the orbital's personnel, fallen in random places. Then, when he was right on the threshold of the maintenance room, he found out what the cause of the creaking sound was.

"Oh shit," he muttered. He passed a warning across the comms channel. "Everyone be absolutely quiet!"

Garcia was right behind and he saw it too. "What the hell?"

The two men stared.

"This is where they're getting in," said McKinney.

"Must be. One of many places."

To the left of the entrance doorway, there was a circular penetration through the outer wall of the *Juniper*, into which a round metal access tube had been pushed. This access tube was six metres in diameter and made of a near-black metal. Its leading edge was viciously serrated, leading McKinney to believe it doubled up as a drill to get through the hulls of whatever the Vraxar brought into the hangar bay of their mothership. He could see all the way along the access tube – pale blue and sickly green lights reflected against the dark metal. There were Vraxar soldiers around the entrance, standing motionless. They gave no sign of having seen or heard McKinney.

"Sergeant Woods, come and take a look at this."

Woods came. "Not good," he summarised concisely.

"How many of them can you count?" asked McKinney.

"Twenty-five."

"Repeater turrets to the left and right, would you agree?"

"They look different to ours, but I'd lay money on them being some kind of repeater, sir."

"That's what I thought."

McKinney stepped back to think. The enemy soldiers were approximately a hundred metres away and standing in no particular formation. The repeaters didn't have a crew, though that didn't mean anything – they could be set to fire automatically based on any number of criteria. One thing was certain – these Vraxar presented a significant obstacle to the squad's progress towards the hangar bay. Even if they could successfully kill the aliens, it would raise the alarm in the mothership. It was certain they'd pour reinforcements through quickly once they realised what was happening.

McKinney wasn't given the luxury of planning time.

"I think I saw something, back here in the storage room," said Whitlock across the open channel.

"There's something coming, Lieutenant," said Munoz.

McKinney heard the discharge of two gauss rifles. The sound was repeated and joined by a third. The non-coms shuffled deeper into the entrance tunnel, squeezing up against the soldiers and pushing them forward. Return fire from the Vraxar pinged and whined as their slugs deflected from the walls nearby.

Whatever good luck they'd experienced so far, it was fast running out and McKinney was determined he wasn't going to fail now. Unfortunately, it appeared as if the Vraxar had other plans for the surviving personnel of the *Juniper*.

CHAPTER EIGHTEEN

WITH VRAXAR ahead and more approaching from the rear, McKinney was spurred into action.

"Webb, take out the left repeater, Musser you get the right. Don't wait for each other. Do it quickly and see if you can incinerate some of the guards at the same time. Roldan, you've got a good arm – try and land a grenade in there once Webb and Musser have fired."

Webb was with Squad A and already near to the front. He spun up his plasma tube and ran towards the edge of the doorway. McKinney continued giving orders.

"Squad D, watch our rear. B and C, we're making a run for that bench over there once Musser's fired his tube. If you see anything move, shoot it!"

The words hadn't left McKinney's mouth before Webb got his shot off. The plasma rocket screeched away and detonated with a thump. Webb jumped away out of sight.

"Direct hit. They know we're here now - Musser, you're going to have to time yours well."

Musser's sour reply indicated he wasn't particularly

impressed with the news. Even so, he got his tube in position and activated its warm-up. He leaned out and fired, before hurling himself away from the edge. A fusillade of enemy slugs smashed into the wall opposite.

"Did you hit?" asked McKinney.

"Negative, sir."

McKinney swore – the bench he intended to use for cover was ten metres away from the doorway. There would be ample time for a repeater to shred anyone attempting to cross the gap.

"Roldan, you'll have to throw blind unless you want get yourself shot."

"Here's a greeting from Tillos," said Roldan, pitching one of his plasma grenades into the room. He didn't need to make himself visible to do the throw and the grenade sailed away, following a high arc.

A few seconds later, Webb's tube was recharged for a second shot and he moved into position. Shots clattered nearby as the Vraxar tried to keep the soldiers pinned down. There was no sign of fire from the repeater turret and McKinney hoped it had been damaged or disabled by the grenade.

Webb started to perform his familiar step-fire-hide routine, which would bring him into sight for only a second. His rocket burst from the tube, at the same time as a Vraxar bullet entered the soldier's chest and exited from his back in a bloody cloud. Webb made a sound of puzzlement and dropped to his knees.

"Grover! Get here!" McKinney bellowed over the comms. He didn't know if Webb's shot was successful and knew he would have to gamble. He ran out of cover into the maintenance room, sprinted five quick paces and then threw himself headlong behind one of the benches. "The rest of you, move!"

"There're plenty coming up from behind," said Woods on the open channel. "Looks like the Vraxar are getting their act together."

From the corner of his eye, McKinney detected the closest members of Squad A preparing to follow. He lifted his head and looked over the top of the bench. The Vraxar access tube was smoking with plasma heat, and his visor sensor detected a shimmering in the air which he hoped indicated the repeater turrets were destroyed.

They were running out of time and McKinney knew it. He saw movement. A group of Vraxar soldiers stood to one side of the access tube, firing their hand cannons towards the doorway. It was sufficient to make the men in the passage wary about emerging. McKinney was a good shot with a gauss rifle and he took aim. The first slug took one of the Vraxar in the head. He changed target, fired and repeated three more times. On each occasion one of the enemy soldiers fell. They hardly even attempted to take cover and he wondered if they were designed to be nothing other than meat shields. *When you've conquered as many races as the Vraxar, you can probably afford to treat your soldiers as disposable assets,* he thought.

A few of McKinney's squad took advantage of the opportunity afforded by his accuracy with a gauss rifle and they darted over to join him. Roldan was amongst them and he threw another grenade as he ran, sending it towards the enemy with a tremendous heave of his arm.

"They're going to start coming through that access tunnel at any moment," said Garcia. "I'll bet they've got a hundred thousand troops on that mothership."

"Best get these ones shot quickly and then we can move on," McKinney replied grimly.

One of the Vraxar grenades detonated with a thump on the other side of the bench. McKinney saw it land but wasn't quick enough to get out of sight. The extreme edges of the blast struck his suit. It wasn't enough to breach the material but it was enough to trigger warnings on his HUD.

For the next few moments, the remaining Vraxar exchanged shots with McKinney's squad. Without assistance from their repeater turrets, the aliens were easy targets and they weren't able to reach the cover of the workbenches without being picked off.

The engagement ended when Musser fired a second plasma rocket into a cluster of the enemy soldiers. The explosion turned them to charcoal and scattered their remains in several different directions.

"That's the last of them, sir," said Musser.

"Until the whole damn lot on the mothership come for us," said McKinney.

He barked out a series of orders, directing the withdrawal of Squad D from the passageway leading into the storage room. Webb wasn't in a good way and he was covered in huge quantities of blood from his injury. McKinney had no idea if the man would survive. The squad medic, Armand Grover had taken charge and he directed some of the non-combatants to assist with getting Webb moving.

"We're going straight for the hangar bay. Squad D will cover our backs."

McKinney urged the survivors on towards the exit from the maintenance area. It was only two hundred metres away, though it seemed like much further given the pressure they were under. He called Bannerman up to run alongside him.

"How long since you heard from the *ES Blackbird*?"

"Back in the storage area, sir. They're still shadowing the Vraxar spaceship."

"It's been about fifty minutes since they first made contact. Another ten minutes and they'll be ready to start firing."

"If everything goes to plan, sir."

Just then, McKinney felt a surge of acceleration, savage and crushing. He stumbled and Bannerman did likewise. The sensation passed quickly and he steadied himself. A few of the squad were picking themselves up from the ground. They threw questions into the open channel.

"We've gone to lightspeed," said McKinney. "I don't know what that means, so don't ask. We're sticking to the plan and going to the hangar bay."

"I don't know if the *Blackbird*'s comms will be able to reach this pack now, sir. Comms don't work at lightspeed," said Bannerman. "I can't detect them as a receptor and we should assume they will have the same problem. We're blind to each other."

"Just another thing to add to the pile, Corporal."

The high-pitched whine of gunfire brought McKinney back to the present.

"Report!" he shouted.

"There's movement at the storage room entrance, sir," said Woods. "They're coming after us."

McKinney glanced over his shoulder. There was no sign of enemy reinforcements spilling through from the mothership – not yet. *They'll come*, he thought, increasing his speed.

They entered the enormous expanse of Hangar Bay One, travelling at little more than a jog. Webb was slowing them up and, in addition, the front squads were required to provide cover to Squad D as those men fell back.

The bay was a stark, cold place. It was partly lit in blue-white, whilst in other places the red warning lights cycled in warning. The external doors were to McKinney's left – they were gargantuan slabs of metal which, when retracted, could allow smaller warships to berth inside the orbital. The wall opposite the bay doors was punctuated by deep alcoves, which were used by the maintenance teams for minor works and also for storage.

There was a Space Corps prospector in the bay, resting on its support legs in the middle of the floor. This model wasn't much more than a few hundred metres long and with a pitted hull which spoke of many years in service. The prospectors were mostly comprised of sensor arrays tuned for geological investigation, along with an engine that was only just suitable for carrying them around Confederation Space. They were rarely armed and this one was no exception to the rule.

McKinney strode deeper into the bay, doing his best to spot the place where T.O. Rhodes had managed to hide not only herself and twenty other technicians, but also an operational shuttle. She'd provided a description on the comms, but it wasn't easy to join her words with the picture.

"T.O. Rhodes. We are in Hangar Bay One. Please update us as to your exact location."

"I can see you, Lieutenant," she said. "I'm waving."

McKinney had already gathered that T.O. Hattie Rhodes was *one of those people.* A person who was perfectly decent and hard-working, but who wasn't quite able to grasp when it was time to be serious.

"This is not the time!" he said. "We are taking fire and Captain Blake is going to blow the main doors open in less than ten minutes."

A figure emerged into view, a good distance to McKinney's right. The figure was waving vigorously in his direction. McKinney suppressed a sigh.

"We're over here, Lieutenant! In this maintenance unit."

McKinney didn't respond immediately. Instead, he beckoned his squad onwards, urging them to make haste out of the maintenance area. Once done, he turned his attention to Rhodes once again.

"What maintenance unit?"

"This one," she repeated, as if it were the most obvious thing in the world.

McKinney was about to make a sharp retort. He held his tongue and stared past her at a section of the wall in the corner of the main bay. At first glance, it appeared as if there was nothing there. When he focused, he saw that there was, in fact, another one of the alcoves, with something squeezed in so tightly there was hardly any room around it. When he realised this, the additional details become clear – this was the square rear-end of an ancient shuttle behind which the technicians must have taken refuge. If you weren't looking and had no need to go any closer, it was very easy to miss, though the hiding place wouldn't have fooled the Vraxar forever.

"Is the shuttle warmed up?"

"Just like you ordered, sir!"

"Start backing it out."

"We can't."

"What's wrong? Is it stuck?"

"No, sir. None of us knows how to fly it."

"Why didn't you say so earlier?"

"You didn't ask."

McKinney gritted his teeth. "Can you at least get the rear door open so we can come onboard when we reach you?"

"Of course, sir. How else could I have come out to see you if the door wouldn't open?"

On any other day, Rhodes might have been entertaining to speak with. On this day, she was particularly infuriating. McKinney couldn't allow himself to be angered by such little things and he did his best to ignore her obtuseness.

Nearby, Squad D completed their retreat from the maintenance area. Sergeant Woods was the last man out and he threw himself around the edge of the doorway between the two zones. Movement in the air suggested a fusillade of shots had followed his escape.

"Looks like we poked them too hard, sir," he warned. "Got a small army of them coming out of that mothership."

As Woods spoke, a Vraxar rocket shot through the wide doorway. It continued across the bay and detonated in a blossom of dark energy against the side of the prospector, leaving a smouldering patch on the vessel's outer armour.

"Definitely time to move," panted Garcia, joining the men and women sprinting towards Technical Officer Rhodes.

While he was running, McKinney saw the entire rear section of the shuttle dropping away, to reveal the interior. The surviving technicians were inside, milling around with the uncertainty of people who had never dreamed their jobs would bring them face to face with murderous aliens. The passenger area was easily big enough to carry everyone, but there'd be a few people standing.

With a burst of speed, McKinney dashed past the lone figure of Rhodes and reached the shuttle first. T.O. Rhodes stopped waving and she turned her head to follow. His feet clanked over the boarding ramp and he barged his way along the central aisle between the bare metal seats as he made for the cockpit door. One of the technicians – a man from his build - wasn't quick enough to move and he was knocked to the floor as McKinney went by.

"Everyone onboard!" McKinney shouted. He wasn't certain if his command reached every one of the technicians. "Are all your group in the passenger bay?" he asked Rhodes.

"Yes, sir!" she replied. Then, with significantly more doubt in her voice. "One of you *can* fly this thing, right?"

McKinney was trained to fly shuttles, though it was a while since he'd been on anything as old as this one. "Yes," was the only response he gave.

The cockpit door had a *No Unauthorised Personnel and No Decaffeinated Beverages* sign on it. The door was attached to the frame by stiff hinges and it shuddered as he wrenched it open. When he saw the cockpit, he felt a momentary dismay at the age of the equipment. It was so old he wouldn't have been shocked to find a reinforced clear windscreen to look through. There wasn't one – only the sloping front inner wall of the shuttle's wedge-shaped nose.

"When did they build this thing?" he asked Rhodes over the comms.

"Seventy-five years ago," she replied proudly. "There are only five of this exact model operational within the Confederation and you're standing in one of them."

McKinney sat himself on the single seat. It had grey cloth upholstery which the technicians hadn't yet got around to replacing and there was something that looked like dried chewing gum on the backrest. The single control panel was battered and no doubt had more than its fair share of coffee spilled on it over the years. It was still functioning and McKinney was relieved to find it was loaded with the familiar Space Corps interface which had seen decades of refinement, whilst remaining recognizable no matter which version you were using.

"Seventy-five years old is a good thing?" he asked.

"I think most people would say so."

"I'm not one of them."

"You're a grouch, Lieutenant. I hope you know that."

McKinney suppressed a grin and proceeded with the standard list of pre-flight checks. The *Juniper's* technicians were capable of fixing pretty much anything in the fleet, so it was no surprise to find the onboard systems were fully operational. He activated the front sensor feed and an image appeared, covering the front inner wall of the cockpit. The screen showed the area in which the technicians had taken refuge – it was a mess of discarded cups, trays and wrappers.

From the sound of it, he could tell it was getting busy in the passenger bay. Only a couple of minutes remained of the hour Captain Blake said he would wait before destroying the outer doors. The timing was tight.

"Are you ready?" he asked on the comms.

"We just got Webb up the ramp, sir," replied Corporal Li. "You're going to need to close this back door before the enemy get around the corner."

The rear door was activated by means of a mechanical switch. McKinney pressed it firmly and heard the whirring sound of motors. The shuttle itself might have been seventy-five years old, but he guessed the original design went back another fifty on top of that. The button light changed from red to green once the door was closed. It wasn't a moment too soon – immediately the shuttle was sealed, McKinney heard the sound of small arms fire against the rear door. The vessel's armour would be proof against the small stuff, but he didn't want to test it against anything heavy.

The shuttle's engines had a coarseness to them – the sort of charisma McKinney admitted was lacking in modern craft. They responded readily enough when he fed the power into them and he was satisfied they'd do the job.

He counted himself a skilled pilot, but there was no way he intended scraping them out of this alcove inch by inch. There was an autopilot option, buried away in a sub-sub-menu. He turned it on, keeping his fingers crossed that the navigational system wouldn't refuse to operate in such a tight space. It seemed that this shuttle predated the safety-above-all era and the autopilot happily accepted McKinney's command to get them the hell out of the alcove.

The cabin shook and the engines rumbled. McKinney heard the screeching sound of metal dragging over metal. Slowly, the shuttle's engines dragged it out of the alcove. The intensity of small-arms fire against the rear door, which had been sporadic at first, increased until it was a constant rattle. An explosive of some type thumped beneath the shuttle, rocking it against the side walls. McKinney swore under his breath and tried not to think about the damage they were taking.

There was a second blast, larger than the first. The shuttle was so old it didn't even have a way of communicating the nuances to the pilot. Instead, it simply flashed a big, red *Warning!* notice on the second of the four console screens.

"It's getting warm back here, Lieutenant," said Corporal Li. "And there's none of us dressed for sunbathing."

"I hear you, Corporal. Steady as it goes and we'll be out of here soon enough."

"Captain Blake's late, sir."

"Yes, he is. Try not to think about it."

At that moment, the shuttle was enveloped in the thunderous clashing noise of a thousand wide-bore repeater projectiles raining against the hull. The comms became filled with curses and a dozen overlapping questions until McKinney shouted for silence. The only thing he could imagine was the Vraxar had managed to haul another repeater off the mothership and brought it to bear on the shuttle.

"We're going to suffer a breach soon, Lieutenant," said Sergeant Woods. "This heap of crap wasn't made to stop bullets."

"Heap of crap?" came the indignant voice of T.O. Rhodes.

"That's what I said, ma'am."

With one final shudder, the shuttle's autopilot guided it free of the alcove. McKinney grabbed the control sticks at once. He hauled the vessel backwards until there was room to turn. He has happy to discover his knack hadn't deserted him and he spun the shuttle around on the spot, turning it to face whatever was firing at them.

He saw it at once - the fourth of the big Vraxar was there. It stood near to the bay doors, its chaingun pointing directly at the shuttle, spraying thousands of rounds into the hull. Other, smaller Vraxar were scattered close by, firing their own guns.

McKinney wished they'd installed nose guns on these old

shuttles. The weapons control software was loaded, but they hadn't thought to fit a chaingun at the same time.

There were two choices. The safest of the two was to use the inactive prospector vessel as a shield and keep it between the shuttle and the Vraxar. However, McKinney wasn't in the mood for running. Seeing the alien standing emotionless as it tried to deny him and his squad everything they'd fought for filled him with anger.

"Let's see how you like this," he growled.

With that, he jammed the shuttle's joystick forward. Part of him expected the action to produce a steady movement across the bay floor. It didn't. With a harsh resonation of overstressed engines, the shuttle accelerated with incredible speed.

The armoured Vraxar had little time to react. The shuttle impacted with the alien at a speed of several hundred kilometres per hour, shattering its bones and organs, crushing its armour. The Vraxar was hurled away by the force, and it slithered over the bay floor until it thudded against one of the walls. It didn't try to get up.

In the cockpit, McKinney pulled the shuttle in a sharp turn, whilst decelerating as quickly as possible. The vessel missed the bay doors by a matter of metres – it was far closer than he'd intended. He brought the shuttle higher above the floor and steadied it over the prospector. He flexed the tension from his shoulders and emptied the air he'd been holding in his lungs.

The Vraxar didn't give him time to settle. Barely five seconds passed before the hammering on the hull resumed. With horror, McKinney realised it was coming from several directions. He saw the cause – there were at least two more of the armoured Vraxar in the hangar bay. He had no idea where they'd materialised from. He banked the shuttle away, hoping to buy them some time. It was no good and he couldn't seem to find a place where the aliens had no clear line of sight to the shuttle.

"They just popped a hole in us, Lieutenant," said Corporal Li without any obvious sign of panic. "Make that a few holes."

"Stay down!"

"The holes are in the floor, sir."

McKinney was starting to ask himself if he was trapped in some kind of nightmare where everything was deliberately weighted against him. He kept an eye on the bay doors, becoming increasingly convinced that something had gone wrong with Captain Blake's brave plan.

At that point, something exploded in the bay. This time it wasn't small-time like a grenade. A thunderous blast rolled across the entire space, filling it with flames. The blast expanded with hideous speed, emanating from an unknown source. The shuttle was picked up by the force of the explosion and thrown across the bay. All the while, McKinney fought with the controls and uttered curses at everything he could think of.

CHAPTER NINETEEN

ADMIRAL HENRY TALLEY was in conversation with Fleet Admiral Duggan when the Ghast battleship *Gallatrin-9* detected them.

"They got a ping off our hull, sir," said Lieutenant Mercer. "It won't be enough for them to pinpoint us, but they'll know we're here."

Talley raised a hand in acknowledgement and continued talking to Duggan. He was aware that each passing minute without action was time wasted and he spoke quickly.

"There's enough Obsidiar to transform both of our civilisations, John. If we try to deny the Ghasts access to it, they may well feel obliged to fight for it. Their claim is just as strong as ours."

"I know it, Henry."

"Neither the *Devastator* nor the *Gallatrin-9* has a way of carrying the spoils. We could likely recover some of the smaller pieces of Obsidiar using our shuttles and a gravity winch."

"Yes – the *Devastator* is a warship, not a cargo vessel."

"It'll need specialist equipment. We may need to cut the Estral carrier open."

"And if the Ghasts won't cooperate, we'll have a real job getting to the Obsidiar," said Duggan. "Especially so since we're currently at war with the Vraxar. The last thing we want is the Ghasts shooting down our recovery vessels."

"Will the Confederation Council buy my suggestion?"

"They won't be given the opportunity to say no."

"You'll speak to the Ghasts?"

"I'll contact Subjos Kion-Tur immediately and put forward the offer. A fifty-fifty split on what's on that Estral vessel in return for their full military assistance against the Vraxar."

"Will they go for it?"

"I think they're waiting for the chance to get involved. What you've discovered on Vontaren is the game-changer we needed."

"What if they don't like the offer?"

"If they play hardball, I'll tell them the *Devastator* will turn Vontaren into a ball of flame that won't cool down for a thousand years."

"I don't know whether to believe you."

"I don't know if I believe me either. Let's not worry about it until it happens."

"I agree. And when they commit to an alliance?"

"Go back to Roban with the *Gallatrin-9*. The Confederation Council has denied the secession, so, for all their idiocy, the people of the so-called Frontier League are still a part of us. We'll do what we can for them."

Time was pressing but Talley couldn't resist asking another question.

"What about the *Juniper*?"

"We don't know. The Vraxar ship carrying it has gone to lightspeed. The *ES Blackbird* was shadowing it and they've gone off the comms."

"Destroyed?"

"No. They're at lightspeed too. I don't know what's happened – I gave instructions for the deployment of an Obsidiar bomb and it seems that opportunity has been squandered."

"Let's keep our fingers crossed."

"I'm getting arthritis from keeping so many of my fingers and toes crossed." Duggan gave a sudden laugh. "I don't know how this is going to end up, Henry and it makes me feel young again. It's like no outcome is yet decided and we still have everything to play for."

"Good luck with the Ghasts, sir."

"You'll hear shortly."

With that, Duggan left the comms channel. Talley looked around at the expectant faces of his crew.

"We've got to try and avoid picking a fight with the *Gallatrin-9* until Fleet Admiral Duggan gets back to us."

"We could disengage the stealth modules," said Lieutenant Johnson. "That might reassure them we have no hostile intent."

"Let's not give up our advantage just yet. Lieutenant Mercer, please open a channel to Tarjos Rioq-Tor."

"Yes, sir. Their captain has been sending out transmissions asking for a response from the moment they detected us."

The connection was soon made.

"Tarjos Rioq-Tor," said Talley in greeting.

"Admiral Henry Talley. What cargo does the *Astrinium* carry?"

"*Astrinium* is the name of this crashed Interstellar?" asked Talley. He wasn't unduly surprised to discover the Ghasts had a way of determining the vessel's name.

"That is its name. What cargo?"

"Haven't the Robanis told you?" asked Talley, uncertain if this Ghast was a master amongst his species when it came to pretending ignorance.

"They have not, though we can guess."

Since Duggan was in the process of telling the most senior member of the Ghost navy about it, Talley didn't see the need to lie. "The Estral were carrying Obsidiar amongst other things. A great quantity of Obsidiar."

"Which you hoped to keep from us."

"No, Tarjos, which we hoped to share with you. Assuming an agreement can be reached by our superiors."

"What will be the price?"

"An alliance against the Vraxar."

Rioq-Tor laughed, the sound reproduced as a mixture of static and white noise by the translation modules.

"They have already attacked your planet Roban."

The Ghost was well-informed. "And together we will drive them away."

"Together we will *kill* them." There was more laughter. "I would enjoy the opportunity to test the *Gallatrin-9* against those who pushed the Estral to the point of extinction. I hope our superiors reach a consensus."

Lieutenant Mercer waved her hands frantically, mouthed a few words and put both of her thumbs into the air.

"I think that consensus has just been reached," said Talley.

A top-priority message appeared at the head of his list. He scanned the contents, which confirmed what Mercer's thumbs-up gesture had already communicated.

"I am receiving instructions from the Subjos," said Rioq-Tor. "It appears I am to put my battleship at your immediate disposal, Admiral Talley. I am to follow your orders."

Duggan had a reputation for fast action in a crisis and here was an example of it in practise. In a matter of a few minutes, he'd formed an alliance that gave humanity a far greater chance in the war with the Vraxar. Of course, the small matter of a few billion tonnes of the most valuable currency in the known universe played its part.

"We are going to kill some Vraxar, Tarjos. My comms lieutenant will invite you to our network and we will share our lightspeed calculations to ensure we arrive in the same place and at the same time. We are going to Roban and we will not leave until we've destroyed every last one of those bastards."

"That is a plan I like."

Less than five minutes later, the *ES Devastator* and the *Gallatrin-9* were travelling at high lightspeed in the direction of Roban.

"That was easily done," said Commander Adams.

"You always did approve of straight-talking, Commander," said Talley.

"I should have been born a Ghast, sir."

"We're actually going to see some action," said Lieutenant Poole.

"You sound unhappy," said Talley.

"No sir, that wasn't my intention. I'm glad we're going to get something done. It's just that this whole thing with the Vraxar came so suddenly. One minute we're travelling towards Roban to head off the threat of a rebellion, the next thing we know, the rebellion's taken place *and* we're fighting an alien species which has wiped out half of the universe for all we know. So, to summarise, it feels a bit strange but also good to be amongst the first to start the fightback."

It was the most Talley could ever remember hearing from Poole's mouth in one go. "We're going to give them hell, Lieutenant."

The conversation reminded him of something which hadn't been a high priority at the time, since he hadn't been expecting it to become significant.

"I saw a notification that the central weapons guidance lab

has issued new software for the Lambdas. Our missiles were somewhat less than effective during our first engagements with the Vraxar. Have we received the new coding?"

"We did receive it, sir," said Adams. "There was an update for the Shatterer launchers as well."

"What about the Shimmers?"

"As far as I'm aware, they have yet to be tested against the Vraxar. They've not received an update."

"At least the particle beams can't miss."

"A couple of double overcharges will see off those bastards," said Ensign Sykes, using her fingers as a pistol, which she aimed at Ensign Chambers sitting nearby.

Not for the first time, Talley set himself a mental reminder to have Sykes moved onto another warship when they got through this. *Maybe I'll have her assigned to Duggan's office,* he thought with great relish.

The return journey from Vontaren seemed to take less time than the journey out. Talley attributed this to the high levels of activity and preparation which happened on the bridge while they travelled. A nervous energy clung to him, enhancing his senses and making the usually stifling bridge feel cold. He paced constantly in order to keep warm.

After a couple of hours, he caved in and ordered the bridge replicator to vend a huge cup of strong coffee, a drink he'd sworn off many years ago. Now seemed like as good a time as any to reacquaint himself with it. It was like finding a long-lost friend.

Lieutenant Johnson gave the standard ten-minute warning, shouting it loud enough to make the crew jump. It was a call for the testing and the checking to end – a time to settle and mentally prepare for whatever was to come.

Talley lay back in his seat and rested his hands on his chest. The captain's console on the *Devastator* was a vastly complicated and intricate affair, but it was so much second nature to him he could assimilate the information and updates with scarcely a glance. The control bars protruded from the centre section, in exactly the same position as they'd always been. Some captains felt the allure of manual control. Not Talley – he'd always preferred to let the computers handle the flight.

"Two minutes!"

"Everybody remains at their station," said Talley. "You know what's required once we exit lightspeed. We're going to find the Vraxar and we're going to destroy their spaceships. There will be no standoff and no caution. We go in with everything and we don't stop until we have achieved victory. Do you understand?"

His crew understood perfectly and Talley received a chorus of acknowledgements.

The *Devastator*'s cluster of processing cores shut down the fission engines, dumping the battleship out of lightspeed at precisely the time predicted. Five hundred kilometres to starboard, the Ghast Oblivion *Gallatrin-9* did likewise.

"One-point-five million klicks to Roban, sir," said Lieutenant Johnson. "Far enough to see the bigger picture, not so close they can shoot us down before we respond."

"Stealth modules and energy shield activated, sir. The *Gallatrin-9* has activated its shields," said Sykes.

"Send the *Gallatrin-9* a message – make sure they're aware we aren't intending to hang them out to dry by activating the stealth modules."

"Yes, sir."

"Nothing on the nears," said Mercer. "Switching to fars."

"There's barely any activity on Roban," said Ensign Harper. "A few lights amongst the larger population centres and that's about it."

"How defenceless we become when the power is gone," said Talley.

"Our own power is still at one hundred percent," said Lieutenant Johnson. "Wherever the Neutraliser is, we aren't close enough to it for them to shut us down."

Talley gave an instruction and the *Devastator's* gravity engines exerted sufficient thrust to get the battleship moving towards Roban. "Steady as we go," he said.

They continued this way for a few minutes, with the comms team frantically searching for signs of the Vraxar. The *Gallatrin-9* stayed on a parallel course, its own sensors sweeping across the skies.

"Some of our gauges are starting to jump around," said Johnson.

"I wonder if they know we're here or if these Neutralising vessels project a sphere that works on anything close enough," said Talley.

"The *Gallatrin-9* has detected a fast-moving object coming out of Roban's orbit, sir," said Mercer. "Make that two fast-moving objects."

"Put them onto the tactical."

They two approaching spaceships were definitely Vraxar. The closest was five thousand metres in length and the second nearer to eight thousand metres. They made no effort to disguise their course – the two enemy vessels sped directly towards the *Devastator* and the *Gallatrin-9*. Behind, a series of smaller spaceships came into sensor view, these ones following the larger craft. There was no sign of the Neutraliser, wherever it was.

"We're outnumbered," muttered Talley. "Let's hope we aren't outgunned as well."

He didn't think it likely his hopes would come to fruition. It didn't matter – Talley was determined to come out of this engagement victorious.

"Load up six cores for short range transits," he said. "Target Shimmers and fire when ready."

The Ghast captain was already ahead of them. The *Galla-trin-9* was equipped with thirty-two Shatterer launchers and each of them spat out a high-velocity missile, aimed directly at the lead Vraxar.

"Let battle commence," said Talley.

CHAPTER TWENTY

ON THE BRIDGE of the *ES Blackbird*, Captain Charlie Blake could feel things slipping away from him. The spy craft's Obsidiar power supply had recharged to maximum and he kept the vessel hovering a few metres above the immense hangar floor of the Vraxar mothership. The aliens had launched a few small rockets at them from maintenance walkways high above. These rockets weren't enough to cause any significant damage, nor enough to prompt Blake to activate the energy shield, though the explosions would eventually whittle away at the spaceship's outer plates.

The trouble at the moment was the absolute refusal of the battle computer to target the *Juniper*. Lieutenant Hawkins had the ability to re-programme Lambda missiles on the fly, but there was plenty of deeply-embedded coding that she couldn't touch. It was this coding that prevented a launch against the *Juniper's* hangar bay doors. The Shatterers were the same – the original design was copied from the Ghasts, but parts of the guidance systems were taken from existing Space Corps tech, which was to say, the Lambda missiles.

To add to the problems, their comms wouldn't reach Lieutenant McKinney owing to their being at lightspeed.

"I *hate* being late," Blake growled.

"We could still, you know...use the bomb," said Pointer. "I don't like the idea of dying, but we've still got the opportunity."

Blake turned in his seat and smiled. "We're not going to blow ourselves up quite yet, Lieutenant. For a start, I have no idea what would happen if we set off an Obsidiar bomb when travelling at lightspeed. I doubt there has been extensive testing."

"It seems likely we'd destroy this mothership," said Hawkins.

"And let the Neutralisers escape," said Blake. He raised a hand. "Don't worry, I've got no intention of backing away from the difficult decisions. We're still alive and we have to assume Lieutenant McKinney is likewise. While that's the case, we're not going to do anything hasty. Besides, I'm curious to learn where the Vraxar are taking us."

"If they're stupid enough to take us anyplace that's significant to them."

"We don't know if they care what we learn about them. They've shown no indication they want to hide in the shadows. Anyway, we need to get through the *Juniper*'s doors. Can anyone hazard a guess what would happen if we rammed them?"

"Not going to work, sir," said Hawkins at once. "They're too thick for a spaceship of this size to break through. In addition, I'm not sure we have the room to gather enough speed, plus the necessary angle of approach would make it almost impossible to strike the doors dead-on. We'd glance away."

"Do the Shimmers have the same coding as the Lambdas?" he asked. "They're a new design – maybe they didn't expect anyone to target Space Corps assets."

"They fire from the forward tubes, sir. The *Juniper* is clamped overhead, so we'd need to sit on our tail and launch straight into the hangar doors from about five hundred metres."

"Will their warheads activate and detonate from that range?" Blake asked. The Lambda missiles had a failsafe to prevent them exploding in their launch tubes. He didn't know if the Shimmers were the same.

"I genuinely don't know the answer to that one, sir," said Hawkins. "What I *do* know is that we will suffer extensive, perhaps terminal, damage should we allow a Shimmer warhead to detonate so close to our hull. I imagine that anyone within the *Juniper* will be likewise incinerated."

"We have an energy shield, Lieutenant."

Hawkins didn't look happy. "Assuming we manage to balance the *Blackbird* on its tail, activate our energy shield and fire a missile at the *Juniper*'s doors, the explosion may occur within the shield itself."

"It might work, sir," said Quinn unexpectedly. "When the shield is activated, any part of it which would materialise within a solid object is simply not generated. In other words, we can rest ourselves right on the floor of the mothership's hangar bay and the shield will extend into the places where there are no walls. If the leading edge of the shield were to reach the hull of the *Juniper* then it wouldn't be created in that space and Lieutenant Hawkins' description of our likely deaths would be accurate. I don't think that will happen. I reckon there are a few metres spare."

"You aren't going to listen to me are you, sir?" said Hawkins.

"That's not accurate, Lieutenant. I'm not going to agree with you. There's a difference."

"What about Lieutenant McKinney? There's no way to predict how much of the Shimmer explosion will penetrate into the *Juniper*'s hangar bay."

"Lieutenant McKinney is blessed with two attributes. Firstly, he has a natural skill for survival. Secondly and most importantly, he's proven time and again that he's lucky when it counts. We're going to blow open those doors for him and get him out."

Hawkins didn't complain further even if her face showed her inner feelings. It was her place to offer the benefits of knowledge and expertise, but the final decision was not hers to make.

"We're going to move quickly," said Blake now he'd made up his mind.

What he intended wasn't in the manual and the autopilot computer evidently thought something was amiss. It refused to accept the instruction, leaving Blake to do the fine-tuning himself. Swearing under his breath at the inability of computers to do as they were told, he moved the *Blackbird*'s control rods gently until the vessel was positioned directly beneath the doors of Hangar Bay One. He made a couple of minor adjustments until he was satisfied. Then, he rotated the spaceship around its lateral axis until the nose pointed straight up. The *Blackbird*'s tail scraped against the inner side of the mothership's hull.

"Couldn't have got it much closer," said Pointer.

The front sensor feed showed how close they were to the orbital. The *Juniper* appeared as a wall of grey, marked here and there by the impacts from minor space debris. The seams of the massive hangar doors were visible as dark, deep lines.

"Confirm our positioning," said Blake.

"The Shimmer tubes are aimed directly at the *Juniper*'s hangar doors, sir," said Hawkins.

"Activate the energy shield."

"Activated."

"Well?"

"Sir, I can confirm the leading edge of the shield does not extend as far as the *Juniper*."

"We're protected?"

Quinn smiled. "Absolutely."

It wasn't the time for further thought or for the seeking of doubt. "Fire Shimmer tube one," said Blake.

"Firing Shimmer tube one," said Hawkins.

The missile shot from its tube, already travelling at several hundred kilometres per second. The *Blackbird's* battle computer turned off a five-metre diameter section of the energy shield for the briefest of times to allow the missile out. With the weapon gone, the battle computer reactivated the missing section of the shield again.

A moment later, the front sensor feed overloaded and turned into a pure, bright white. Gauges on Blake's console jumped and warnings vied for his attention. The Obsidiar power source maintaining the energy shield took a big dive. When the front sensor array adjusted itself to the high levels of input, it revealed the extent of the damage – there was a hole in the *Juniper's* hangar doors that was several hundred metres across. Plasma fires raged across the metal and the edges sagged, dropping thousands of tonnes of molten alloy onto the *Blackbird's* energy shield.

"I'm detecting signs of small-arms fire within the bay," said Pointer.

"That can only be a good sign," said Blake. "Find out who is shooting at who."

"There's a shuttle!" said Pointer excitedly. "And about three hundred Vraxar on the ground firing at it."

Blake watched the sensor feed, trying to make out the details. He could see many small shapes moving around inside the *Juniper,* along with what appeared to be several much larger Vraxar. The angles looked entirely wrong – because the orbital was on its side, the floor was at ninety degrees to the floor of the mothership's hangar bay. It appeared as if those fighting inside should simply fall to their deaths. Blake knew the only explanation for them remaining in place was for the mothership's life support to extend to everything within its bay. This life support was somehow keeping the entire interior of the mothership's bay pressurized, even with the breach in the outer hull and this new breach into the *Juniper*.

The *Blackbird* wasn't equipped with full-sized Bulwark cannons owing to the constraints of its size and the requirement to fit other hardware into the places a Bulwark might otherwise be installed. It did, however, have a total of eight heavy repeaters mounted in various places about its hull. These were adapted versions of ground artillery guns intended for use against light-to-medium armoured vehicles, though they would happily mow down anything they were aimed towards.

"Set our repeaters on auto," Blake instructed.

"We've only got two turrets with a firing angle," said Hawkins. "Setting those to auto."

The moment of truth. "Will they fire into the *Juniper*?"

"Yes, sir. They're acquiring targets."

"Good. Let's see how the Vraxar like it."

The sound of the *Blackbird*'s repeaters was audible on the bridge as a distant pulsing. The effects within the hangar bay were more immediate. The guns raked a great swathe through the enemy soldiers. Where bullet impacted flesh, there was no subtlety in the result, nor any chance of survival. The Vraxar were smashed away, their bodies flung towards the far walls of the bay.

Blake watched impassively as one of the larger Vraxar succumbed to the onslaught. It was clad in armour of some sort. Its protective coat didn't help and the creature was punched dismissively to the floor, a hundred slugs reducing its body to something unrecognizable.

"Where's that shuttle?"

"Near to the prospector vessel, sir. They're full of holes and I can see where our Shimmer blast caught them. I don't recognize that type of shuttle either. When I spoke to Lieutenant

McKinney earlier he said it was an old model. He wasn't wrong - it looks like it came straight from a museum."

"Is there anything we can do to get a message to them? Even if I have to stand on the *Blackbird*'s nose and wave a flag?"

"No, sir. They can't have failed to notice our arrival. It's down to them now."

The *Blackbird*'s repeaters didn't let up and they killed every Vraxar in line of sight. There were others – they hid to the sides of the hole in the *Juniper*'s bay doors and they attacked from the rooms adjoining the hangar.

"Come on," said Blake. "Take the chance and escape."

McKinney remained true to his type. With the crew of the *ES Blackbird* urging it on, the shuttle emerged from the far side of the prospector. It paused briefly as if it needed time to gather its energy and then it accelerated towards the hole in the doors.

"They've taken too much damage," said Quinn. "Look at the state of it."

"Positive thoughts, please," warned Blake.

The shuttle came under a fresh barrage of gunfire and it lurched to one side when a low-yield explosive burst against its underside. Still it came, flying onwards until it exited through the rapidly-cooling hangar doors. Behind the shuttle, Blake saw a large, elaborate object slide into view. He swore when he realised what it was – it was a mobile missile launcher.

The *Blackbird*'s repeaters opened up again, pummelling the missile launcher with several thousand rounds of hardened Gallenium. The crew cheered when the launcher broke into pieces. A second later, it exploded, spilling a cloud of caustic, dark energy in a wide area around it. The shuttle was unaffected and it completed its escape from the *Juniper*. Once it was clear of the doors, Lieutenant McKinney changed course to take it out of the firing line as quickly as possible. The crew on the *Blackbird* cheered again.

"Should we move into a better position for him to dock?" asked Pointer.

The best place for McKinney to take the shuttle was the rear docking iris – there were closer ones, but they would be in view of the Vraxar on the *Juniper*.

"We're not moving an inch," said Blake. "Once he's through our shield, he should be safe enough from any of these Vraxar rockets."

The next step was uncertain. The Space Corps had only introduced docking irises forty years ago and they required a compatible spaceship in order to latch. Subsequent revisions had seen the release of what were termed *universal* docking mechanisms, meant to work with anything in the fleet. The designers probably hadn't expected the end product to be tested against anything quite so old as McKinney's shuttle. The small vessel came closer, its course erratic. The *Blackbird*'s battle computer made a hole in the energy shield and the shuttle flew through.

"I can't tell you what model engine they've got, but I can definitely tell you their power readings aren't very high. Their propulsion system is failing."

"Will they make it?"

"I don't know."

"Maybe you should land the *Blackbird*, sir," said Pointer. "We could lower one of the boarding ramps."

"We'll give Lieutenant McKinney a chance to succeed at Plan A."

The wait was a nervous one. The *Blackbird*'s sensors showed the shuttle coming in close to the iris. McKinney was clearly flying on manual for whatever reason. His first three attempts to make the connection failed and on each occasion the shuttle bounced away from the iris. There was no way to be certain if these failures were caused by an incompatibility, or if it was because the shuttle was so badly damaged it couldn't hold steady enough to latch.

Blake was just about ready to change his mind and set the *ES Blackbird* down, when the fourth attempt saw the shuttle hitch onto the iris and remain in place.

"Yes!" roared Blake. "See if we've got comms!"

The hull-to-hull connection created a route for the internal comms system. Lieutenant Pointer got a patch through to the shuttle's cockpit.

"There's no one there," she said.

Blake's heart fell until his brain registered Pointer's follow-up words.

"I'm picking up fresh life signs entering through the rear iris," she said.

"How many?"

"They're still coming. They're in a real hurry to get off that shuttle."

"I'm sure."

After a couple of minutes, the last of the new arrivals entered the *Blackbird*'s rear airlock. The numbers were both a triumph and an incredible disaster at the same time.

"There are forty-six additional people onboard," said Pointer.

"Out of how many on the *Juniper*?"

"Ninety-one thousand five hundred and twelve according to the Space Corps' database, sir."

"Forty-six is something?" he asked, numbness spreading through his limbs at the enormity of the loss.

"It's infinitely better than nothing, sir," said Pointer. "I figure we still owed Lieutenant McKinney after Tillos."

"There wasn't much between us on the scales."

"And now there's nothing between us."

"A debt I'd gladly have weighing me down if we could have rescued another few hundred from the *Juniper*."

"Better that it had never happened at all, sir," said Hawkins. "We need to prepare ourselves for whatever comes next."

"You're right, Lieutenant. Our next challenge is how to escape from this mothership and deliver the Obsidiar bomb without killing ourselves and everyone else we've just rescued."

Blake tried his best to avoid dwelling on the downsides. They'd accomplished something, even if it could be taken away from them at any moment. The Vraxar knew the ES *Blackbird* was inside their hull – the situation would definitely become interesting once they got to their destination. Blake mulled over the idea of trying to send the spy craft to lightspeed to see what happened – there were proven instances of the transition allowing a vessel to ignore such trivialities as physical objects. On this occasion, escape was still secondary to finding where the Vraxar were going and then destroying them.

Unable to leave his seat in order to visit the new guests, Blake sent a message to Lieutenant McKinney to welcome him onboard. McKinney reported casualties and advised he would come to the bridge as soon as he was able.

With nothing to do other than wait, Blake remotely activated the purging mechanism on the rear docking iris. The attached shuttle dropped away and crashed to the floor below. He stared at the smoking, bullet-riddled shell for a long time. It seemed a shame to treat it with such contempt, but there was no way he was going to leave it attached to the side of his spaceship.

Meanwhile, the Vraxar mothership continued with its flight, taking them to a place Blake was sure he would rather not arrive.

CHAPTER TWENTY-ONE

THE ENGAGEMENT BETWEEN THE *DEVASTATOR,* the *Gallatrin-9* and the Vraxar ships was in the opening phase, and already it was looking like it would be a hard clash of technologies. The Ghast captain Rioq-Tor had thrown his vessel into the fray with an unsurprising joy. The Ghasts were a military race and they'd been at peace for a long time. Missiles spilled from the *Gallatrin-9*'s launch clusters in their hundreds, crowding the skies as they fought to reach the closest of the Vraxar warships. The range was extreme and Rioq-Tor was evidently trying to saturate the enemy countermeasures and then overcome their shields.

On the *Devastator*'s bridge, Admiral Henry Talley looked at his tactical screen, trying to make sense of the hundreds of objects crowding the display. Amongst the chaos flew a total of six Shimmer missiles, those being the *Devastator*'s sum contribution to the total.

He felt as though his preconceptions of space combat were already being tested. In the scenarios played through in his mind and in the simulators, it was like a strategy game with much higher stakes. Each piece on the board moved in real time, with the captains of the warships doing their best to anticipate and counter. He'd spoken about his methods with Fleet Admiral Duggan over late-evening drinks on occasion. Duggan usually just laughed the laugh of a man who truly knew. *It'll come as a shock to you Henry. Space combat is harsh and it can be utterly unfair. Sometimes I think I must be the luckiest man ever to have lived. Give it everything you have and pray that luck is on your side.*

Inside, Talley felt something click. It was as clear in his mind as two pieces of a metal jigsaw snapping into place. Rioq-Tor knew exactly the way to play it, whilst Talley was tiptoeing around, timidly looking for an opening when his opponent wasn't going to give him that chance. The only openings were the ones he made for himself.

"Target Shatterers. Focus on that lead Vraxar. If we can knock it out before the rest engage, we'll have this battle half-won. Give them every available Lambda X cluster. Tell me the moment we come within particle beam range."

"Yes, sir!" said Commander Adams. "Sixteen Shatterers launched. Five minutes to impact. We have only a thirty percent success rate on Lambda X launch, which makes two hundred and forty in flight."

"Prepare Splinter countermeasures and I want shock drones ready to deploy."

"Sir."

"Try hitting them with a full sixteen-chain disruptor chain as soon as our Shimmers come close. This is the Space Corps' first engagement with this type of Vraxar ship. I'd rather we counter any surprises before they spring them on us. Lieutenant Johnson – do we remain undetected?"

"I can't tell you for certain, sir. They know we're here

because of our weapons launch. I doubt they can target us directly yet."

"Good. Keep me informed."

"The Ghasts don't seem to have any targeting problems, sir. They've launched another nine hundred missiles and a second wave of Shatterers," said Adams.

"They've always been ahead of us when it comes to guidance systems," Talley replied. "I'm not surprised to find there's no change."

"I've launched a second round of Lambdas. Waiting on reload for Shimmers."

At this point, the space between the two sides was filled with missiles, all of them heading in the same direction. There were sufficient warheads to take a big chunk out of even the strongest shield, Talley felt sure. On the other hand, he realised it was foolish to expect the Vraxar to fly meekly into the storm.

"Wait on Shimmers," he warned sharply. "They'll do a short-range transit once we've committed half of our missile stocks."

"Waiting," Adams confirmed. "Looks like the Ghasts are doing the same, sir."

"Lieutenant Mercer, let's have a look at our enemy."

"Bringing the lead Vraxar battleship onto the main viewscreen. It's hard to fix on them."

The smaller of the two Vraxar battleships appeared on the main bridge display. It was V-shaped and built from near-black metals. The outline put Talley in mind of some of Old Earth's earliest aircraft, except there was nothing noble in the alien design. The Vraxar ship's hull was covered in round lumps, along with thousands of short-protruding antennae and dozens of rotating turrets. Its armour crackled with filthy green-blue energy and sparks of it leapt out into space like greedy tendrils seeking life. Every few moments, its outline blurred and it disappeared, before reappearing a few thousand kilometres closer.

"I wonder if they've mastered a way of jumping to lightspeed when it suits them," said Talley.

"I don't think that's the case, sir," said Johnson. "There's no energy build-up, nor any sign of a fission expulsion. Whatever this is, it's a different line of tech to anything I'm aware of."

"The smaller spacecraft look identical to the ones which engaged the *ES Lucid* over Atlantis," said Mercer.

"What about this biggest ship?" asked Talley, watching the second Vraxar battleship on his tactical screen.

"I've just about got lock on them...there!"

The view changed to show the largest of the Vraxar battleships. At eight thousand metres long, it was larger than anything in active service in the Space Corps. It didn't look much like the smaller battleship. This one was a long, bulky cuboid with rounded edges. A series of flat, square wings were fixed along its length. It was equipped with many particle beams and there were two, much larger, squared-off turrets at the top. Its nose curved down slightly, which was the only way to distinguish the front from the rear.

"I don't like the look of those turrets," said Adams.

"Ask the Ghasts if they have any idea what they are."

"They're in the dark the same as we are, sir," said Mercer when she'd finished speaking to her counterpart on the *Gallatrin-9*. "They recommend we don't find out."

Talley kept his eyes on the tactical screen for the next few seconds, wondering when the Vraxar would make their move. The swarm of missiles closed rapidly on the V-shaped battleship, but still it made no effort to evade them.

"Fire another two hundred Lambdas," he said.

"Two hundred Lambdas on their way, sir."

"There's a power surge on the front battleship," said Johnson. "Make that all of the enemy spaceships."

"Here they come," said Talley. "Make sure the Ghasts know it."

There was no time to communicate the details with the *Gallatrin-9*. Simultaneously, the two Vraxar battleships and the four smaller escorts vanished into lightspeed. They reappeared a fraction of a second later, arranged in a semi-circle around the *Gallatrin-9* and at a distance of less than fifty thousand kilometres.

Immediately, the Ghast battleship began spilling missiles from its launch clusters. On one of Talley's status displays he saw needles jump to indicate the discharge of high-intensity particle beams from both the *Gallatrin-9* and the Vraxar warships.

"Holy crap, the Ghasts must have been holding back earlier," said Lieutenant Poole. "I count eighteen hundred missiles in that wave."

"Let's help them out," said Talley. His tactical screen showed there were only two Vraxar support vessels within range of the *Devastator*'s overcharge. "Split front and rear overcharge between those two," he ordered. "Fire immediately. Launch our second wave of Shimmers, stick with the original target."

"Overcharging particle beams, firing," said Adams.

The overcharge was technology stolen from the Estral by Fleet Admiral Duggan several decades before. It used the power of Obsidiar to magnify the strength of a particle beam, allowing it to ignore the protection of an energy shield and to inflict incredible damage. The only downsides were the short range and the immense power draw.

Two wide, invisible beams flickered from the *ES Devastator*'s beam domes, draining several percentages from the battleship's Obsidiar reserves. The effect was instant. The closer of the two cruisers turned from near-black to bright white. Its alloys expanded far quicker than they could cope and the Vraxar ship split into many different pieces, each as bright as a distant sun for a few seconds until the heat ebbed into the chill of space

The second Vraxar ship fared no better. The overcharged beam plunged through its energy shield and into the flattened cylinder of its hull. The rear two-thirds split from the front and spun wildly away, sending showers of incandescent sparks in an oscillating spiral for hundreds of kilometres all around. The crew of the *Devastator* cheered loudly.

"The remaining Vraxar vessels are trying to put some distance between us," said Mercer. "I don't think they liked that."

"They fought the Estral and will know the limitations of the overcharge technology," said Talley. "Commander Adams, tell me when we can fire them again."

"They've got a while yet. Firing Lambdas."

"Keep up the pressure on that first battleship."

Although the Vraxar peeled away from the *Devastator*, they remained in range of the *Gallatrin-9*. The *Devastator*'s instrumentation picked up constant particle beam fire between the two sides, along with a different type of weapon which the Vraxar had deployed against Space Corps warships previously. It was known to be a disintegration beam of some kind, though as yet it hadn't brought down the *Gallatrin-9*'s shields.

"First wave of Ghast missiles about to detonate," said Adams. "No sign of enemy countermeasures."

The Ghast missiles streaked in towards the smaller Vraxar battleship. When they were within ten thousand kilometres, the Vraxar ship demonstrated something new. A vast wave of invisible energy erupted from it, forming a perfect, rapidly-expanding sphere. Where this energy struck the inbound missiles, it burned out their onboard processing units. With their guidance systems destroyed, they were unable to track the moving battleship. Most of them missed their target entirely, whilst others crashed into the Vraxar energy shield without exploding.

"Crap," said Adams. "That's a kick in the balls for us."

The Ghost Shatterer missiles were more robust than the other warheads and these flew through the anti-missile sphere, exploding in a series of enormous blasts of roiling plasma far larger than Talley was anticipating. He stared in wonder at the size of the explosions - the Ghosts had somehow managed to fit a much, much bigger payload to their own Shatterers than that on the Space Corps' version of the weapon. In fact, they seemed to be similar in size to the *Devastator*'s Shimmers, six of which exploded a moment later. It wasn't enough and the Vraxar battleship twisted and turned as it sought to bring its own weapons to bear.

The next few minutes saw a thundering exchange of fire. The Ghosts seemed eager to test their strength and Talley joined them, with battle rage swelling in his chest. The *Gallatrin-9* turned a hundred and fifty Vule cannons onto the Vraxar. White streaks burned across sixty thousand kilometres of space, each one joining the two battleships. The Ghosts fired their disruptors in short, irregular bursts as they sought to bring down the enemy shield. All the while, they fired missiles and particle beams.

The *Devastator* unleashed its full arsenal. One hundred and twenty-eight Bulwark cannons poured out tens of thousands of slugs each second. Missiles and particle beams added their weight to that of the *Gallatrin-9*'s onslaught. Talley ordered the battle computer to get them close enough to use the overcharged particle beam, but the Vraxar hopped from place to place, making it hard to get within range.

The Vraxar did not stand idle under the combined attack. Their primary weapons were particle beams and the dark energy weapon. In addition, they had fast-firing turrets of their own which spilled out in response. The larger of the pair was armed with two huge guns, which fired fifty-metre balls of Gallenium at an incredible velocity with a constant thud-thud-thud. The smaller warships darted around, trying to divide the firepower of the human and Ghast vessels.

"How long can they hold their shield?" said Talley, not sure if he was referring to the Ghasts or the Vraxar.

He checked the status of the *Devastator*'s energy shield – they hadn't taken anything like as much damage as the *Gallatrin-9*, but their shield was close to fifty percent. Something had to give and it did.

"The Ghasts have lost their shield, sir," said Lieutenant Johnson.

With its shield gone, the Vraxar particle beams struck against the Oblivion's hull. Great swathes of its armour glowed with the heat and two huge sections of its hull crumbled and fell away. Still the Ghast captain kept his ship in place.

"I want a short-range transit," said Talley. "Bring us right on top of that Vraxar battleship and then hit them with both overcharges."

The timing was tight. The *Devastator* flashed into lightspeed, covering sixty thousand kilometres in a time so short there was no instrument accurate enough to measure it precisely. The battleship reappeared within five thousand kilometres of the enemy vessel.

"Front overcharge beam firing."

The Vraxar had evidently been waiting for exactly this move. Before Commander Adams could fire the rear beam, the enemy warship vanished into lightspeed, appearing another sixty thousand kilometres away. It hadn't escaped in time and the single overcharge beam had ruptured its underside, leaving a rough-edged, burning, two-thousand metre hole. Unrestrained green-blue energy spat out through the heat in jagged spears.

"Again!" shouted Talley.

Once more, the *Devastator*'s Obsidiar cores hurled the vessel into a lightspeed transit. When it reappeared, both the *Gallatrin-9* and the two Vraxar battleships had vanished.

"What the hell...?" Talley began, with no time to wonder how the Ghasts had managed to reach lightspeed with no Obsidiar power left. "Find them!" He scanned the tactical quickly – the two Vraxar cruisers were still in the vicinity and they resumed firing upon the *Devastator*. "Blow those bastards away!" Talley snarled.

"Rear overcharge firing," said Commander Adams.

The rear particle beam dome whined and thumped in a discharge of energy that could have powered the whole of Roban for a month. The target Vraxar warship wasn't designed to withstand so much punishment and had no way to dissipate the heat. Its fate was the same as the previous two destroyed by the *Devastator* and it became a searingly hot chunk of melting alloy which burned fiercely as it tumbled towards Roban.

"That's going to land bang in the middle of their main land mass, sir," said Ensign Banks. "I estimate thirty minutes and it'll probably be enough to kill half of the people on the planet."

"It'll have to wait," said Talley. "Where're those damned battleships? And why is that Vraxar cruiser still shooting at us?"

"I've got it targeted, sir," said Adams calmly. "Lambdas on their way and our Bulwarks are already firing."

The Vraxar captain wasn't stupid enough to duke it out with the *Devastator*. With a sudden expulsion of fission energy, the Vraxar cruiser vanished into lightspeed, leaving the Hadron temporarily alone in space and Admiral Talley nonplussed.

"Got them!" yelled Mercer. "Our sensors have just picked up the *Gallatrin-9* - it's going across the surface of Roban's moon at more than a thousand klicks per second."

"It'll burn up in no time!" said Talley.

"The two Vraxar battleships are there as well, sir. They're trying to keep up."

Talley opened his mouth to give the order for a short-range transit to assist the Oblivion. Two events occurred before he could speak the words.

Firstly, something detonated on the red-dust surface of Roban's moon. It began as a tiny deep-red pin-prick on the *Devastator*'s sensors, which expanded rapidly. It looked small from this distance, but Talley could only imagine the incredible size of the blast. It continued to spread, growing like it would never stop. Within the space of five seconds, the whole of Roban's single moon was ablaze, like a meteor with a four-thousand-kilometre diameter.

Talley wasn't given the opportunity to assimilate and act upon this development.

"I think the Neutraliser has decided to show its face," said Lieutenant Mercer.

A new object was on the tactical display. It was a spaceship in excess of eighteen thousand metres long and it was flying at high speed from the cusp of Roban and directly towards the *Devastator*.

Split off from the Ghasts, with Roban's moon ignited and a Vraxar Neutraliser approaching, Talley stood frozen while his brain frantically tried to think what to do for the best.

CHAPTER TWENTY-TWO

"WHAT'S HAPPENED to Roban's moon?" Admiral Talley asked. "Quickly!"

"An incendiary, sir," said Commander Adams. "I've never seen the like before."

"It's the Ghasts," said Talley. "Ignore the Neutraliser. Lieutenant Johnson, I require a short-range transit to bring us with twenty thousand klicks of the moon."

It took Johnson all of two seconds to enter the coordinates. "Activating," he said.

The *Devastator*'s engines grumbled and the battleship travelled almost a million kilometres before it arrived within a few hundred metres of its intended destination. Roban's moon was alight. It burned fiercely, without a significant source of oxygen and apparently without fuel. The flames reached upwards for hundreds of kilometres in a conflagration of monumental proportions.

"Whatever they've used, it's done something to the surface," said Mercer in disbelief. "They've altered the makeup of the rock and set off some kind of chain reaction."

"Where's the Oblivion?"

"I think they're still in there somewhere, sir."

"Get them on the damned comms!"

"I can't reach them, sir. They must be out of comms sight, else there's something in this fire that's interfering."

"What about the Vraxar? Have they been stupid enough to follow the Ghasts into the middle of it?"

"I'm not sure," said Mercer. "They circled around the planet and they haven't come into view again. I don't know if I'll be able to lock onto them through all this flame."

"It's touching four thousand degrees at the mid-point of the fire," said Lieutenant Johnson. "Our hull will melt at four thousand two hundred degrees."

It wasn't entirely clear to Talley if the Ghasts had been stupid, brave, foolhardy or a mixture of all three. They'd managed to lure the Vraxar battleships into chasing them around this small moon and then used some kind of weapon to set it alight. *Surely they aren't going to stay in there until they burn up?* Talley thought.

No sooner had the thought formed when a shape burst away from the moon's surface. It exploded outwards only a few hundred kilometres from the *Devastator*.

"That's the *Gallatrin-9*," said Mercer. "I have no idea how its holding together."

The Oblivion accelerated with smooth, crushing power until it peaked at rather more than two thousand kilometres per second. There was nothing visible of its hull, since it was completely alight. Orange and white-hot flames clung along the whole of its length and as the battleship reached maximum velocity, it left a beautiful trail across the *Devastator*'s sensors.

"Captain Rioq-Tor," said Ensign Banks dumbly.

The Ghast captain's voice was piped through the bridge speakers. He roared with laughter, as if he'd found the entire meaning of existence in this single encounter. "This is how we fight, Admiral Talley! Let us test their shields now they have tasted the heat of our flames!"

The Vraxar warships came into sight, emerging from the flames with equal speed. Their shields were gone, burned out by the *Gallatrin-9*'s incendiaries. The smaller of the two burned brightly from the heat and the damage from the overcharged particle beam was clear to see. The larger Vraxar battleship was also alight, though only in small patches here and there across its hull. It was evident they hadn't detected the *Devastator* and they were comfortably within the fifty-thousand-kilometre range of the Hadron's particle beams, which they were about to discover.

"Fire," said Talley.

"Overcharged front beam fired," said Commander Adams. "No angle for the rear."

The *Devastator*'s battle computer caught up and spun the warship around in a circle so tight it made the hull creak and groan.

"Firing rear beam," said Adams.

The smaller Vraxar battleship was ripped into pieces. There was nothing graceful about its destruction – it broke into a thousand pieces of vaporising metal. The force of their disconnection from the whole was such that they were thrown in a wide arc away from the moon's surface. Here and there, sparks leapt from the larger pieces, as if some of these separate parts continued to generate power after the death of the parent vessel.

Meanwhile, the dogfight continued. The *Gallatrin-9* sprayed missile and Vule cannon slugs at the pursuing Vraxar ship. Whatever the name of the countermeasures system the enemy had used to destroy the previous missiles, it was either burned out or on cooldown and the Ghast missiles detonated in their hundreds on the Vraxar hull. In turn, the Vraxar turrets launched their own projectiles, which smashed into the heat-softened armour of the

Oblivion, punching huge holes into the metal. At the same time, beams of dark energy stabbed across the intervening space, causing large sections of armour to disintegrate and scatter in scorching clouds of white-hot dust particles.

Talley watched it all, this short experience of combat a thousand times more real than a decade in the simulator or talking tactics with his officers. Duggan knew it – this was the life he'd lived for years. He'd tried to make Talley see the reality - that without having once been in the middle of it, all the words were as nothing. *Now I see, old friend.* He was gripped by a feeling of profound sadness which lasted for only the shortest of moments. Then it was swept aside by something different and stronger. His mouth and tongue moved, activated by the primal part of his brain he thought himself completely separate from.

"Fire everything we've got," he intoned. "Bring them down."

"Launching. Shimmers, Shatterers. We've got a full Lambda X launch, sir. Whatever they've been using to screw with our guidance systems isn't working any longer."

"Don't stop."

What had started off tentatively, became bloody and terrible. The *Gallatrin-9* was little more than an indistinct form of molten metal and flames. Still it fired, wave upon wave of missiles. Vule fire – much more sporadic now - tore into the Vraxar spaceship.

The *Devastator*'s missiles took only seconds to reach the enemy ship. Such was the quantity that exploded, it appeared as if the whole length of the Vraxar battleship was engulfed in plasma. When the fires died, its hull was a patchwork mess of impact craters and in one place there was a hole greater than a thousand metres across and five hundred deep.

The enemy weren't finished and they pursued the *Gallatrin-9* as the Ghast Oblivion spun off along a trajectory that would see it skim across the edge of the dying fires of Roban's moon. The Vraxar's rear turrets and particle beams took aim on the *Devas-*

tator and began firing, each successful strike draining a significant portion of the remaining Obsidiar power reserves.

"Follow them!" shouted Talley. "What's the status on our overcharge?"

"Ready whenever you are, sir," said Commander Adams. "It'll take our power close to zero and once that's gone…"

"No shields, no engines and no hope."

"We should hold off with all the beam weapons, sir."

"Understood."

The *Devastator's* battle computer selected the most efficient course and gave the colossal engines full thrust. Even with the life support system fully operational, Talley felt the acceleration push him into his chair. He stared at the retreating tail of the enemy and dared to hope they might emerge victorious. A different thought intruded, one he didn't welcome. *Where the hell is that Neutraliser?* He hadn't quite forgotten about this largest of the Vraxar vessels, but he'd somehow imagined it would take some time while it sailed across on its gravity engines.

"Where's the Neutraliser?" he asked.

"I can't see it, sir," said Mercer. "We've got this moon between us and Roban."

Talley swore. "We need to finish this battleship off."

"The Vraxar cruiser we shot down will crater on Roban in approximately twenty minutes," said Ensign Banks, reminding Talley how much there was riding on the outcome of this encounter.

It wasn't the Vraxar who were defeated first. The *Gallatrin-9* had suffered catastrophic damage and it suddenly lost power and plummeted towards the moon's surface a few hundred kilometres below. The moon was cooling, though still hot, and it had a reflective sheen in many places. The Oblivion fell and the Vraxar pursued. The *Devastator* maintained a withering assault of missiles and particle beams, whilst the Vraxar returned fire.

"Some of that dust has fused," said Ensign Lewis. "It's the only moon made of glass I've ever seen."

"Sir, we're going to need to turn off our shields," said Lieutenant Johnson. "Each hit on them is taking away the power we're going to require for our engines."

"You're right. Turn off the shields," said Talley. "That's what the plating is there for, right?"

As soon as the shield was switched off, the enemy projectiles began crashing into the *Devastator*'s nose. The armour plating was angled in such a way that the attacks were deflected, but the impacts still resulted in significant damage. Particle beams raked into the metal, along with one of the dark energy beams. Talley watched the list of damage reports speeding across his screen and did his best not to think about them.

"How many missiles is it going to take?" said Commander Adams, the first indication he was losing his composure. "We've hit them with more than a thousand Lambdas!"

"Don't let up."

The *Gallatrin-9* crashed down at speed and at a shallow angle. It skipped up, turned in the air and then spun wildly over the rocks, pulverising a series of stone peaks and leaving a wide scar across the surface that stretched for many hundreds of kilometres. Talley wasn't sure if he imagined it, but he thought he saw the shockwaves ripple away from the main points of impact.

"Come on, come on!" said Adams.

Talley turned his attention to the tactical display. A thick wave of the *Devastator*'s missiles was within five seconds of the enemy warship. It had to be enough.

The Vraxar used their anti-missile countermeasures again. Many hundreds of Lambda missiles screamed high and wide past the warship, their guidance systems no longer functioning. Talley felt something clench in his stomach when he realised what had happened.

"No!" shouted Adams, thumping his broad hands against his console.

However, not all of the missiles were affected by the Vraxar countermeasures. Six Shimmer missiles reached their intended target. The rear of the enemy ship was hidden by the size of the explosion. A total of sixteen Shatterer missiles followed, the detonation of their payloads adding to the heat and light.

"I think they're breaking up!" said Mercer.

"Their power readings are all over the place," said Johnson.

"They're still damn well firing at us!" shouted Talley.

"Lambdas launched," said Adams. "They can't have anything left in the tank."

The Vraxar vessel was tough and Talley wasn't too proud to admit it. For the next few seconds, the enemy turrets pounded the *Devastator*'s armour with slugs until Talley became worried that mutual destruction was to be the outcome of the engagement.

On this occasion, Space Corps metal came out on top. Hundreds of Lambdas crashed against the enemy hull. This time there was no doubt and it broke apart. Commander Adams fired another wave of missiles, dividing them amongst the larger pieces of the Vraxar battleship. Huge chunks rained down upon the moon's surface, striking it with immense speed.

When it was over, Roban's moon covered in craters ranging from a few hundred metres wide, to some which were three or four hundred kilometres across. Talley wondered what it would take for the moon to break up and destroy Roban. It didn't happen, though the damage was extensive.

With the battleships destroyed, Talley turned his attention to the next problem on his neverending list – the missing Neutraliser.

CHAPTER TWENTY-THREE

THERE WAS no sign of the largest of the Vraxar warships. The *Devastator* continued its low orbit of the moon, hunting or running, Talley wasn't sure which. If the enemy vessel was close by, it was only a matter of time until the two of them met.

"Did our sensors pick anything up that we missed during the fighting?" Talley asked. "Could they have given up on Roban and gone to lightspeed?"

"There's not even an echo of a fission cloud," said Johnson. "They could have gone to lightspeed on the exact opposite side of this moon and with a vessel that size we'd know about it. Anyway, we're still tapping into the Obsidiar core, which means it's in range to keep us offline."

"It's out there somewhere."

"And we're in no fit state to deal with it," said Adams. "We need another twenty minutes for the Obsidiar core to recharge."

"They must know we'll be a lot harder to deal with if they allow us the time to recover," said Talley. "Lieutenant Mercer, try and reach the *Gallatrin-9*. See if our allies are alive."

"They can't have lived through that?" Mercer said.

"If their life support was active, they can live through pretty much anything," said Talley. "Find out when they'll be operational."

The *Devastator*'s Hynus comms arrays were able to pierce through small planets and moons such as this one, so there was no need to be directly overhead. Mercer got on with her job and attempted contact.

The Ghast captain was alive, though the Oblivion wasn't going anywhere soon.

"This is not time for talking, Admiral Talley. Our sensors tell us the main enemy vessel is still operational. Go."

The Ghasts were similar to humans in some ways and distinctly different in others. Talley realised he had a lot to learn – Rioq-Tor wasn't interested in his life, he wanted to be on the winning side and didn't expect any consideration until the conflict was brought to a full conclusion. Talley cut the channel without further response.

"Pass on a verbal update to Fleet Admiral Duggan," he said. "Let him know the situation isn't yet resolved."

"The Vraxar have disabled our main comms and we're on backups, sir. The message won't reach him until next week."

Talley bit his tongue to stop from swearing. "Send it anyway."

"Yes, sir."

Until the main comms were restored, there was no choice other than to get on with things.

"Fifteen percent on the Obsidiar core," Talley mused. "Not enough to sustain our shields through any sort of extended engagement. We have to stay hidden."

"We should be able to activate the stealth modules shortly," said Johnson.

"Good – keep me updated. How long until the wrecked Vraxar cruiser comes down?"

"Fifteen minutes until it impacts, sir," said Banks.

"Maybe we should deal with it first," said Lieutenant Johnson.

"We've got time and I don't want to get caught in the open," said Talley. "In truth, I don't want to lure the Vraxar back towards Roban in case they start taking pot shots just for the hell of it."

The Hadron was equipped with various satellites to use in situations like this one – the idea being to drop them behind in order to monitor the enemy when they came into range. Unfortunately, these satellites were fitted with Gallenium engines and power supplies. The Neutraliser's effects reached them in their launch tubes, rendering them offline and useless.

"What are we going to do against the Neutraliser even if our power source recharges to maximum?" asked Adams. "We're a minnow in comparison. I'm willing to give it a go, but I don't think we can knock them out."

"We're only a minnow in size, Commander. We know little about the Neutralisers' offensive capabilities and it could be their primary function is to disable Gallenium power sources, whilst they themselves are only lightly armed."

"If it wasn't carrying weapons, it would have run, sir," said Adams, pointing out the obvious.

"We don't know it's the last Vraxar ship left at Roban, either," added Lieutenant Poole.

"True. On the other hand, it seems unlikely they'd have drip-fed their forces in our direction in order that we could pick them off piecemeal."

"That's hardly what happened, sir."

Talley could only agree and he fell quiet in order to think. The last two or three minutes had a bizarre feeling to them, as though it was the calm both before and after the storm. He found himself in a position where he didn't want to locate the enemy, yet he needed to face them in order to bring some stability to this area of Confederation Space. There was one possibility, which he hadn't confided with his crew. *Now's the time.*

He entered his command codes into his console. The *Hadron's* battle computer required verification, which he also provided. "Commander Adams, I'm giving you access to one of the *Devastator's* hidden weapons systems."

"I see it, sir."

"We're carrying an Obsidiar bomb. One of three the Space Corps currently possesses."

Adams' eyes widened. The bombs were top-secret, but the rumours still went around in certain circles. "What's the blast radius of this model, sir?"

"Unknown. These things are largely theoretical and there have been only two recorded uses of the weapon. Our entire stock was built forty years ago under orders from one of Fleet Admiral Duggan's predecessors. Let us settle on the word *huge* to describe the likely radius."

"It's got hardly any propulsion system on it, sir. We'll have to drop and run."

"We won't be dropping it anywhere near Roban or its moon."

"Exactly how *huge* do you mean?" asked Adams, looking bewildered.

"It'll be in the files somewhere. Definitely enough to take out a Neutraliser." Talley smiled without humour. "Even if it happens to be a considerable distance away."

Two short minutes passed, during which the *Devastator* continued in a low, slow orbit of Roban's moon. Talley wondered if he should simply withdraw for a period, in order to take stock and plan. He dismissed the idea quickly – the Vraxar were an unknown and he didn't want to present them with an opportunity to make an unmolested punitive strike against Roban. It was better to keep close and hope to avoid detection until the battleship was prepared. They'd suffered damage and a number of missile clusters and Bulwarks had been disabled, along with a secondary particle beam turret. The Hadron would need repairs to bring it back to full operational capability, but with the Vraxar threatening the entire Confederation it didn't seem likely it would be in a shipyard any time soon.

As time passed, Talley began to think they were going to make it to full shield strength. The Obsidiar core's reserves built up until they climbed past thirty percent. The moon rolled by beneath, its surface temperature still a few hundred degrees higher than normal. Talley ordered the stealth modules be activated in order to give them the advantage when they stumbled upon the Vraxar.

The warning, when it came, was too late.

"Sir, I've located them," said Lieutenant Mercer.

The main tactical display populated with details of the Neutraliser. There it was, stationary on the moon's surface a few thousand kilometres below, waiting for them to pass overhead.

"Have they detected us?"

"Yes, sir, they have," Mercer replied. "They're lifting off."

She got a sensor fix on the enemy spaceship and the sight drew Talley's eyes. He'd seen the file images, but the reality was somewhat less pleasant. The Neutraliser was long and almost delicate in appearance. Its black-metal front and rear nullifying spheres crackled with an unknown source of energy. The trapezoidal central section was as long as the *Devastator*, so although the Neutraliser looked fragile, it was in fact nothing of the sort. It rose from a flat plain of red-tinged glass, slowly, yet with increasing momentum.

Contrary to Talley's hopes, the Neutraliser was more than adequately armed. A dozen energy beams raked through space, hunting the cloaked Hadron, whilst concealed turrets spewed out heavy projectiles. The *Devastator* was equipped with surface incendiaries – nothing like as effective as those deployed by the Ghasts - and Talley ordered them launched. A series of huge cannisters tumbled from the Hadron's bays. They ignited the rock for the second time and scattered their fires for hundreds of kilometres around.

"Not quick enough," said Mercer. "They've climbed too high."

"Fire everything we've got, damnit!"

Missiles exploded from their launch clusters. Once again, many of the Lambdas and a few Shatterers refused to target. Those which did launch were met by the same scrambling wave of energy which the Vraxar battleship had used. The guidance systems on two hundred Lambdas were fried, rendering the missiles useless.

"Use the overcharge!"

The familiar whining thump vibrated through the walls.

"Direct hit. Firing the rear."

Another thump.

"Direct hit."

Both strikes were against the front sphere of the Neutraliser. More than half of this sphere burned with a hundred different hues. The metal sagged and flowed in huge rivers, giving the damaged area of the Neutraliser's hull a flattened appearance. Through it, the sparks leapt with undiminished energy. Talley's hopes that he could somehow disable the Neutraliser's nullification field were dashed and the battleship's Gallenium engines remained offline.

"Keep firing!" ordered Talley. His voice was strong, but his heart was heavy. The *Devastator's* primary shock weapon had clearly done a great amount of damage to the enemy ship, but now it required time to recharge.

"Firing missiles," said Adams. "We're going to need far more than another two rounds from the overcharge to take them down."

"Agreed," said Talley.

"Recommend deployment of the Obsidiar bomb, sir. Before it's too late."

"There will be no deployment of the bomb so close to Roban's moon, Commander! I thought I made myself clear."

"Yes, sir. As soon as their weapons systems pinpoint us through the stealth cloak, we are going to lose. This would be a good time to retreat."

"And give them free rein over Roban?"

Adams was teetering on the brink of argument and he backed down with a nod of his head. "Launching missiles."

The Neutraliser was able to use its anti-missile energy wave much more frequently than the Vraxar battleships. Each second wave of Lambdas was countered, cutting the Hadron's offense significantly. All the while, beam weapons danced to and fro between the two vessels. The *Devastator*'s advanced particle beam technology ignored the Neutraliser's energy shield and each discharge struck the enemy hull. Unfortunately, the standard particle beams didn't have anything like the power to inflict a fatal blow on a spaceship as large as the Neutraliser. To make matters worse, each use drained the Hadron's power supply a little bit at a time.

The Shimmer missiles worked as intended, along with a number of Shatterers. Bulwark cannons roared out a constant steam, pounding against the Neutraliser's shield. It wasn't going to be enough.

"They're getting closer," said Adams. "Their average miss distance is below five klicks."

"Ten minutes until the Vraxar cruiser impacts on Roban," said Banks.

Talley felt like he was caught in a vice. Their energy reserves were falling fast and the *Devastator's* energy shield wasn't even activated. The Neutraliser was so big it looked as if it could mop up standard particle beams all day and its own shield wasn't troubled by the few missiles which got through its countermeasures. On top of that, Talley knew he needed to act soon to prevent half a billion deaths on Roban. He was left in the unenviable position where there was no apparent path to victory.

Two of the Neutraliser's slugs pounded against the *Devastator's* starboard side. The battle computer spun the ship and lifted it a few hundred kilometres higher to try and fool the enemy targeting. Another slug punched into them, leaving a crumpled dent in the armour plates.

"They've got a lock on us, sir," said Adams.

A particle beam lanced into the same place where the projectile had recently connected. The structure of the ship was designed to channel the heat away, but there was only so much it could do. A few of the plates burned and others fell away into space.

"Sir, I recommend an immediate withdrawal," said Adams.

"Fire the front and rear overcharge, Commander. Target their front sphere."

"We'll have hardly any power left if we discharge both, sir."

"It's my call, Commander. Fire."

"Front and rear have fired."

The front sphere on the Neutraliser was ravaged by the attack. It hadn't started to cool down from the previous overcharge strikes and these two new ones heated parts of the metal to several million degrees. A billion tonnes of molten alloy slid away, cascading towards Roban's moon. A moment later, the central strut attaching the sphere to the rest of the ship bent downward. It looked as if it might snap under the stresses, but it did not. The Neutraliser remained in place at an altitude of ten thousand kilometres, and continued firing.

"The stealth modules have deactivated through lack of power," said Adams. "We've got just enough to keep our critical systems running. The disruptors are unavailable and we've only got a few shots left with the standard particle beams."

Talley saw the warnings on his console. There were too many to count – it was the kind of thing they threw at rookies and experienced officers alike in the simulator. They called it the no-win situation, informally known as the *dead man's choice*, to see how a person would react to failure. Talley was in that position right now and it was infinitely worse than being in a simulator where you knew you could get out when it was over and discuss the results with your commanding officer across a table.

The one lesson you were expected to learn from the dead man's choice was that you should never give up, no matter how bad the situation.

"Don't let up on them, we might force them to run."

It wasn't looking likely – it was as though the Vraxar had claimed Roban as their own and they weren't going to relinquish it for anything. The *Devastator*'s hull was a mess of heat and impact damage, with several areas crumbling from the dark energy weapon the Vraxar employed.

"Sir, we are going to break up," said Adams.

"Roban is going to suffer a catastrophic event in the next few minutes," said Lieutenant Mercer. "If we let ourselves be destroyed, a lot of people will die."

Talley realised it was time to listen to the advice of his crew – the lesson of the dead man's choice was a highly-nuanced lie. Reports of previous encounters with similar vessels to this Neutraliser had indicated they usually broke away from the engagement if they were put under sufficient pressure. He'd gambled on the same happening here. In fact, he'd taken it to the edge and looked over the precipice into the infinite depths below. His attempts to be bold had failed and now it was time to run. Before he could give the order, there was another development.

"Sir! I'm reading a fission signature! There's a spaceship inbound!" shouted Lieutenant Johnson.

"One of ours?"

"No, sir. I don't know what it is. It's a vessel of significant size."

"Commander Adams, let us see if this new arrival is more susceptible to our missile technology than this Neutraliser. Prepare to target and fire. We might catch them by surprise. As soon as we've launched, activate a short-range transition towards Roban."

"Yes, sir, preparing to target."

"Readying the SRT. We'll go on your order, sir."

The new spaceship dropped into local space only thirty thousand kilometres from the combat, as though it had been somehow forewarned of what to expect. Talley closed his eyes and bowed his head when he saw what it was.

"It's the *ES Rampage!*" said Mercer.

At three thousand three hundred metres long, the *Rampage* was one of the first generation Galactics, laid down at the height of the Ghast war and still in service after forty years of combat, repairs and extensive refits.

"What are they going to do?" asked Ensign Chambers. Everyone knew what she meant – the captain of the *Rampage* had declared for the Frontier League. In theory, the heavy cruiser's crew no longer fought for the Confederation.

In the end, there was no doubting what action the *Rampage* would take.

"They've launched missiles," said Adams. "They're having the same problems as we are with the Lambda targeting."

It wasn't only Lambdas which came from the *Rampage's* launch tubes.

"What the hell are those?" Adams continued.

"Nuclear missiles," said Talley.

"I thought they were banned?"

"The Space Corps keeps its secrets. The *Rampage* is the last ship in the fleet carrying a stock as well as a mechanism for delivery."

The Vraxar Neutraliser emitted its energy burst again, treating the *Rampage*'s Lambdas as dismissively as it had those from the *Devastator*. The nuclear missiles – ten in total – came from a much earlier line of ballistic technology and they weren't relying on a direct hit. When they came to within a few hundred kilometres of the Neutraliser, they detonated. The vacuum of space ensured their explosions were comparatively small, but it wasn't the blast which was intended to do the damage. Huge areas around the Neutraliser were saturated with immense quantities of gamma radiation. It enveloped the Vraxar ship, interfering with its shield generators and burning out many of its critical systems.

"Their shield has gone down," said Adams. "Targeting our missiles and away they go."

The gamma radiation shut down not only the Vraxar's shields, but its missile countermeasures and target lock interference systems. The *Devastator* got away a full launch from its Lambda clusters. Hundreds of the missiles twisted through space before crashing into the Neutraliser. Six Shimmers followed, striking the enemy ship near to its glowing front nullification sphere. The high-yield explosions tore the spaceship into two separate pieces and the sphere broke away entirely. It plummeted downwards, still sparking with unrestrained energy.

"The *Rampage* is firing again, sir. Conventional missiles and particle beams."

Incredibly, the Neutraliser was still operational. It climbed rapidly upwards, rotating as it did and trailing liquid metal in its wake.

"They're charging for lightspeed," said Johnson.

"It's too late for those bastards," said Talley grimly.

It was a close-run affair. A huge series of plasma bursts ripped into the Neutraliser's hull. It attempted to escape into lightspeed, but the damage was too great. It leapt forward a hundred thousand kilometres before its engines failed and it was dragged back into local space. The *Rampage* activated a short-range transition immediately and appeared five thousand kilometres away from the stricken Vraxar ship. Talley checked his console. The *Devastator* only had enough power remaining for a single SRT.

There was no need to assist. The *Rampage* showed no mercy and subjected the Neutraliser to a sustained bombardment, pursuing the larger pieces until there was nothing significant remaining. The crew of the *Devastator* didn't see it, since they had departed this area of space in order to pursue the wreckage of the Vraxar cruiser they'd shot down earlier. Mercer quickly found it.

"There they are, sir."

The sensor image was both beautiful and terrifying. The planet Roban turned almost imperceptibly in the background, bright greens and azure blues, whilst the Vraxar wreckage hurtled onwards towards it. The Space Corps was equipped to deal with incidents such as this one, though usually the threat came from asteroids instead of alien spacecraft. Talley activated the Hadron's in-built interception routines and the *Devastator* pursued the falling object, closing until it was visible to the naked eye.

With a series of targeted missile and particle beam strikes, the Vraxar wreckage was reduced into progressively smaller pieces. Many of them were deflected away from Roban, whilst others burned up on entry into its atmosphere. Other pieces refused to succumb and they crashed into the surface and the oceans. Talley could only hope they'd done enough and that the casualties would be few.

It wasn't over yet. The *ES Devastator* was battered, though not yet broken, and with its Gallenium engines slowly coming online. With its Obsidiar core drained, it wasn't in a fit state for combat.

"The *ES Rampage* has locked onto us," said Commander Adams.

Talley sighed. "Will it never end?"

"Captain Lana McBride wishes to speak with you, sir."

"Of course. Bring her through."

"Admiral Talley," she said in a voice so husky it had to be an act.

"Captain McBride. Why have you locked your weapons onto us?"

There was a long pause, as if McBride had instigated the conversation without having a clue what would come from it. The *Rampage* disengaged its weapons lock.

"It would be best if we talked first, wouldn't it?" McBride laughed, the sound as husky as her words.

For the first time in what felt like weeks, Talley knew he was talking to someone sensible and relief washed over him.

He took his seat. "There is a lot to discuss," he said.

CHAPTER TWENTY-FOUR

AFTER A TOTAL of thirty-six hours travelling at lightspeed, the Vraxar mothership shuddered and grated as its gargantuan fission drive deposited it into local space.

On the bridge of the *ES Blackbird*, Captain Charlie Blake was taken by surprise. He'd been on edge for so long, waiting for this moment, that it took his brain a few seconds to register the event. He felt sharp and alert, but underneath the disguising veneer of synthetic stimulants and adrenaline he was pumped full of, he knew his body was exhausted and desperate for sleep.

The journey had been as uneventful as one could reasonably expect when one was stuck in the cargo hold of a forty-one-kilometre hostile alien mothership. The Vraxar had spent most of the time attacking the *Blackbird* with a variety of artillery weapons from the maintenance walkways above and to the side. The automated response from the spy craft's repeaters kept them from getting too bold and the *Blackbird*'s Obsidiar shield was able to recharge as quickly as these minor attacks whittled it away. It had been a tense period, though not ultimately one in which the Vraxar had been able to press home their obvious advantage.

Blake had a plan, worked out during the time at lightspeed. *Plan* was a generous term for his preparations. The reality was he'd tried to cobble a few ideas and best-guesses into something which might work out under the right circumstances. Part of him believed he'd blown his mission – there'd been an opportunity to destroy three highly-significant Vraxar assets and, for various reasons, he'd failed to take the chance. Another part of him was content that he'd done the right thing and that the rescue of the *Juniper*'s survivors was worth the gamble.

Now he had to make it back home, whilst doing as much damage to the Vraxar as possible. *Else it's a court martial for me,* he thought. It wasn't actually the court martial he feared – it was the look of disappointment he imagined on Duggan's face at being let down by the captain he'd trusted with this important mission.

"Does everyone know what we're doing?" he asked the others, as soon as it was apparent they were back in normal space.

"Yes, sir," they responded in unison, though without a great deal of enthusiasm. It didn't require a master strategist to spot the multitude of flaws in what Blake intended. Since none of them had any better ideas and since they weren't in command, Blake felt content in proceeding.

"It looks as if we've discovered a flaw in the Vraxar defences," he said, repeating what they'd previously discussed. "We're inside what is likely to be one of their most powerful ships – if not *the* most powerful ship – and they lack the means to destroy us while we stay here."

"Which means they have to flush us out," said Lieutenant Hawkins.

"And to do that, they will open these cargo doors and have a number of their other ships waiting to hit us with particle beams. We will escape from them and leave behind an Obsidiar bomb as our parting gift." He looked at Pointer, inviting her to spell out the largest obstacle to their success.

She duly obliged. "Because we don't know where we are, we cannot immediately go to lightspeed. We will require a short period for our sensors to calibrate and for our positioning system to update."

"Which will definitely not take very long," he finished.

"In an ideal world," she added.

As it happened, Blake had no intention of waiting around for the cargo doors to open – he was going to take control instead of sitting around and waiting to see if the Vraxar did as he anticipated. Having entered through a hole in the mothership's hull, he was going to utilise this same breach on the way out. The edges of the missile penetration through the bay doors had hardened with the cooling of the metal. There was no way the *Blackbird* would be able to force its way back out without further action.

Taking care to avoid a collision with the *Juniper* overhead or the side walls of the cargo bay, Blake piloted the *Blackbird* upwards and backwards. He was sure they were running out of time, so he sacrificed precision for speed. Proximity warnings flashed up on his screen repeatedly, distracting him from the controls. The external sensor feeds showed the bay from various angles as he manoeuvred the *Blackbird* along. An occasional explosive flash showed that the Vraxar hadn't given up their attempts to disable the spy ship.

There was a rumbling through the bridge walls and Blake noticed a slight resistance on the control bars.

"We just hit the *Juniper*," said Pointer. "Took out the tertiary backup comms antennae."

"I don't think they'll be needing it again."

He hit something else and this time Pointer kept her mouth shut. There was no need to worry about a few bumps and scrapes against the orbital. If Blake's plan worked, it wouldn't be going into back into service.

Another proximity warning appeared, this being the one he was waiting for – it told him the *ES Blackbird* was as far along the cargo bay as it could go. He brought the ship to a stop.

"Target the area of the hull breach with our last Shimmer missile."

"Targeting."

Hawkins went quiet for longer than expected.

"What's the problem?" asked Blake.

"Sir, the Shimmer won't accept the command to lock on."

Blake swore. "Why not?"

"It won't target because the *Juniper* will get caught in the blast."

"We just blew the *Juniper*'s doors open with a Shimmer missile!"

Hawkins huffed and puffed, as she tried to figure out what was wrong. "Damn. This last Shimmer missile has more recent software on it than the others. They must have added additional targeting routines to prevent accidents."

"You're kidding me?" asked Blake, knowing she wasn't doing anything of the sort.

"Sorry, sir. We won't be firing this Shimmer anywhere near the Juniper."

"We'll have to wait and see if they open these doors," said Pointer.

"I've had enough of waiting," said Blake.

There was no choice other than to sit it out. Minutes passed and the cargo doors didn't open. The crew fidgeted and shifted at their stations.

"What if they're in no hurry?" said Hawkins at last. "We can't harm them and they can't harm us."

"We're carrying a huge bomb. Of course we can harm them," said Blake testily.

"They don't know that, sir."

After another ten minutes, Blake was beginning to doubt his predictions and his brain cast about wildly for new ideas. It came up blank and a whispering voice began to suggest that he should simply detonate the Obsidiar bomb and have done with it. He wasn't scared to die, but it somehow felt wrong that he should have taken part in the daring rescue of the *Juniper*'s survivors, only to sacrifice them when freedom was within their grasp.

"Any luck with the comms?" he asked.

"Still nothing, sir. Until the sensors calibrate with something outside, I won't know where to point the arrays."

Blake gritted his teeth with the frustration and didn't answer. The whispering voice was just beginning to increase in volume and insistence, when he was suddenly rescued from the inevitable death it offered.

"Look!" said Pointer. "The bay doors are opening."

That got Blake's attention and banished all thoughts of suicide from his mind. "Is the bomb ready?" he asked.

"The timer is set at two minutes, sir. I won't start the countdown until you say."

They watched the cargo doors. At first, they opened a crack and then stopped for a time. The *Blackbird*'s sensors tried to make sense of what lay beyond but could only pick up darkness.

"Come on!"

The two doors resumed opening, retracting with effortless smoothness into the walls of the mothership's hull.

"Activate our stealth modules."

"Stealth modules active."

Blake double-checked the energy shield was still active, since it would be a disaster if it was not. There were no errors and the shield was still in place, keeping them protected from the onslaught he expected would begin any moment.

"Prepare the Obsidiar bomb for deployment. Do *not* activate the timer."

"It's ready when you are, sir. Once the timer is set, it cannot be stopped or overridden."

The unlocked file pictures showed there was nothing elaborate about the Obsidiar bomb's appearance – it was a dull grey cube with rounded edges, a little more than twenty-five metres along each side and contained in a chute underneath the *Blackbird* specifically designed to house it. The Space Corps had built five such bombs and the registration number on this one was 000002. The first time he saw the number, Blake asked himself how many they'd been planning to build – how many would have been built if there was sufficient Obsidiar to fulfil the perceived need.

There was a nameplate on this particular bomb and whenever Blake read the words, it made him feel like he was staring at a pile of a billion sad-faced corpses. *Inferno Sphere.*

The cargo doors opened further, until the gap was wide enough that Blake reckoned he could squeeze through. They stopped again.

"I think that's it," said Quinn.

"I can see shapes outside," said Pointer. "There's something waiting for us."

"They must have an angle to fire at us if they wanted, but I can't believe they'll aim their weapons into the hold of their mothership," said Blake. "They want us to come out."

He was right. The cargo doors opened wider, until the depths of space beyond became clearly visible. The sensors detected many shapes and Blake began to wonder what the hell they'd got themselves into.

"Have the sensors calibrated yet?" he asked. "I can see stars in the background."

"No, sir. They're still working."

With a final, unhesitating movement, the cargo doors slid all the way open, revealing what lay beyond. It was worse than Blake could have imagined. Having committed this far, it was not the time to back down or try to think of an alternative.

"Start the timer and deploy the bomb."

"Acknowledged. I have started the timer," said Hawkins.

The bomb dropped from its chute beneath the ES *Blackbird*. It had a rudimentary propulsion system – one which specifically did not draw its power from Gallenium. The bomb floated gently towards the floor of the cargo bay, where it nestled – a tiny object, lost in the vast expanse of the mothership.

"The Obsidiar bomb is now deployed. We have two minutes to get as far away from here as possible."

A timer appeared on a screen to Blake's left and began ticking downwards. He gave the *Blackbird*'s gravity engines maximum power and pushed the control bars hard along their runners. The spy craft was amongst the most agile vessels in the Space Corps and it burst forward, carrying them out of the mothership's cargo bay and into space.

Immediately they emerged, Lieutenant Pointer set the *Blackbird*'s sensors to the task of pinpointing their location in order that they could go to lightspeed as soon as it was required.

"Oh crap," she said.

Blake saw what she meant and he too swore at the details brought up by the sensors. It looked as if the mothership had returned to its fleet and the *Blackbird* had emerged right in the middle of it. There were Vraxar warships everywhere around them – Blake had no time to count, but he saw what must have been ten Neutralisers parked in a row. Nearby was a similar number of battleship-sized vessels, lined up in the same way a child might do with his or her toys.

Clustered around the mothership were other Vraxar ships – a hundred or more of them.

"Our welcome committee," said Blake.

The firing started. Particle beams flashed through space and hundreds of ultra-heavy gauss turrets opened up. The *Blackbird*'s advanced stealth modules were enough to make the spy craft an elusive target and although many of the inbound projectiles came close, not one of them hit.

TIMER: 110 SECONDS TO DETONATION.

"They're holding back," said Lieutenant Quinn. "We're too close to the mothership. The further away we get, the more we'll have directed our way."

It was a tiny advantage, though one Blake was more than happy to accept. He spun the *Blackbird* around in the tightest of turns, bringing them closer to the mothership. This wasn't a show of bravado, he was simply giving the sensors the best possible view of the surrounding area in order that they could calibrate as quickly as possible. He wanted to be at lightspeed long before the Obsidiar bomb went off.

"Where are we, Lieutenant Pointer?" he asked.

He guessed the answer himself, just as he saw this solar system's vast sun appear on one of the port sensor feeds.

"Cheops! We're in the Cheops system!" she yelled.

"I can see that myself."

It made sense – this was the place they'd picked up the mothership in the first place. There had been no opportunity for an extensive search at the time, but it looked as if the Vraxar had mustered a significant portion of their offense fleet here.

Judging by its perceived size, Blake guessed Cheops-A was many millions of kilometres away. He could see they were close to a planet. Once you'd flown through space for long enough you developed a knack for gauging where you were in relation to other celestial objects and he assumed this planet was the closest one to Cheops-A. From his memory, he dredged up the planet's name: Tarnor. It was a hot rock with a diameter of thirty thousand kilometres and two moons. The Vraxar fleet was parked near to Tarnor at an altitude of approximately eighty thousand kilometres. There was nothing special about this particular place as far as Blake could tell. Doubtless a computer had chosen it and the aliens had come.

TIMER: 95 SECONDS TO DETONATION.

Without a better idea, he levelled the *Blackbird* out and aimed towards Tarnor. His brain worked out the numbers – approximately eighty thousand kilometres away at the *Blackbird*'s top speed: twenty-five seconds.

"Lieutenant Pointer, we're running out of time. We need lightspeed and we need it soon. It'll take nearly twenty seconds for the cores to do the maths."

Pointer had only bad news. "There's a problem. We can see it's Cheops, but the navigational systems still aren't able to place us within Confederation Space."

"What?"

"She's right, sir," said Lieutenant Quinn. "The options to enter lightspeed coordinates are greyed out on my panel. We're not going anywhere until the navigational system catches up."

"This is the most up-to-date tech in the Space Corps, backed by sixteen Obsidiar processors. Why are we waiting for it to catch up with what our eyes can see?"

"I don't know, sir. Quantity of data perhaps," said Pointer. She crinkled her nose, the expression able to distract Blake even in these most trying of circumstances. "We're sending pings everywhere and none of them are coming back," she said.

"The Vraxar can jam our guidance systems and block our

comms. Could their ships be interfering with our positional systems?"

The same answer came back. "I don't know, sir."

The *Blackbird* hurtled through space towards Tarnor. The planet came steadily closer and Blake realised he'd underestimated the distance. In the initial few moments after the *Blackbird*'s emergence from the mothership, the Vraxar struggled to lock onto the spy craft. Now they were adapting and their rate of fire increased. A hundred particle beams stabbed through nearby space, along with thousands of high-velocity projectiles.

TIMER: 70 SECONDS TO DETONATION.

Tarnor was close. Its surface was incredibly hot, though not enough for the rock to become molten. On the sensor feed he could see the pockmarks from a billion years of meteorite strikes. There were mountain ranges, harsh and rugged, with rivers of flowing lava. A vast canyon cut from left to right, like the scar across the face of a god. The two moons were to the left and to Blake's eye they were so close to each other it was almost as if they were touching.

Having realised their crude trap was in the process of failing, the Vraxar fleet started moving out on their gravity engines. This wasn't what Blake wanted. In his discussions with Pointer, they'd agreed the sensors would only take seconds to calibrate and then they would be out of here – a maximum exposure to the Vraxar forces of thirty seconds, before they vanished into lightspeed, leaving the aliens to make the acquaintance of the Obsidiar bomb. In fact, the *Blackbird* wasn't going into lightspeed and the Vraxar were following them.

"They've stopped," said Pointer suddenly.

"What do you mean?"

"They're returning to their original positions."

"That's got to be a good thing," said Quinn. "They've given up."

"Except they're still firing at us."

TIMER: 50 SECONDS TO DETONATION.

The *Blackbird* came to within ten thousand kilometres of Tarnor and Blake took the spaceship along a course which would take it around to the far side.

"I'm reading a power build-up on the mothership," said Quinn. "Their output has climbed by over a million percent and it's still rising."

Blake had no idea what they were planning, but he was sure he didn't want to find out. "I don't think they've given up," he said.

The *Blackbird* flew on. Far behind, the Vraxar mothership's power output reached a peak and then steadied, as if they were waiting for something to happen.

CHAPTER TWENTY-FIVE

BLAKE KEPT the *Blackbird* low to the planet's surface in order to shorten the distance it would take to hide from the Vraxar. Just when he thought they would escape to the far side of Tarnor, a particle beam connected with their energy shield. The *Blackbird* was carrying a big lump of Obsidiar, but the hit knocked thirty percent off the power reserves. Another beam came within a whisker and a barrage of Gallenium projectiles raked across the planet's surface, kicking up high plumes of hot dirt and adding their own craters to those already etched into the rock.

TIMER: 40 SECONDS TO DETONATION.

"We're going to make it," said Hawkins.

"Got it!" shouted Pointer. "Our coordinates are updating!"

Blake watched as the details flooded into the guidance system. He punched the air. "Yes! Good work Lieutenant! Get us out of here. Anywhere, I don't care where."

Lieutenant Quinn was distracted by something else. "The mothership is going to..."

With the ES *Blackbird* right on the cusp of sight, the Vraxar mothership fired. A beam of pure darkness came into being from a dome positioned in the middle of its uppermost armour plates. The beam was thick and formed a perfect line between the Vraxar and the planet Tarnor. For several seconds, nothing happened.

"Oh crap," said Quinn, fumbling to choose a destination. "You need to get us out of here, sir. Fission drive warmup is a little slow since the navigation system is still catching up. We'll be out of here in twenty-eight seconds. I don't know what the hell the Vraxar have done."

TIMER: 30 SECONDS TO DETONATION.

"Perfect timing," said Blake.

He checked how much distance they'd put between themselves and the enemy. They were more than one hundred and twenty thousand kilometres away from the Vraxar and twenty thousand from Tarnor. They'd come far enough around the planet that he was able to keep it between the *Blackbird* and the enemy fleet. With Tarnor as a shield, he kept the spaceship pointed in the opposite direction to the Vraxar in order to get as far away as possible.

It was not to be so straightforward.

With its core ruptured by the Vraxar energy beam, Tarnor exploded. It began lazily enough – a few large pieces of lava-drenched rock tore away from the surface and out into space. After the tiniest of pauses, the rest of it followed. Blake watched in horror as a hundred million objects appeared on his tactical screen. The utilisation on all sixteen of the spaceship's cores hit the maximum the tactical system was permitted to access – fifty percent on each processor.

From the corner of his eye, he saw the unimaginable destruction on the rear sensor feed. The entire planet fractured and great plates of surface rock – some of them two thousand kilometres across – were sent into space. As they spun and tumbled out into the void, the pieces crumbled and seemed to gather pace. Within seconds, the fastest sections were level with the *Blackbird* and then they were far ahead.

TIMER: 20 SECONDS TO DETONATION.

"We're going to make it!" Blake shouted, as if his willpower alone would make it happen.

Before he knew it, the *Blackbird* was amongst a storm of rock so dense and thick, all of the sensor feeds showed a variation of the same thing – lumps of fiery rock of infinite different sizes and shapes. They streaked by, some of them travelling at fifty thousand kilometres per second and leaving glowing orange traces across the background of space.

A cloud of red-hot dust particles enveloped the spy craft. Where these particles hit the energy shield they left behind motes of red, until the spaceship looked as if it was held in the centre of a sphere of glowing, sparkling flames.

Several parameters governing the warship's battle computer were breached and it switched itself to automatic. The *Blackbird*'s heavy repeaters sprayed projectiles at the nearest of the rocks, jumping from target to target. The craft wasn't anything like sufficiently armed to destroy so many objects and the defensive system was overwhelmed. It continued firing, the cannons producing a low thrum audible to the crew on the bridge.

Blake wrestled with the controls. His brain was overloaded by the quantity of information and he pulled the *Blackbird* left and right. The energy shield sustained a series of heavy blows, taking huge chunks out of its power bar. *Hand off to the autopilot, you idiot,* he thought.

The autopilot didn't want to know. The palm of Blake's hand smashed down twice on the activation pad. The autopilot system had calculated their chance of escape to be exactly zero percent and in those circumstances, it was programmed to remain unavailable.

TIMER: 10 SECONDS TO DETONATION.

Swearing loudly, Blake hauled the spaceship hard to one side, narrowly avoiding a boulder which was eight hundred kilometres across. He thought for a second they'd made it, only for two smaller pieces of rock to collide behind them. The collision threw out a single, massive chunk which hurtled straight at the *Blackbird*. Blake's brain realised the inevitable and he prepared for impact.

The huge dull-glowing section of Tarnor's crust crashed into the *ES Blackbird*. This boulder was nine thousand metres in diameter and vaguely spherical – Blake didn't want to guess how many trillions of tonnes it weighed. The spaceship was exceptionally dense and heavy for its size, but it was hurled to one side without affecting the boulder's trajectory.

"Oh shit," said Lieutenant Quinn. "Our shield's offline."

Blake's console lit up with a hundred warnings. His hands moved towards the panel, before he realised there was no point. An arrow-shaped section of Tarnor hit them side on, scraping away a hundred thousand tonnes of armour plating and sending the spaceship off on a new, unwanted course. Again and again they were hit. It felt to Blake as though time had slowed down, whilst his brain operated at its normal speed and tried desperately to figure a way out.

"Everything's shutting down," said Quinn, his words as slow as treacle.

"Activate the fission engines."

"Critical failure, sir."

TIMER: 0 SECONDS TO DETONATION.

OBSIDIAR BOMB DETONATION SEQUENCE ACTIVATED.

There was a moment when the bridge was utterly silent – the briefest of instants between the sounds of the alarms and words of the crew. The air felt heavy and with the smell of chlorinated water. Blake's mind continued working. *We're one hundred and eighty thousand klicks from the centre of the blast.* He was able to find humour of a kind in the situation. *It won't be the explosion which kills us,* he thought with a bitter laugh.

Deep within the cargo hold of the Vraxar mothership, the Obsidiar bomb exploded. The huge spaceship wasn't merely torn into pieces – it simply ceased to be, every atom disconnected from those surrounding. The blast grew with hideous speed – a ball of energy darker than any Vraxar weapon. It engulfed the alien war fleet and continued outwards. The closest Vraxar warships, including Neutralisers and battleships – which were in the process of moving away from the destruction of Tarnor - suffered the same fate as the mothership. Their energy shields held for infinitesimal moments before they collapsed and the spaceships beneath them were unmade.

There were other Vraxar warships, further from the centre of the blast sphere. These ones were simply destroyed, their armoured hulls peeled away by the force of the explosion. A few of the larger ones were hurled outwards with the force, spinning uncontrollably as they disintegrated.

The effects of the detonation did not stop there. The sphere grew still further, beginning to weaken at its extremes. This weakening was relative and the dark energy washed amongst the remains of Tarnor. Where rock and dark flames met, the molten pieces crumbled, their fires quenched. In places, tiny fragments of Obsidiar were formed.

On the bridge of the *Blackbird*, the crew could only stare in dumbfounded shock. The fires of the Obsidiar bomb came to them through the debris of the shattered world, breaking up rocks which would have destroyed the spaceship. It touched the ruined armour of the *Blackbird*, reacting with the metal and corroding it so that it scattered away like the foam from a windswept ocean.

The flames receded. As quickly as they'd come, they dissipated. In the aftermath, the *ES Blackbird* was left damaged and amongst the thinning rubble of Tarnor. Blake had not for a single moment abandoned his efforts to pilot his ship to safety and he continued unabated. The control rods were heavy and unresponsive, and the gravity engines were jumping rapidly between offline and online.

"Give me a status report," he said. His voice sounded distant, as if it came from elsewhere.

"Life support critical and in a borderline failure state," said Quinn. "We've lost plating and engine mass from our rear and port sides."

"Weapons systems critical and offline," said Hawkins. "I might be able to get the repeaters back."

"Three of our main sensor arrays have failed," said Pointer. "We're not blind, but it's not good."

The tactical display was a confused mess of objects, which jumped around on the screen as the remaining sensors did their best to carry the load for the offline arrays. Much of the debris was far ahead of the *Blackbird* now and the slower pieces had either been destroyed by the Obsidiar bomb or weren't moving quickly enough to overtake them. The treacherous thought formed in Blake's head. *We made it.*

"Sir, the furthest parts of the debris have reached the closest of Tarnor's two moons. I'm reading numerous large impacts," said Pointer.

Blake growled with anger. He had enough on his plate with the exploding planet and bomb – the thought something might happen to Tarnor's moons hadn't occurred to him.

"Show me," he said.

The front sensor array wasn't in perfect focus and the image flickered erratically. It was sufficiently operational to show the turmoil on the closest moon. There was a crater several thousand kilometres wide, with a blurriness to the image which he guessed was a fountain of dust thrown up into space.

"There have been two catastrophic impacts and dozens of minor ones," said Pointer. "The most distant rocks are just about to strike the second moon."

The sensor feed changed, now showing the pristine surface of the second moon. Something collided with the moon dead-on. The object was too small to be seen, but the results of its impact were not. A crater formed, appearing as an area of darkness on the red-liquid surface. Moments later, a second, much larger crater appeared.

"They no longer have anything to orbit," said Hawkins.

"What's our distance from the closest moon?" asked Blake.

"A third of a million klicks."

"Calculate the trajectory of both moons. The *Blackbird* isn't responding well – it's like flying a brick and I don't want to go through that same crap again."

"That one's breaking up," said Quinn in wonder.

He was right – a series of huge fissures ran around the circumference of the moon, emanating from the largest crater. The moon fractured into three pieces. It was nothing like as violent as Tarnor's destruction and the separate sections drifted apart, spraying the contents of their molten cores into space.

"Get your eyes off the sensors and try and bring those fission engines online!" snapped Blake.

"They aren't coming back any time soon, sir. Some things you can fix quickly, others..." Quinn shrugged.

"Lieutenant Pointer, can you suggest a course for me to follow that will get us out of this?"

"Yes, sir. I'm feeding the details over to you now."

Blake needn't have worried. The courses of the two moons would take them far from the *ES Blackbird*. A few of Tarnor's smaller rocks continued striking the rear of the spacecraft and he altered course to avoid a cluster of larger pieces. It wasn't exactly plain sailing, but he permitted himself to think his earlier thought again. *We made it.*

"There's an eighty percent chance the intact moon will collide with Cheops-A at some point in the next thirty days," said Pointer. "The pieces of that other moon will drift forever."

The next ten minutes took all of Blake's concentration. Gradually, he managed to steer them onto a course where he was confident they wouldn't be struck by any debris of significant size. There were still pieces of rock which were moving faster than the *ES Blackbird*, but these were easy to avoid. In fact, the autopilot permitted itself to take over, allowing Blake to remove his hands from the control rods. This respite allowed his body to catch up and he felt the tension in every muscle of his body.

"Get on the comms, Lieutenant Pointer. Let Fleet Admiral Duggan know the news of our success."

"We're on the backups, sir. The signal will take a while to reach its destination. I don't recommend you attempt a live conversation."

"No matter. Make him aware."

With the autopilot in control, Blake was able to evaluate the multitude of damage reports on his panel. The stealth modules had failed totally, but the life support systems remained operational, though at reduced efficiency. The weapons systems remained offline and the failed sensor arrays would need complete replacement. There was some good news – the Obsidiar core was undamaged and it recharged at its usual rate.

"Even if we're stranded, we'll still have our shields," said Pointer.

"How long to reach the closest Space Corps outpost on our gravity engines?" asked Blake.

"It's not too bad. A few months." Pointer laughed. "If we're lucky, they might send someone to help us out."

"They'll need to bring a long tow rope," said Hawkins.

"None of the replicators have failed, so we won't go hungry."

Blake wasn't sure what made him notice it. There was an object on the tactical display which the sensors had flagged as just another rock. This one was travelling on a course that wasn't quite a straight line from the centre. That in itself wasn't unusual – many pieces of debris had collided with others and deflected onto new trajectories. However, the speed of this object meant that it should have overtaken the *Blackbird* several minutes ago.

"Lieutenant Pointer, can you give me some more information on Tactical Object #318224578? It's two hundred thousand klicks to our rear."

"One moment, sir, I'm not able to get a clear view of it." Pointer furrowed her brow and then swore loudly. "It's a Vraxar ship."

Blake wasn't a man to give up, but at that moment he felt something akin to despair. "Have they detected us?"

The answer was no surprise.

"Yes, sir. They are definitely heading our way."

"What is it?"

"I don't think I can believe it. It's the battleship that accompanied the mothership the first time we shadowed them around Cheops-A."

"Activate our energy shield."

"Shield online," said Quinn.

As the Vraxar battleship came through the rubble, the *Blackbird*'s upper sensor arrays resolved more details. The enemy ship was badly damaged, with huge chunks of its plating burned away and the rest of its hull blistered. The fact it hadn't entered lightspeed in order to close the gap suggested it no longer had that capability.

Usually, Blake would have fancied the *ES Blackbird* in a race against pretty much anything. At the moment, it was so much down on power, the enemy battleship was closing on them – slowly, yet inevitably. Watching the aliens draw near, Blake felt his hatred for them rise. Whatever his emotions, he couldn't escape the truth of his helplessness to avoid what was coming.

A particle beam struck the ES *Blackbird*'s energy shield.

"Not much power behind that one," said Quinn. "Maybe their ship will fail before they reach us."

The Vraxar fired a second particle beam.

"Why can't they just piss off?" said Pointer.

"They don't know when they've been beaten, do they?" said Hawkins.

"How are you getting on with the fission drive, Lieutenant Quinn?" Blake asked loudly, cutting across the inconsequential insults directed towards the Vraxar.

"Give me six hours and I'll give you ten minutes at light-speed, sir."

It wasn't going to be enough. The Vraxar battleship forged onwards, leaving a trail of metal dust and positrons behind it. Blake was sure it was too badly damaged to defeat anything larger than a fleet destroyer, but it was going to be more than enough to destroy the ES *Blackbird*. There was no real benefit for the aliens in this pursuit and he wondered if the Vraxar experienced emotions such as anger and the need for vengeance.

The particle beam stabbed across the intervening space again and again. The *Blackbird*'s energy shield fell steadily - each attack it absorbed removed eight percent of its total. Death was coming and it was coming soon. The crew worked hard to figure out how to get something from the fission engines. It was no good – as Lieutenant Quinn had said, it was going to take hours to bring them online.

"There's no point in running any longer," said Blake. "Who wants to go down in a blaze of glory?"

"Not particularly," said Hawkins. "I was hoping to die on a

sun-drenched beach somewhere, next to an empty plate of lobster tails in garlic butter."

"How about death caused by ramming a Vraxar battleship at high speed?"

"No lobster tails?"

"Sorry."

"Let's get on with it, then," she said.

"Any other objections? I don't think it's a good time to ask the *Juniper*'s survivors."

"No objections, sir," said Pointer. "It's been nice working with you all."

He smiled. "Yes, it's not been too bad, has it? We got a few things done."

Blake didn't say anything more. He grabbed the control rods and pulled them over to the side, shutting off the autopilot in the process. The *Blackbird* grumbled and the metal flexed and groaned. It wasn't anything like as nimble as usual and it took a painfully long time to come around. With their nose pointed back the way they'd come, Blake took aim at the Vraxar ship.

"There's a fission signature, sir," said Quinn. "Correction: there are overlapping signatures. We have several spaceships incoming. They'll land close by."

Blake knew the answer before he asked the question. "Ours?"

"No, sir." Quinn's voice climbed an octave. "I think it's Ghasts!"

The Ghast vessels materialised into local space. Pointer got a sensor lock and brought them up on the main screen. The crew could only stare in awe.

"Oblivions," said Blake. "They sent three Oblivions."

"With Obsidiar cores," said Quinn.

The Ghasts were not an artistic species, at least not in the same way as humans recognized the word. However, there was something about the design of their spaceships that captured a harsh, terrible menace and beauty. Their battleships were incredible to behold – streamlined wedges of metal, bristling with turrets and missile clusters. The Ghasts were far less numerous than humanity, yet their weapons and spaceships were a match for the best in the Space Corps.

The Oblivions began firing upon the approaching Vraxar battleship. As well as their missiles, they used something Blake had not seen before. The Ghasts were masters of incendiary technology and this new weapon caused the vacuum around the Vraxar ship to erupt in blue-tinged plasma flames. The Ghast particle beams darted into the fire, igniting the already-damaged hull of the enemy ship.

The Vraxar didn't even attempt to break off. It was so obvious they were utterly outmatched that they continued on their same course, firing the same single particle beam at the *Blackbird*. *We're the consolation kill*, thought Blake as he turned the spy craft onto a new heading.

The enemy battleship failed. It quickly broke apart under the bombardment and its burning wreckage split into many pieces. The Ghasts didn't stop and they continued firing until there was nothing recognizable left of the Vraxar ship.

Blake glanced down at the state of the *Blackbird*'s energy shield: five percent.

"Can we speak to the Ghasts?" he asked.

"We have inbound comms, sir," said Pointer.

"Patch them through."

"Captain Charlie Blake, I am Tarjos Gor-Lon." The Ghast laughed without a hint of mockery. "You have caused much destruction. It has brought us great pleasure to see the aftermath."

For some reason, Blake couldn't see the funny side. The Obsidiar bomb had obliterated a huge number of Vraxar warships and an entire planet had been destroyed. There were positives to the situation, but he didn't feel like laughing.

Blake couldn't think of a suitable response, so he kept it simple. "I'm glad you arrived. Thank you."

"We are allies now, Captain Charlie Blake! The Confederation and the Ghast Subjocracy. Before we are finished, these Vraxar will wish they had lost to the Estral!"

The conversation didn't last long and when it ended, Blake stood and faced the others of his crew.

"That was by far the hardest week of my entire life. Now that it's over, I don't know whether to laugh or cry," he said.

To his surprise, Lieutenant Pointer burst into tears.

REFLECTIONS

Fleet Admiral Duggan sat in his chair. The evening sunlight flooded in through his window, lending a brightness to one half of the room and leaving the other half in gloom. In a way, it reflected his mood.

"Why must every success have a failure to counterbalance it?" he asked. "Who makes up the rules?"

"The *Juniper* is gone," said his wife. "The Vraxar took it and they paid the price. They had enough ships at Cheops to take out half of the Confederation and now they're destroyed."

"A steel toecap in their metal balls," said Duggan with a sudden laugh. "That's how Captain Blake described it."

"You like him, don't you?"

"I see the potential."

"He's the same as you and different at the same time."

"He's a carefree version of a younger me. The man I could have been."

"Is it how you wanted to be?"

"No. We are who we are and I don't regret my past."

She smiled, casting her own rays of light upon him. "I'm glad to hear it. Now what is next for the Confederation?"

"We're hearing the right noises from Roban and Liventor – the Council are confident they'll return to the fold. It'll be stormy for a time, but fear of the Vraxar will keep them in line. The Obsidiar was their only bargaining chip and we've taken that away from them."

"Was the price worth paying?"

"For a full military alliance with the Ghasts? They'll be worth every ounce of the *Astrinium*'s Obsidiar."

"For the first time in my life, everyone's pulling in the same direction. I mean not just pretending – really going for the same thing. We're going to win."

"I've always loved your optimism. It's the perfect foil for my dwelling on the negatives."

"When will the evacuation of Atlantis begin?"

"Tomorrow. The projections guys reckon there's a good chance we've cleared the Vraxar out of the area. The Interstellars should get the time they need on the surface."

"After that?"

"We wait and we prepare. The Vraxar aren't gone. They've beaten every species they've encountered up until now and they have no choice other than to keep at us. Once they've defeated us, they can use the bodies of our dead to replenish their numbers and begin the cycle again."

"The Space Corps has the right man for the job," she said.

"I was beginning to have doubts. Those doubts are fading and now all I feel is anger. We have Obsidiar and we have the Ghasts. Captain Blake's victory at Cheops buys us some time. When the Vraxar return we will give them much more than a bloody nose."

The voice of his personal assistant Cerys intruded. "Councillors Stahl and Dawson wish to speak with you, Fleet Admiral, about a matter of some urgency."

"Aren't all matters urgent?" Duggan replied. "Bring them through to my communicator."

His wife stayed for a while, listening to the conversation. Duggan had always been a man with his inner demons. When the time came, he always fought through. As he spoke to the two councillors, the tones of his voice were strong and confident. Whatever the Vraxar brought, they were going to find in Duggan a wall of solid iron which wouldn't flex an inch and wouldn't break. This was going to be a war they would wish they never started.

Follow Anthony James on Facebook at
facebook.com/AnthonyJamesAuthor

ALSO BY ANTHONY JAMES

The Survival Wars series

The Obsidiar Fleet series

38275917R00164

Printed in Poland
by Amazon Fulfillment
Poland Sp. z o.o., Wrocław